THE
INDUSTRY

Natasha Rocca Devine

New Generation **Publishing**

I would like to thank immensely each of my teams; 'Authoright PR' in London and New York, 'Invoke PR' and 'Tara O'Connor PR' in Dublin and 'New Generation Publishing' in London for all of their help and hard work in creating 'The Industry'.

To my family and friends, I am eternally grateful for your support. In particular my parents, sisters, brother, niece and aunts. Thank you all.

For everyone who I have met to date, you have each contributed to my work, so thank you.

Last but not least, I want to thank and commend everyone working in 'The Industry'.

Wishing you all lots of light!

Natasha Rocca Devine (NRD)

Chapter 1

Tweet: @*AStar Looks like a girl, but she's a flame,*
So bright, she can burn your eyes.
Better look the other way,
You can try but you'll never forget her name.
She's on top of the world,
Hottest of the hottest girls say X @*CStar* @*Alicia Keys*

June 2013, V-Bar, City, London

'One, two, three, and off I go,' Alanna mumbles under her breath whilst the burly security guard opens the heavy iron-laden door.

She enters the infamous *V-Bar.*

'Welcome to *V-Bar.* Can I help you locate your guests?' offers the pint-size host in a skin-tight Lycra dress. She has tanned skin, blonde hair, blue eyes and freckles framing her proportionate face.

Alanna awaits acknowledgment while the 'host's' eyes are clearly fixating on her iPhone, rather than the job at hand.

'I am here for the private event. Can you tell me where it is?' Alanna requests in her thick Kerry accent.

The host's green glitter-shadowed eyes look up immediately. 'Oh, ooh, oh the private event.'

'Yes, indeed, indeed you are,'

'This is located in the cocktail room downstairs, miss'.

'Susan has requested you go straight down upon arrival. The event is expected to begin soon,' the host says in her Essex accent with an assuming smirk on her face, as if to say she knows why Alanna has come tonight.

'Thanks,' says Alanna, disregarding her. She smiles and walks on through the beautifully lit glass tunnel ahead.

***

Looking around, she is immediately impressed with the stunning round room filled with carefully placed bankers, blondes, and brunettes, each elegantly dressed. It was picture-perfect. She had seen the bar in many magazines, but it was much more stunning in reality, and the people were too. Glass chandeliers and pendants of sunburnt orange reflected against the theme of velour and leather-buttoned banquet seating.

Glass tables circled the space, along with mirrors reflecting back the bar – a sight akin to a 1950s movie.

A further glance took in the array of *Louboutins*, pearly teeth, suits, skirts and stockings, all fitted around the French style booths and high-perched glass stools. Here the standard was high. Higher than she could have ever have imagined.

Tweeting *a photo:*

@AStar@V-Bar – Stunning, when you see this scene it's clear why people move to London.

***

Alanna, naturally drawn to the music, moves her eyes to the small stage on the left of the bar which is managed by the curvaceous, black-haired, pale-skinned jazz singer. She is moving her body in sync with each beat. Closing her eyes, she is enjoying every moment, in her own world and mesmerizing to watch.

Continuously looking around with a mother-like smirk, she notices the older men enjoying the fresh bait of the new international youthful ladies. Feeling the vibration from her iPhone, she sees Carlton's face pop up.

'Darling A, where are you?' he screams down the phone in his Brooklyn New York accent, so loudly that it would appear that it was him placed in a crowded bar, not her.

'Ye know where I am,' she reacts just as loudly.

'I posted up a song just for your blog. Check it out, ha ha ha.'

'Well, yeah, maybe later. I am kind of busy!' she reminds him.

'Alanna, the reason why you have an agent is because of our blog, so don't start dissin' it!' he screams.

'OK, Carlton,' she responds dismissively.

'So, how does it feel to wear a camera? Are you feeling all Bond and superhero-like?'

'No...'

'Sista, get out of this negative mood and up your tempo. It's a Friday night. We young, we fine and we in London to have a good time, ha ha ha,' he laughs. With no reaction to this, he continues, 'Remember, we are in showbusiness, Queen A. So this is your job, but if you don't love it, then GET OUT QUICK!' He screams, 'I told you what Momma always tells me: 'Darlin', you in a SHOW business, so you always on show...' It may be pretty on the outside, but it ain't always a pretty picture behind the red curtain. Your job is you gotta keep the audience happy or else they ain't got no reason to watch you. Get with the program or sign out.'

He hears no reaction. 'Plus Alanna, you don't gotta do anything you don't want to... but I suggest you do,' he laughs in his own cheeky way.

***

6

As Alanna continues looking around the room for signs to the downstairs bar, she listens but remains evasive.

'Look, it's only a job. If you are worried, you call me if it goes wrong. I got your back. I will be over there as fast as the *Kardashians* release their next publicity stunt,' Carlton says.

Smiling, Alanna listens closely to the sound of Beyoncé and lots of people screaming to *Single Ladies (Put A Ring On It)* coming down the phone as background noise.

Recognising the song, she asks, 'What is that noise? Where are ye, Carlton?'

'Queen A, didn't I tell you? Being the professionals we are, myself, Julian and some guys from studio are practising our routines. Mainly picking our songs for the show. I start with mine and since you ain't here Julian is stepping in.'

'Carlton, don't lie. I bet ye's are doing a *Wii 3-D Dance-Off.* Sure, any excuse to perform to Beyoncé's tracks? Ye've been caught. I saw the playlists and sparkle and shimmery outfits before I left,' she laughs out so loudly that the people she walks past notice.

'Well, yeah. Hope you don't mind? I've got the best tunes: *Ring On It, Independent Woman* and *Sweet Dreams.*'

'Sure, but only if you promise to record. It would be a good one for me to watch tomorrow. Oh, and keep *Fever* for me. That's my tune,' she smiles, which Carlton notices immediately.

'That's more like it. Enough about my Lady B. Lady A needs my love on her big night. Oh, and I took some of your clothes and make-up to get into character. Do you mind? No, didn't think so. Did I tell ya? I am also considering *X-Factor* auditions…'

'*X-Factor*? Sure we can't do anything like that with class, or Francesca's head will combust. If she hears that, ye'll never graduate. Anyway, why would ye bother after all yer hard work and sure...' she reminds him.

'I know, I know, against class policy, blah blah blah, but we ain't there much longer... and I ain't one for waitin. Speaking of which, gotta run, Justin is taking over my main stage.'

'Stage? Ye call that a stage? Ha ha. Sure, ye couldn't swing cats in our place, so do what ye can do,' she says encouragingly.

'Ha ha. Fo sho. Show them what they don't even know they want, sista. Laters.'

He cuts off.

***

Meanwhile, Alanna manoeuvres her red dress and curves through the *V-bar*. She manufactures a smile too – a smile still seductive enough to cause every man a chance to double-glance at her. She never understood nor enticed this blatant attention from men – and women at times. All she knows is she could get whatever she wanted by the way she moved her body.

She was not always sure of the power of her prowess. She never did anything to stop them looking. Yet, she enjoys people underestimating her, followed by her proving them wrong. All she does understand is that she gets further in life once she glances at a man. He would fall at her feet. Literally. She believes her appeal might help her case on this night, and so whatever it was, she is keeping it up.

On first glance, people see her red fiery hair, 5' 11'' femme-fatale figure and rounded face with a seductively placed mole over her plump lips. Her piercing green eyes give anyone enough reason to double-glance at this Irish goddess.

On a deeper level, her dance skills, dry wit, Irish accent, intelligence, ambition and remarkable innocence are enough to have anyone pursue her with sincere interest. Her voice and musical abilities are her best assets, yet these are something people had to earn the right to eventually discover.

***

Alanna moves towards the appropriately lit bar, people parting at her presence, conversations stopping as if noting that she was a lady of importance. Continuously looking around for any evidence of signs to the event, she takes a seat. Her palms are moist. She can feel her heart pacing profoundly, as if someone is close enough to see her camera, just above where her heart is racing. Perching herself on the glass stool, she immediately hears, 'G'day, what can I get you, beautiful?' from the chiselled young Australian barman.

'Dry Martini, please, sir,' she requests with her sarcastic flirt.

Showing off his bartender skills while flexing his pecs under his white shirt, he prepares her drink while his eyes are drawn to her lips and chest. She watches his muscles contract as he prepares the shaker.

It is a fair deal.

At a glance, she notes the lit neon sign to the cocktail bar. Once handed the drink, she brings it close to her lips and knocks it back in one go. Before the barman has time to turn around, she drops the glass and moves on, leaving fifteen pounds on the bar – ten for the drink and five for the man who has calmed her nerves. With no time to waste, she paces forward for a 'pit stop' in the ladies' room.

***

London, so busy and brilliant, has many people with the same qualities. The competition is fierce, particularly in terms of dating.

Standing in front of the wide and brightly lit mirror, Alanna can't help but notice two other woman double-glancing each other. From the outside, it is as if they are in a boxing ring, landing punches on each other through the evil looks in their eyes. Back and forth, back and forth, the punches are thrown, all three continuing in the alpha-female bathroom routine that causes endless queues and confusion worldwide. The routine is easily broken into various stages: peeing, pouting, bitching to and at other females, texting, 'Whats App', taking photos, tweeting, calling, Facebook-photo uploading, re-tweeting, re-applying lipstick, adding dusts of shimmer to the appropriate points, mascara re-touch, hair flick back and toss back, tears falling *Pending; Happy or sad, perfume spraying, re-adjusting dresses and last but not least perking up breasts and checking the mirror before entering back into the wild.

Depending on the alcohol intake, the process can be slower and much tougher. Alanna notices the blonde lady on her right, who is struggling with stage four: mascara.

Covering all stages, including adjusting the secret camera on her left chest, Alanna is ready to go back out. Moving into the bar, her dress appears tighter than normal, as if it were her new undergarment. The camera is her new weapon, but, like a rash, she has to touch it although she knows it will only make things worse. She looks down and checks that it is on, knowing that from this moment she is constantly on show, accepting her fate whatever may come.

The next steps go slowly, following the sign downstairs, marking the private function '18 Members Event'.

Chapter 2

Tweet: *@AStar I've got my eyes on you…*
Because you're a good girl and you know it.
I can't get over you, You've left your mark on me
@Drake
;) xxx CStar

V-Bar, 18 Members Event, City, London
In her eight-inch heels, lycra skin-tight dress and smirk, Alanna arrives downstairs. She sees a room full of dynamic-looking individuals in a twin of the bar upstairs, but less crowded. The group appears much more interesting than the one upstairs, and she walks on with a smile. At a glance each person is nervous and yet hopeful, some with glasses filled with wine, cocktails and beer, others glassless and sober – or perhaps they'd wisely had pre-event drinks.

This doesn't feel right yet. They need me to get this done. Sure, what's the worst that could happen?

Ordering another drink from an equally attractive young man with a London accent, she has no time to think as the sound of a glass tinkling brings everyone's attention towards the bar. Everyone including Alanna moves their eyes to a svelte middle-aged blonde woman looking slightly worn out but glamorous in her plum dress. Her killer legs perch upon her impressively high heels.

***

'Welcome, everyone. As you will all know, I am Susan, the founder of 18 Members Only Club. It is my pleasure to invite you all to tonight's exciting event. This is your chance to meet your Prince Charming or your Bella, so give each other a chance. With nine dates each, after each meeting you must score your partner on the iPads provided. You have only five minutes with each date, so ladies, please, let the men talk. Don't be a one-way street.' She laughs at her own joke then moves back to a serious tone too quickly for everyone to know whether to react or not.

'When you have completed your scoring, please move to the next table and on to your next date. We shall break midway for a short interim and then at the end I will be notifying you all. In any case, let's start very soon, so arrange a drink and get seated. Oh, if you have any questions, just shout. I'll be at the bar. Enjoy the evening, my darlings,' she says, turning her back to the barman, who was the sole focus of her attention from then on.

***

Like children during musical chairs, the mature adults run to a seat, each forgetting that every person has a space… indeed, they have paid for one. Minutes later, everyone is on one side of a leather-buttoned booth facing a person of the opposite sex, placing their drinks next to two iPads, which appear part of the modern glass table architecture. Within a few moments, the buzzer signals to mark the start of the event.

'The race is on!' hollers Susan from the bar.

The sound of voices soon fills the previously strained room, drowning out the jazz music playing.

Alanna begins her prepared speech in a thicker-than-normal Kerry accent. 'I am Alanna, a dancer and singer from Kerry – ye know, Kerry in Ireland. I am very traditional, especially with dating, but "When in Rome…", as Mam says! London and this city life… well, it's all new to me, so I would like to meet a man, one who can show me around really. And how 'bout yerself?'

Alanna's first date, from a physical standpoint alone, is every woman's dream. His suit is tailored to perfection, his shirt – crisp as if it came direct from the packet – complementing his dark hair and eyes. With a charming smile set in his strict jawline, he was the Machiavellian Italian man.

Jaysus, this isn't a bad start at all!

'Piacere! I'm Marcello. I'm honest. Kind. Funny. You-a take me as I am and I take you... where I want,' he laughs earnestly. Yah. So I am a footballer. I am here with my friend Jack,' he points to the Light-haired man sitting three booths away. 'We are working hard but playing harder.'

Alanna smiles in acknowledgement.

'Yah. So, I come from a small town in Italy. I was one of the lucky ones who made it, but I love Italia. I love all the great things in life: football, family, food and women, *hahaha*. Oh, and Alanna, I have no problems dating, but I always try new things so I come-a here-a, yah. Capisco.'

Not realising his own actions, as his eyes were blatantly wandering up and down her chest. Alanna feels he may not know it is her face he is meant to talk to.

His hands move around so often that Alanna believes he must have managed an orchestra concerto in another life. Despite this, his impeccable style and passion for life make up for his broken English and frivolous behaviour. The buzzer goes and each have a moment to vote before exchanging seats.

'Ciao, bella,' he smiles, his racing eyes forward to the blonde ahead.

***

Alanna moves to her next table to meet with a tall man with dark hair and green eyes, in the most expensive outfit she has seen this evening. His face is rounded and plump but well suited to his frame. Alanna shares her speech with her usual genuine smile, already feeling at ease with him.

'How do you do?'

'It's a pleasure to meet you, Alanna. Ireland is a beautiful place. The people too,' he continues. 'I'm Harry. I own my own company, all in and around technology. Based between London, New York and Hong Kong, wherever my job takes me. But mainly I run the ship from London. I came this evening with my best friend Hugh, who sadly has just broken up with his fiancée.'

Alanna continues listening to him. He has the poshest London accent in the room.

'Honestly, Alanna, I have no interest in these events. Truth be told, I am an old romantic, so would never pick up a woman through these means. Yet often in life an opportunity presents itself and when a friend is in need I must step in. At least the bar is beautiful - remarkably beautiful, one might say,' he says, looking at Alanna, his eyes deep into hers, making it very obvious that his compliments were directed nowhere near the bar.

'I'm glad you think so,' she responds, her cheeks blushing.

He returns her smile and a slight blush appears in his cheeks too.

The buzzer cuts them off in their special moment.

Harry takes his time to leave, and with his height and stature looks down directly into her eyes. 'It has been a pleasure to meet you, Alanna,' he says, as he lifts her right hand and kisses it.

'Likewise.'

'Have a wonderful evening,' he adds as he moves off, but he looks back every step of the way.

***

A mousey-brown-haired young man is seated at her next table. He's strikingly attractive, well-dressed in a shirt and t-shirt, and peeping out underneath are leather bands on both arms and a piercing on his left eyebrow. There are also some signs of tattoos, but Alanna does her best to not stare at his arms and chest.

Alanna shares her general speech while he follows suit.

'That's cool. Hey, I'm Josh. An actor and model from LA. I came here to shoot a pilot, but it never took off and I got an agent here, so I never went back. I don't like cities much but I am here working as a personal trainer in a gym for a year or two. I'm saving up before I go back to the States to film my own show.

'I miss it there. In LA I spent most of my time on beaches, being a lifeguard during the day and then some PT work on the side. Here, I keep up my training and audition in between. All good in the hood.

'Like you, an Irish lady, I love outdoors. I grew up on a farm in Kentucky. I love anything wild and adventurous.' Alanna smiles as she looks into his blue passion-filled eyes, reminiscing about her love of the outdoors life and the simplicity he spoke of – the simplicity she too had left behind.

'I see life as a daily adventure. London is my latest one,' he shares. 'Life is good. I date lots, but today I just came for fun.'

The buzzer goes off. They vote again and move on.

'See ya around, Alanna. By the way, you are one of the hottest ladies I've seen here… In London, I mean.

Here's my card. Let's hook up.' He places it in her hand, winks, and moves on.

***

As soon as she is seated, she looks up to see the next guy is dressed smartly. He is the youngest of all. Brown-haired, blue-eyed, fresh, and too innocent to be at such an event, never mind living in London.

Alanna repeats her speech, which is met with, 'Hi, Alanna. I'm Philip, a marketing exec from Dublin. I'm working in the city on a graduate scheme. Well, it happens that the guys in work dared me to do this as part of my inauguration – either this or a breakfast run everyday at 6am for God knows how long. A no-brainer. I took this. Anyway, nice to meet another Irish person. You do miss the accent when you're away, don't you?'

'Yes, I do,' Alanna agrees.

'Well, I'll craic on. I'm from a nice family... good stock, as we say in Dublin. Not sure how you put it in Kerry.'

For such a young man, he speaks non-stop as if he is in olden-day Ireland, where each person would have a dowry. The bigger your dowry, the better chances you would get as a potential mate.

He must have had a big one. Or he is compensating.

She smiles. 'I understand. It's something similar in the country.'

In every country, I'm sure, lad.

'Oh cool. Well, like you, I moved to London for work, mainly. It's great here, lots of options. I am young but have high expectations. I aim high, and always reach it. Plus my folks have an apartment in Kensington, which is cool. Nice pad, ya know. I travel when I can, I like food, clothes, and the usual manly things like sport. Work late but love my job. Well, the money is good, so that's fantastic.'

He smiles again, with not a mark appearing, showing once again his innocence.

'Oh, I play rugby on the weekends. You know, I gotta keep in touch with the lads. So it's a tough life, but no complaints' he says in well-spoken accent.

Speaking so fast and without any filters, it was clear his nerves have taken over, yet his smile and the light in his eyes are sweet. London hasn't broken his spirit. Not just yet. The buzzer goes again while they look up, exchange goodbyes and score up.

***

'Everyone, we will have a short fifteen-minute break to allow time to freshen up and get another drink,' Susan calls out from the bar.

'Nice to meet you, Alanna. Would you like a drink? I would hate to see a lady paying for herself,' Philip suggests.

'Sure. That would be great, Philip, thanks.'

As they both make their way towards the bar, it's clear that everyone has already lightened up, as laughter echoes amongst them all. All new, all mixed, all typical of a London get-together.

Drinks pouring, glances and words exchanging, fifteen minutes passing very easily until another announcement comes up: 'Everyone, please make your way back to the same seat. Although you may wish to remain with your previous dates, or not, *hahaha*,' Susan laughs. 'Please do ensure that you are seated with new members.' On that note, just as before everyone quickly retreats into their new booths, preparing themselves for stage two. Alanna is ready as ever as part two of the race continues.

Chapter 3

Tweet: *@AStar Hey I just met you*
And this is crazy
But here's my number
So call me maybe
@CarlyRaeJepson

V-Bar, 18 Members Event, City, London
As Alanna sits down again, she meets a handsome and extremely well-dressed man – a man who is ridiculously drunk judging by the way he was leaning on the bar throughout the entire break. He was stumbling around, and up-close he is slightly foaming beer or alcohol at the mouth. Another giveaway is a drink in each hand – never a good sign on a first date. After a minute or so, Alanna, hearing his accent, realises it is Harry's friend, the newly single man.

What a catch. Wonder why she left him? she thinks to herself.

Alanna continues with her plan as per usual, while he follows with, 'I am Hugh.' He slurs his words while closing his eyes in the effort to form a sentence. 'Well, no news. No news other than my fiancé just walked out on me last week.' As he knocks back another part of the pint, he rolls his eyes back. 'She's in love with her agent. He's sixty-three – or eighty-three, who knows? Also, half my size in height and near double in weight. So, I am great, JUST GREAT!' He screams so loudly that one or two of the guests look over, including Harry.

She smiles awkwardly, unsure what to say.

'Free as a bird. Who needs her anyway?' he continues. 'Oh yes, what else? Oh, work. Well, I work in fashion as a buyer. Well, I buy and sell shares and own a couple of stores. All exciting to say, but it's business at the end of the day. It is not all it's cracked up to be,' he says while drinking more of his left-handed pint.

'Nothing in life is what it seems, Alanna. Learn that young.' He knocks back the end of his drink and looks into his glass with pity.

'Especially love.'

The buzzer goes.

Votes are being made, but in this case Alanna has to pass as she is assisting Hugh over to his next seat. Ordering him water and taking the second pint away, she knows he will thank her tomorrow.

***

Moving to her next booth, she is sitting across from a slim guy, impeccably groomed with his hair styled as if in an ad. Again she makes her speech and awaits his response.

She expects another banker, another city story, but she is met with, 'Jaysus, another Irish person. How are ya, Alanna? This place is bleedin' massive, can't get me head around it. I've always wanted to come to one of these nights. Didn't really believe dey were real. You see it on MTV or RTE or one of those stations, but its bleedin' great to try it. Oh, I'm Jack, a footballer from Dublin. I'm playing in Manchester United and we were playing up the road at Fulham. Not sure if ye'd know it or not? Anyway, me ma and da and all me family are at home. All da players are nice, but they all have their families and birds, so I said I'd come to meet new people. I came wit me mate, the Italian fella. The lads say it would be craic.'

'Nice to meet ye too. That's great for ye, playing for Man U. My dad supports them. Fair play to ye,' she says sincerely. 'So, do ye like it here? Huge change, isn't it?' Alanna asks.

There are a few seconds' silence while Jack goes pale and Alanna, not knowing how to react, looks around the room.

After a few seconds, he admits, 'OK, Alanna, I have to tell ye da truth. I actually have a bird, but me mates told me she was flirtin' with her ex Damo. Loadsa times since I moved they've seen them in da local pub and she's makin' a show a me. So, I was tryin' to make her jealous. The lads booked me in here to get started. She won't move over as she can't leave her ma, so I told her I was coming tonight and she was DEVO. She's raging but I hope she'll think about movin' now. What do ya think? Anyway, Ireland is small and I thought ye might know her so I had to tell ye as I can't really date ye. Ye're real pretty, though. Da prettiest here, and I feel bad lying to an Irish person.'

Alanna laughs at his speech.

'I am a terrible liar, amen't I?'

'The worst,' she admits, but then looks down to the camera placed on her chest, feeling a pang of guilt at the ease with which she herself is lying. 'Yes, yes, you are. Best ye stop the games and get things sorted out with yer lady.'

Ye, yeah, yer right. I just think it's too hard with the distance. Maybe I should let her go and I can get on with things here? That's what all de players and me ma and da are saying. I know I have to break up, but it's hard, Alanna, real hard,' he says with his sad eyes.

'Do what ye think, Jack, always do what makes ye happy. Most people do in the end, whether it hurts people or not,' she guides him.

'Yeah, yer right, Alanna. Yer so rite. Oh, and don't tell Susan. She looks like she'd break me in two for lyin'.'

Immediately both look to the lady at the bar flirting with the barmen half her age, laughing in agreement.

The buzzer rings.

They vote.

'Let's keep in touch. If ye ever need anythin', Alanna, ye give me a call. This city isn't easy for young ladies. Ye hear me? Any messin' and I'll be over to help ye,' he says in a protective way as he kisses her cheek.

'See ya soon.' Alanna feels his sincerity, thinking he would be the kind of friend she would appreciate, particularly in London.

***

Alanna now sits across from an attractive Pakistani man with the kindest eyes. He wears a shirt, tie and sleeveless jumper, as she shares her story with ease.

'Nice to meet you, Alanna. I am Aman. My family comes from Pakistan, but I travel a lot. My mother is from Switzerland and father from Pakistan. So I've been living in Europe all my life but go to Pakistan often.

'I was a writer in Pakistan, but sometimes it got dangerous, so now I run my own publishing company here. It includes all sorts of books. I love to read and write, as I believe it opens up our lives to new dimensions and places we may never get to visit. Without these gems people may not understand the rest of the world. And vice versa. Just my opinion, though.'

'It is a great opinion,' she states.

'London is a world of opportunities if you just make it work for you, Alanna, never forget that.'

She smiles in agreement.

The buzzer goes off; they both look down to vote.

'Lovely to meet you, Alanna,' he says, smiling back at her.

'Same to you,' she says and moves on.

***

As Alanna moves around, she repeats her speech to the designer-dressed, happy and kind-eyed Asian man sitting oppoite her. His demeanour is extremely polite and clear, mirroring his sharp dress.

As she finishes, he begins, 'Hallo, I am Chen from Hong Kong. I work in the City. London is lovely. I like to work and party so it is good here. Like you, I like to meet lots of new people. Also, someone in work says about tonight and so I came. Nice place. You like it?'

'Yes, very much so,' she responds.

The buzzer goes and they vote.

'Nice to meet you, Alanna, very nice,' he says, moving on.

***

As she moves to another seat she is met with her final guest, Peter, a blond man with blue eyes. He is dressed practically and acts slightly jumpy, looking around a lot. He is the most nervous of the night, judging by the sweat dripping down his face and his armpits, which have rings around them. It is clear he is shy, and Alanna empathises.

He is like Brendan.

She says her part and then lets him take his turn.

He reads his speech in a monotone, looking straight ahead as if he has prepared this all day in front of the mirror. 'Hi, I am Peter from Germany. I work for a car manufacturing company. I am the lead engineer, which is nice. I like to keep my life organized, but then sometimes I just book a flight and go somewhere random on the weekend. I like to live on the edge.'

Living on the edge. If only he knew.

As the buzzer goes, they vote and say their goodbyes while everyone moves to the bar.

***

'Thanks to each of you for joining us this evening,' Susan calls out. 'You shall receive your report via email this evening. As agreed prior to the event, you have given members the opportunity to contact you by phone, email or on Facebook and Twitter pages, depending on your choice. If there are any changes in your decision, please let me know before you leave. No lawsuits, please.' She laughs at her own joke again. 'I hope you all had a wonderful evening, and no matter what happens, it is all experience – one that remains private between the 18 Members Only.'

Each person gathers their things, and some move towards the bar, indicating they will remain there for some time. After a few minutes others move upstairs, mingling with the even busier crowd who have moved in from the street. The event is now over, hair flicked, glances exchanged, too much beer, expensive cocktails and wine drunk, jokes told, uncomfortable silences played out. Sparks flew, sparks burned out, all appropriate to a first date.

***

Alanna, not realising how drunk she is, moves herself immediately up the stairs, through the bar and out of the door. Luckily, cabs are lined up outside, so she gets in one and moves away. On her route home through the bright lights of London she looks out of the window and then down to her iPhone to make an *Evernote*:

Dear Sally... My little sister.
Tonight was unreal. I can't believe I did it.
Shocked at how easy it was for me to be a new-age
spy. Makes me think we are all actors in life. Sure, who
else was telling the truth or were we all lying?
Looking at the young crowds out my window, bare
legs, stumbling outside clubs, couples new and old
holding hands, people screaming, it is a Saturday scene
night in London. I am thinking of each person I have
met, and how each had their own dress and personality.
They all came and left in their 18 unique ways: by foot,
on the Tube, in Ferraris, by push-bike, buses,
Mercedes, Volkswagens, Mini Coopers and even a
Vespa.
18 together, now 18 apart.
You were with me all the way, sister.
Love ya,
X

***

While taking off the camera, she is distracted by her phone buzzing, so she takes the call.

'Congratulations, Alanna, just calling to let you know that you have received "Top Scorer" in this evening's 18 Members Speed Dating Event. Courtesy of 18 Members, you shall receive a free voucher to *Gaucho* for a three-course dinner with one of tonight's guests. I must book this in for some time this month, so please let me know who you choose?'

Without hesitation she responds, 'Josh, Josh from LA, please. I've not met many Americanos in Kerry. Oh, and can we say in two to three weeks, over a weekend? That suits me best.' She is booking this so

26

casually, as if it was she is midway through a takeaway order.

'Wonderful. Consider it booked. Dates, times, etcetera, will be emailed to you tomorrow and I will send Josh details too. We are so happy you found love with us. Please do refer us.' London-like and determined to create a connection, Susan doesn't leave time for a response. 'Thanks for coming. Ciao.' The phone goes dead.

Alanna looks at the phone, smiling. Being very traditional, this is all a first for her. *When in Rome...* she thinks, then she remembers her cheesy speech and looks out of the window at London, laughing at the night's event.

Chapter 4

Tweet: @CStar Love,
Love don't come easy, no no @DianaRoss

Alanna and Carlton's apartment, Earls Court, London
Alanna awakes in her apartment to the sound of Motown. She gets out of bed with a blinding headache, hair matted and make-up all over her face. Moving into the living room-come-kitchen in their 1950s dated apartment, she heads to the kitchen.

Within seconds she looks over to her laptop on table to see Dennis pop up via Skype.

'Why did we set up this automatic Skype?' she mumbles under her breath, while she smiles and looks up.

Clicking the button to accept she smiles Dennis, his face behind glasses smirking back.

'Hi, darling. Congrats on last night. Top scorer. You did very well. Very well indeed. You know I'm running the tape by the producers. These are the top guys in LA. I've checked the event list, forget the losers, Harry is our man. You need to work out how to meet him again.'

'You know the contract. I have to see each clip before anything goes out,' Alanna says in a serious tone.

'Sure, Alanna,' Dennis agrees. 'Now head to that casting, it sounds promising. Also, I have a DJ, in fact a few of them, who I want you to meet. Sky Bar soon?' he asks.

'OK, see you later,' she says, and at the same time he cuts out.

While walking towards the kitchen Alanna hears another Skype call ring in. Seeing her mothers' face she moves back towards the laptop. She answers the call. 'Hi darling. Dennis and the school say you're doing great and have some castings lined up. Well done. We are so proud of you!'

'Thanks, Mam,' Alanna replies.

'Remember, Alanna: no matter you do, we are proud.'

'Hi Brendan, my favourite brother, how are ye getting on?' Alanna ignores her mum and directs her attention to Brendan. Unbeknown to herself, Alanna's voice returns to a Kerry accent when she speaks with her family.

'Hi, Alanna,' he says, whilst looking up to the sky, spacing out yet smiling.

'Brendan, I hear you're doing very well in your classes, Mam says you're doing amazing.'

'Yes, I am. I am very smart,' he says. 'I miss you, Alanna. You left me... you left me, you left me!' he shouts.

As if he were a son of her own, Alanna has tears welling up in her eyes. 'I can't bear to see you upset, Brendan. Mam, I can't do this.

Brendan, I am working hard to get you into you're the best Austistic school so you will shine. Ye, hear me. I promise I will,' she says while wiping away the tears.

With perfect timing, Carlton walks past and sits next to Alanna on the couch. 'Hi, Mrs O. What's up?'

'Hi, Carlton. Lovely to see you,' she responds, smiling.

'You're looking great, Mrs O. It must be all those dance classes you teach. You a hot momma!'

Blushing and unsure of what to say, Alanna's mum replies, 'Oh Carlton, you're such a character. Thank you.'

He winks and glances at a message that has popped up on his iPhone while suddenly moves himself off the couch. 'Well, I gotta run. Have places to go, people to meet. Love to you all,' he says as he moves around the screen and grabs his bag. 'Bye, A. Let me know how you get on?' he says as he winks at Alanna.

'Sure.' She smiles at him in his tight crisp shirt and trousers as he closes the door tight.

***

Alanna, moving her hand through her wavy hair, tries to untangle the knots that have developed overnight, while her mother continues. 'You know Simon is asking for you. His sister isn't well.'

Alanna goes silent trying to block the feelings that this evokes, emotional once again. She looks up. 'Poor girl, I'll light her a candle.'

'His mam and sisters say he misses you terribly and hasn't been the same since you left.'

'OK, Mam, I think I'll deal with my love life myself.'

'Sorry, Alanna. Everyone here just wants you to be happy, and he is such a nice man. I want you to have a nice man like your father. London is a dangerous place and I know a Kerry man would take care of you.'

Looking at her mam's porcelain face and the kindness in her blue eyes, Alanna feels a wave of guilt, mixed in with anger. *Sure, load up the pressure, Mam. If only ye knew.* 'I understand, Mam, but I'm a big girl and can decide what I want and who I want to be with.'

'Lani, I know you're not like the others, but you've barely made it past nineteen and you've been through so much. You need a nice man. A man to take care of you. If not Simon… well, why, why aren't you and Carlton an item? What a lovely lad.'

'Mam, I'll explain another time, but let's just say Carlton isn't available. He gets off at the other bus stop.'

'What bus stop?' Mairead asks.

'Forget it, Mam,' Alanna sighs.

'OK, Lani, well, he is a lovely lad, he is. You should bring him back for Christmas. We'd love to meet him.'

'He may be in New York with his own mam, but I'll ask him. He has always says he'd love to see Ireland, so I'll keep you posted.'

Just then in her bedroom she hears her iPod alarm go off and knows she is late. Plus, it's an excuse to bow out. 'Anyway, Mam, that's my alarm again. Real sorry to be rude, but I have to go. I have a meeting. It's a casting and I can't be late.'

'Oh, of course, love. Have a lovely afternoon and call us when you get a chance. As always your dad sends his love, but work calls. He says he will call you over the next day or so.'

'Send my love back to him. I will call you over the next day or so and let ye's know how I get on. Tell Dad I would love to chat to him too.'

'Sure, Alanna. We'll make sure Dad is here for ye next time.'

'Bye Brendan,' she says, looking at her brother who remains staring at the ceiling.

'Bye Alanna, good luck, good luck, good luck,' he repeats.

'Bye, Mam. Lovely to talk and have a nice day. You take of yourself too,' she says, knowing that every detail of her mam's day was caring for her class, Brendan, and then preparing the dinners, arranging laundry and probably a visit to the grave. Knowing this, Alanna wants in any way possible to give her some hope. 'Ye know, Mam, I will help you out with Brendan's fees and we will get him into a great school and give ye time off. I will help with this, don't ye worry.'

'Alanna, don't pressure yourself, my dear. Ye're doing amazing.'

'Don't you worry about me, I am well able. Lots of love, Mam.'

'Love back, Lani. Bye.'

The Skype call quits and Alanna is overwhelmed with many feelings surfacing. She moves her head down between her legs as if close to tears. While looking down, she realises she has less than an hour to make it across London.

'Crap! Crap! Shit! Holy shit!' Alanna screams as she runs to the bathroom, stripping en route, soon forgetting her family, friends and past as she prepares for her future.

Chapter 5

Tweet: @ *London Guide to Transportation*
'It will save you stress,
money, time, shoes and maybe even your marriage.
Purchase now.' @AStar

Earls Court to LUCE Studios, London
Alanna steps into the underground world. It is hard to believe that just over a year earlier she had relocated from Killarney and stepped on her first Tube.

Yet, after countless numbers of castings, training and spending most of her time in transit, she has become a pro. She has earned this black belt. So much so that she is willing to share her Tube and transport with ninjas in training – particularly the new students entering her studio – those who can't speak English, and, of course, the sensitive types.

God help the sensitive souls, Underground.

In transit she reads over her notes, confident that she's earned this position.

London's Tube and Transport Guide 2013:
(Copyrighted Material – A*STAR):

Tube Bible:
•Do accept that the Tube is not a class divider. Moreover, unless you're a top-earning dancer, singer, actor, model/WAG, footballer, banker, CEO, director, agent, TV producer/director, even at that you will more than often be taking the Tube until you reach any of the above. With that in mind you may as well embrace the next twenty years underground.

•Do accept that even a 'Jedi Knight' would find this underground experience tough.

•Do prepare your fitness levels, as there will be many sprints involved, particularly in rush hour.

•Do purchase and top up your Oyster card in advance, unless you wish to befriend non-European tourists while celebrating their first trip to London with their extended family of twenty-five who are mesmerised by the European currency. Worst of all: being behind students who have no change.

•Never stand close to people, otherwise they will think you want to permanently take up residence there.

•Do not ask for directions from anyone other than the stationmaster, as most people just want to get you out of the way or are just visiting. Neither group cares.

•Do plan, plan, plan in advance, and also plan another route in case the Mayor of London decides to have a wonderful day of re-fixing the lines when you have a mere thirty minutes to get to your destination.

•Do expect that no matter how much you plan you will get lost and end up across the other side of the city, at least once. Only once, if you're lucky.

•Do not breathe; there's a viral infection just waiting to attack you.

•Do not make eye contact with anyone, even the elderly, underground; they are not to be trusted.

•Do not smile or give out your number to people; they will follow you home.

•Do not believe anyone who says they are an agent and you will be the next Kate Moss, particularly if you don't have blonde hair or a size-zero frame.

•Do not believe a man or woman (no matter how attractive) who asks where you are from and then offers to show you around London. Fast-forward ten years: 'Dear kids, Mam and Dad met on the Tube when Dad was hitting on young, vulnerable girls from out of town.' Although love at first sight is possible, probably not a good story to share with future generations at Christmas festivities.

•Do not get offended that no one talks. In fact, the quieter they are, the more 'normal' they are.

•Do not look back at the married man who is eyeing you up while his wife is punching him in the back; can evoke serious rage and awkward moments for the entire cabin.

•Do your make-up on the Tube; it appears everyone else does.

•Do realise that no one cares on the Tube. So, laugh at a joke on your phone or a funny moment in your book.

•Do bring hand sanitisers.

•Do not stand under the fans thinking you will get cool air. In fact it is circulating air and the breath of thousands, which will be filmed onto your skin and require facials for ten years to follow.

•Do accept that you will be flustered and sweaty; even the most glamorous of women will be hit.

•Do stock up with music that will calm you, or else Jay-Z so you can play it loud and fend off any thieves or perverts (back to the Kate Moss comment).

•Do learn a sentence in a new language to translate 'I don't speak English', preferably in Latin so that the probability is they won't speak it back. Case closed.

•Do wear stilettos, but also expect that they can get stuck and it can prove embarrassing to climb back on the reverse moving stairwell with one shoe and one bare foot to retrieve this.

•Do smile at the train driver.

•Do not laugh at the people who get stuck in the doors. One day it will be you.

•Do cry if you wish to: no one will even notice.

•Do not leave any bags; they will be taken off at the next stop.

•Do not wear anything too see-through or low cut, particularly hot pants. What goes down must go up and that applies to the escalators too.

•Do read the ads posted above; most are very humorous and underrated.

•Do look around to see a glimpse of top catwalk fashion tips, on your doorstep.

•Do expect to see mice on the tracks. Screaming will only group you in the mad list, so accept them.

•Do not expect any man to provide his seat for you; chivalry is disengaged underground.

•Do not accept someone rubbing your ass just because it is a tight space. Unless you want them to, of course.

•Do not fall asleep; you may wake up at Heathrow.

•Do not stand to the left of the stairs or you will be crushed, elderly inclusive.

Accept that you are in one of the most cosmopolitan, fast-paced, largest cities in the world, and Tubes are part of the experience. Acceptance is key, time will pass and it will get you there in the end.

Alternative modes of transport:

Bus: Most of the above applies to the bus, but prepare to be rained on, splashed and take longer in transit.

Walking/running: You can run, but when it comes to London you can't hide (from the crowds).

Cars: Ideal if you work off-peak hours, are not prone to traffic rage and generally have cash to flash.

Bike: This depends on the sexes:

Men: suitable for all men except those who wear Prada loafers. A no-go.

Women: Two types of women, A or B.

A.A woman who rides a bike.

B.A woman who doesn't.

*Decide on one of the above – simple.

Cabs: Fantastic if you are the owner of a Swiss bank account. Otherwise back to alternative options.

Helicopter: Same as above.

Motorbike or Piaggio Vespa: Can cover up your legs but still retain the speed of Titan and the dignity of a lady.

Always expect the unexpected; it is London, after all.

To Carlton: My transport guide is on sale and I will become a self-made millionaire based on a sincere philosophy: 'It will save you stress, money, time, shoes and maybe even your marriage. Purchase now. Credit cards accepted.' We shall be rich soon. X AStar

OMG, sounds fab - Especially since you still owe me rent, sista ;) See ya in class. CStar

With no job per se, Alanna has been resolved to go via Tube – for now at least.

Stepping out of the Underground, she smiles, thinking of all the ways that she would spend her fortune: on a house, car, Brendan, shopping, her own helicopter. She walks on with confidence that things will pick up sometime soon.

Chapter 6

Tweet: @CStar I wanna leave my
footprints on the sands of time.
Know there was something that,
and something that I left behind. @Beyonce

LUCE Studios, Convent Garden, London
Prior to her first audition, Alanna knew LUCE Studios was top-of-the-range, the best in London – by far. Luckily Christina, Alanna's aunt, being a broadway star has the chance to open up many doors for Alanna, including the door to the audition. Christina who arranged the casting was indefinitely 'the best aunt I could have asked for' would 'only have the best for my A'. She stood to her word. As did LUCE Studios. It truly lived up to its name 'Light' Studios, and even Christina was blown away by the light and sound technology when she arrived. With varying rooms of different sizes, combined with the prestige (they had access to a stage in Soho Theatre for their term performances), Alanna was determined to get accepted. It had high ceilings, mirrored walls, perfectly laid wooden sheets on the floor, spotlights, glass, mirrors, screens and laser spotlights for added effect when doing exams. It was remarkable.

She rose to the challenge, singing, dancing and acting along with the hundreds of Spanish, Italian, English and worldwide candidates who took part.

She knew her audition performance had to match up. Luckily, it did.

She was accepted and left Killarney to start in LUCE Studios four weeks later.

***

38

'Today we are here to watch clips of your first day in the studio. I want you to take the same song and re-create the performance.' Francesca speaks succinctly, strictly and always with purpose.

As Francesca watches each student move, Alanna vividly reminisces about day one when she'd made things clear: 'From now, you are a dancer. We are not here to talk and make friends. We are here to perform. We are here to become the best we can be. I want each of you to introduce yourself through dance. Show everyone where you are from through the music and moves you make. Alanna and Carlton, our scholarship students, shall go first.'

Alanna now recalls Francesca's harsh expression as she looked at them both. 'Come to the stage and pick a song from the list.'

Francesca, a top ballet dancer from Russia, believes that 'the only way to learn and be your best as a dancer is through discipline, consistency and hard work. You must decide between you both who shall go first,' she continued.

Carlton had kindly offered. The music sounded as he danced to R 'n' B music and moved his body in ways that seemed impossible for a man of his height and shape as the light followed him and the glitter he had painted over himself. He ended in a breakdance and gave everyone a hard act to follow. Alanna's performance of Irish dancing, mixed in with modern and some hip-hop, set an equally high standard.

One by one, each of the twenty-five students had showcased their culture though pirouettes, pumps, dives and even breakdancing. Alanna observed the standard and believed that each person was deserving of a place, herself included. Today they would do the same, yet far more advanced and competitive.

***

Alanna watching the clips, reflects back to her first day. From day one, it was clear from the expressions on faces and postures of her class that there were plenty of large personalities. All in all, Alanna had sensed only trouble. Little did they know Alanna had got this scholarship from Francesca and Nic, along with Carlton from NYC. Not only did this allow her access for free, but they provided accommodation and a small allowance. She had been told to not discuss this, as it would draw unnecessary competition.

As part of the rules, it was decided that none of the students were allowed to work during terms unless they had an agent set up before day one. Alanna, always one step ahead through her blogs, had tenaciously caught the attention of her agent Dennis. Nic, the Greek owner of the studio, having lived in LA for ten years, had heard of Dennis through friends. Even so, he had warned her: 'Keep your cards close to your chest'. She needs the money so badly, trust wasn't even on her cards.

***

On this first day and ever since, when they went for lunch Alanna remained quiet, accepting that she was not going to be friends with any of these people. They had fierce competition written all over their faces. As soon as she'd found out about Dennis, Francesca had also told everyone that Alanna had an agent, creating green-eyed monsters of the rest – all except Carlton, her new roommate, the eldest and clearly a team player. She decided it was better to keep her distance and do the best she could in school and with Dennis. It was work, after all, and she wasn't there to make friends.

Each day in LUCE, they arrived in studio for 6.30-7.00am and rehearsed sometimes until late into the night, whatever was necessary. Plus, Carlton and Alanna, as part of their scholarships, had to teach day students lessons in between their own. Some days they barely got to eat, and Alanna joked that with such short breaks it was either 'stuff or starve' in the city of London. 'Work hard or get eaten alive... by the starving ones!' Both laughed but wholeheartedly agreed.

'The Industry' was not for the faint-hearted.

***

Alanna now getting up to go stretch looks up to see Francesca walking very close to her

'I saw your blogs, nights out and 'fans'. You can do as you vish outside of class, but if I ever see it affect your work, you will be replaced. Without discussion. Don't forget you are a dancer, singer, artist – not a celebrity. Success is not about fame. Fame comes and goes. Talent remains. Keep working hard and you will be known for your talent,' Francesca says, sharply walking on with her perfect posture and ballet points noted at each step.

'We both know I can have both!' Alanna screams back. 'And I will,' she says with fearless determination as she moves back to the bar to stretch.

***

Once changed, the students enter into Studio, and Alanna sees Nic wave over to her.

'Kalimera!' he calls out, as per usual mingling with the young students, mainly ladies of course. From day one, with his Greek-Italian nature of 'Vapiano', he was notably laid back in comparison to Francesca, yet his dancing makes up for it. Either way, Francesca is the boss, and no matter what, Alanna knows she can't get on Francesca's bad side. Taking her words seriously, she moves into studio and begins her class.

'OK, ladies, enough talkin'. Let's get to work. One, two, three...please, get on the bar to stretch. Come along, ladies. Time to get to work.'

***

'Great work' they call out as she wipes her face with the towel and walking towards the changing room, she sees Aunt Christina's face pop up on her iPhone.

Immediately she answers.

'How are you getting on?' Christina asks.

'All great, can't complain,' Alanna responds, smiling.

'Good stuff. Very pleased. How's the bod? The training? The man? The men?'

'Good, great, fab, fun,' she laughs.

'You're doing great, darling. Oh, how I would love to be where you are. Pop into *Harrods* and enjoy a few cakes and purchase some shoes with me.'

'Sure, well, I am a student so I will only have tap water, hahaha,' Alanna jokes.

'Are you sure you're OK for money? It also kills me to hear you're in Earls Court. Very displeased you didn't take my loft. You must do once you leave this student life.'

'Look I'm happy as I am and don't need help,' Alanna assures her. 'You've done enough. I'm in the Academy and that's all that matters. Anyway, if you

42

want to help, I wish you and Mam would talk. I hate seeing you argue!' Alanna reacts.

'Alanna, we are different people. Anyway, we should meet soon. Lunch on me.

Oh I hear the door buzzing. It must be flowers. I ordered them for myself. I so deserve them.'

'Hahaha, yes, ye do. God, if we all had your confidence!' Alanna jokes.

'Darling, don't talk negative. Just focus on you and your greatness.'

'Will try. Sometimes I wonder how you and Mam are sisters.'

'Let's not go there, I feel the same. Anyway, must dash. Food has been served. Husband number three is very clingy. Chat soon, darling. Call if you need me for anything. Will sends his love.'

'Send my love back.'

'Ciao!' Christina calls out.

'Ciao…' Alanna responds.

Chapter 7

Tweet: @BStar 'And we'll never be royals
Let me be your ruler,
You can call me queen bee
And baby I'll rule, I'll rule, I'll rule, I'll rule
Let me live that fantasy' @Lorde

Great Portland Street, Sky Babe Station Studios, London

With music blaring in her iPod, Alanna runs, as fast as possible in heels, out of the Tube station and down Great Portland Street. She looks at her phone to ensure she is not late for this big casting.

Flustering up the street, she sees a call coming through and picks it up.

'How are ya?' she answers, assuming it is Dennis as she continues glancing up and down for the number of the studio door.

'Hi, Alanna, I was wondering if I could take you for a coffee or some lunch sometime soon?' a man announces loudly, with an obvious nervousness to his tone.

Realising it isn't Dennis or Carlton, she looks down to see if she recognises the number. 'Sorry, who's this?' Alanna responds, perplexed.

'Harry. It's Harry. Harry from *V-Bar*. Apologies – have I caught you at a bad moment?'

'Hi, Harry, no. Well, yes, I'm just running into a casting. Could I call ye back?' she says, gasping for air from her exertions.

'Of course. I was wondering if you'd like to do coffee and brunch tomorrow or sometime during the week? Love to meet you again face to face.'

'Sure, that would be great. Could we make it some afternoon next week as I have a busy weekend? I'll call ye after and we can make a plan.' As she speaks, her eyes look up and down anxiously trying locate the door to the studios.

'Wonderful, Alanna. Most wonderful. We shall meet around Sloane Square? I have a nice place in mind. Good luck in your casting. I am certain you will do great.'

'Thanks, Harry. Talk to ye later.' She hangs up smiling and facing the door to the casting.

***

Entering through the door, Alanna is anxious and knows she must contact her sidekick.

Alanna: Carlton, I have butterflies in my tummy. As Dennis points out, working with Sky will be the biggest moment in my career, and this replays over and over in my mind. Help me! x

She continues walking past the wooden doors.

'Welcome to Sky Babe Station. Take a seat and Andy will be with you shortly,' the dark-haired secretary says. She is wearing the shortest and tightest possible dress, which leaves little to the imagination. She struts back to her desk, as they say in Kerry, 'catwalk-style'.

Glancing around, Alanna can't help but notice that surrounding the desks are calendars and posters with glamour models – not dancers or presenters, at least. Before she has time to read Carlton's message and re-consider calling Dennis to check if she is in the right place, a loud scream comes from behind the partition.

'Hello, my darling, welcome! Welcome, I am Andy.' The new babe says while pointing to his chest. 'It's juzzt stho nice to meet you. Dennizth has told me everything about you.' He looks her up and down as he continues, 'Wow. You are much more beautiful in pertshon. Much more.'

'Thank you.' Andy was a handsome man, flamboyant and evidently gay, but for that reason she appreciated his compliments even more – at least, those that she could comprehend through his deep lisp and Russian accent.

Before having a chance to ask questions about where the Sky Studios were placed, her feet are moving behind his. Pacing through various small corridors and up some stairs, she receives a brief introduction from Andy.

'Well, we think you are gonna be the next BABE! You have such a classy look and that is something we are going for this year. The ratings prove the szlutty babes aren't getting as much full exposure as they uzed to. Szo, we think you have a hot but still very classy style. Dennizth called it a 'burlesque look', and we agree.'

At this point wondering what was going on, she does her best to listen intently, remembering that no matter what, everything would work out.

If all else fails, I have Carlton or the eight-inch heels down below.

***

'So, here we are.' Andy directs her into a room with a couch, two HDV cameras and a small crew. 'Alan and Karl!' he screams. 'Please meet Alanna! Our babe 2014.'

'Nice to meet you, Alanna,' reply the two short and stout men with unfathomable accents.

'She is such a babe. Look at her, guys. Babe, babe, and babe!' Andy announces to the room and anyone within a twenty-kilometre radius.

Having danced with many gay men and now living with one, this reminds her of a lesson Carlton taught her on their first night in London: 'Gays are the worst critics, sista. You wanna keep on their good side. If they love ya, they will LOVE ya, but if they hate ya... well, ya may as well forget it. Move cities if you have to!'

Andy continues, 'Szo, the plan here is I give you a szcript and you can take a few minutesz to prepare yourself. Then you can do a run-through in the outfit. Dennizth gave us your measurements. You have a fine pair, if I may say so,' he says while pointing to her chest as if he was pointing to a weather chart.

Outfit? Where are the big studios? Big lights? Crew?

'Oh, I'm gay, szo don't worry, and these two don't have a brain cell between them,' he whispers.

Just in case the purple fur pumps and Elton John glasses aren't obvious enough, thinks Alanna.

'Here is the script, and here is your attire.' As Andy leans over, he pulls hot pants and a shirt from the rack beside the couch. 'Voila.'

Her mouth drops in shock, and close to tears with amusement, Alanna flashes to a scene with the locals in Killarney if a photo of her in this outfit was ever released.

Headline: Local girl Alanna has been announced 'Babe 2014' as she shares herself with the world on live TV. The lady who went to London and caught the Mad Cow. Literally.

***

At this point the two men are gaping at her. Alanna, unsure whether to laugh or cry, decides to keep calm.

'Andy, before I prepare, can you please help me?'

'Of coursth, darling.'

'Dennis didn't tell me too much, so please can you show me exactly what it is that I have to do?'

'My pleasure,' he says as he lays down on the couch. Alanna is fixating on Andy's uncanny ability to reference female sexualities. Had she been a man, or rather a gay man, she may have been enjoying such a moment. Yet she is not.

Off Andy goes: 'Welcome to Babe Stzation. Tonight I am here to ansthwer all of your queztionz and make all of your dreamz come thru.' It was like she was sitting in on an intimate moment – as if he has waited for this moment his entire life. She considers whether he is living vicariously through his training babes! Deep down they all know that 'Andy is the biggest babe of all.'

As he moves his groin and touches his chest, he re-creates a semi-pornographic scene.

Other than music videos, Alanna has only once seen anything like this, when, as a child, she moved through the X-rated channels on TV by accident on holiday in Spain. Her mam had told her, 'Success is keeping ye're clothes on and getting attention for your voice or dancing or your intelligence. I tell ya, if ye or Sally ever look at this again, you'll be banned from dance and music classes. And if I ever hear you doing this stuff, ye'll be shot. Ye hear me!'

That had been enough to scare her. As a dancer she could perform, yet ever since that moment she had never encountered this kind of sexual exploitation again. To think she was now in a position to be one of those ladies: a doll for men and competition for loyal wives and girlfriends whose husbands wanted such quick-fix pleasures.

This is not talent.

She may not have been in the business for long, but in this studio she knows she is by far the toughest.

I would rather run in a chicken suit through Oxford Street than succumb to worldwide exploitation and shame on my family, or worse, the local parish.

***

Looking over again, Andy is making a reference to his groin. 'Yes, you are exciting me, you're a bad boy, my big bad boy...' he continues.

Alanna, always finding it difficult to hold back emotions, particularly laughter, interrupts his precious moment with a yelp. 'Ah! Oh, I am sorry, I truly am, but I have to leave.' Holding back the laughter, she adds, 'Ah, ye must be out of yer bleedin' mind. This is just not for me. There has been a big mix-up here. I gotta go.'

She darts out so fast that he has no time to react. However, a side-glance of his face tells her enough to know that she is now on his hated list.

Note to self: hated by gays. May have to consider relocating from London.

As fast as possible in her heels, looking left and right she finds the exit, passing many 'Babes in waiting' on her way out. In her usual sarcastic tone she shouts, 'Best of luck, ladies! you'll need it!'

Reaching Great Portland Street, she breaks down in laughter, mainly from shock.

***

Within a few moments, there's a call from Dennis.

'What have you just done, you stupid lady?'

Cutting him off, she bites back, 'Stupid? Stupid!? Babe Station, Dennis. Burlesque, bras on television. You need to cop on. I am a dancer and can sing and I have brains. What are ye like? I think you must be out of your mind! I am already strappin' a camera on me tits for ye so ye need to cool the jets. I mean it.

You try that once more and I am off your books. We both know I am better than that crap.'

She hangs up. Both of them in awe of her fearlessness, they know this is the beginning of her career. She's had to survive the Tube, crowds, lack of support in London and Sally – nothing was worse than Sally – but now she is ready for 'The Biz'.

She moves her curves down the street, past all of the paparazzi outside *BBC Radio,* with a strut and a newfound smile. They all stop and look at her, along with the men she passes.

She was a real babe in the making.

They know it.

Everyone knows it.

It is only a matter of time before the world knows it.

Chapter 8

Tweet: @Artur
You know I'm bad, I'm bad,
you know it @MichaelJackson

LUCE Studios, London

'OK. One, two, three… go!' Nic calls out in his Italian-Greek accent.

Alanna flips her body back across the floor and moves her hips, hands and mouth to hit each beat. In her tight Lycra leggings, neon runners, loose top and hair up, she tips her feet on the ground at the exact point her voice reaches her notes.

Everyone watches her, drawn to her passion. In the back of the room, the class watches and learns, though equally they critique.

'Hey, Art, I know she's my wife an' all, but don't you agree each day that sista is getting better and better?' Carlton whispers to Artur.

'I do agree,' Artur responds in his German accent. 'It is clear her skills are improving. I do agree, Carlton. I really do,' he smiles like a proud father while crossing his arms.

As she moves up and down, flipping her hips, her body comes to life. There is a light in her eyes and everyone can see it. As soon as the music stops, Carlton runs towards her 'Dang, sister, you is on fire!' he screams. 'You killin' that routine. Killin' it.' He high-fives her.

'Now it's your turn,' she says breathlessly.

'You better believe it. I gotta make my queens A and B proud.'

Laughing while placing a towel over her forehead, she joins her other classmates in the corner. Carlton does his breathing exercise, prayer to God and indicates, 'three, two, and one' to Nic to hit the music.

Single Ladies (Put A Ring On It) plays out across the studio. He moves his hips in sync with every moment, playing Beyoncé, yet with his own touches to add his *C Star* spark.

'Carlton sings every word with passion, doesn't he? Some man, I tell ya!' Alanna says to Art.

'Alanna, one could say you are looking right at the video. He gets every little movement.'

'Yes, he has it spot on.'

'What did you say?' says Artur.

'I mean he is very accurate,' Alanna clarifies.

Oh yes, very accurate' he agrees. 'I look forward to seeing you do your piece. You're a great dancer,' Alanna confirms.

'Oh, thank you, Alanna, Thank you so much.'

She smiles back while patting him on the head.

As soon as Carlton is done, he runs over to the other studio members as if he has just come off a stage. 'Thank you, thank you all!' he screams with his eyes closing, as if calling out to fans.

'Fair play to ye, man. Beyoncé would be signing you up sure if she saw ye there.'

'Aw, thanks. I know B is watchin' over me! Bless you, B,' Carlton gestures up to the sky.

'Artur, you're next,' Nic calls out.

'Sure.' Artur efficiently walks onto the floor and is ready to go. *Bad* by Michael Jackson plays in the background.

'He really nails that Michael Jackson move, I tell ya. For a white guy, he ain't half bad,' Carlton says in amazement.

'For a straight-laced white guy, ye mean!' They both laugh as Artur moonwalks to the sounds of the beat.

'So you gonna come out with me to the *G-A-Y Bar*?'
Carlton whispers.

'Hmm… not tonight. I want to get some writing done.'

'All partied out, it seems.'

'You could say that. Actually I have a casting in Essex.'

'What's with the late-night castings? WE-IRD.'

'I have to try it all. Dennis said it's a modelling thing.'

'That agent is all talk. Well, the guys will miss ya…'

'Send my love. Gonna get showered, so if I don't see ya, I'll see ya back home.'

'If you're lucky,' he winks to her.

'Only if you're not, I should say!' she says, and winks back.

***

Earls Court Tube Station, London
Stepping off the Tube, she looks through the crowds, everyone coming and going to a different place. Before having time to think, as if expecting a call, she picks up her phone.

'How are ya, Alanna? This is Jack, just callin' to say tanks a mill for yer advice. I have broken up with me bird. Well, now I am free, I'm wonderin' if ye…'

'Sorry, who is this? I think ye have the wrong number.' She holds the phone closer to her face as she couldn't hear him with the crowds.

'Jack, ye know from the 18 event,' he calls out.

'Ah yes, Jack… sure, great to hear from ye. Sorry to hear about yer break-up, but I'm sure it's for the best,' Alanna assures him.

'Ah yeah, you were right, Alanna. It had to be done and we are still best mates.'

'That's great,' she smiles as she walks through the crowds and up to her door. 'So, how's the old football going?'

'Deadly, bleedin' deadly. I've been scoring a few goals and making a few quid, putting Ireland on the map. Most importantly, Lani, doing me family proud,' he says.

'That's great. I'm delighted for ye! I really am.'

'Thanks. So how are you, Alanna? How's that music career coming along?'

'Ah sure, I'm tipping away. Nearly finished this course and then sure I'll head to the States for a bit.'

'The States? Which part?' he asks.

'LA. I have a TV show lined up…'

'Wow, Alanna, that's great. Ye're a bleedin' superstar! I'll have to get yer autograph. Only buzzin' off ye. Sure will yer family not miss ye, though? My ma is bleedin' crying with me being an hour away. She'd be on a bleedin' stretcher if I moved that far.'

'Ah sure, they'll live. I need to survive.'

'You're a tough one, Alanna.'

'Ah, I dunno. Anyway, speaking of mams, I better head off as my family are trying to call me. It was great talkin' to ye. Sure I'm delighted everything is going well for ye,' she insists.

'Ah thanks, Alanna. I was wondering if you'd like to come out with me soon. Or ye could come to one of me games in Manchester? Or in London? Then ye can come out meet me and the team after.'

'That sounds great. Thanks, Jack. Sure text me on the details and we can make a plan.'

'OK. Savage! 'Looking forward to seeing ye again,' he continues.

'Me too,' she responds.

'I'll be in touch with a plan. Talk te ye soon.'
'Talk soon.' She hangs up.

***

Alanna and Carlton's apartment, Earls Court, London
'Hi, Mam. Sorry I'm running late,' she says to Mairead who is dialing in from Skype.

On the other side of the screen she hears 'Hallo, hallo.' Bright, brown-haired, pretty and petite, Elizabeth pops up.

'Liz, what a ya doin' there?' Alanna questions.

'Well, I drove down to see Mairead and she said she was Skyping so I hung around. So great to see ya. I love our texts, but sure, I wanna hear all the gossip!'

'Ah, I miss ye so much, Liz. You're lookin' great!' How's yer family? John? Job?' Alanna asks.

'All great. They're all flying! The salon is doing great too,' Liz says, smiling back and looking pretty with perfectly applied make-up, as always.

'I'm delighted for ye. I can't wait to see ye all soon. Can't wait to see you. You would love it here, Liz.'

'I love London, Lani.'

'Sure we'll have to hit the markets and then the hot clubs!' Alanna suggests.

'Lani, we're all dying to see you in your show. Forget the clubs… and then I'll book yer flight and get ye back to Kerry. Ye can get a job teaching all the kids your stuff, then have ye're own. We all know sure Kerry is where you belong,' Liz insists.

As the call continues, the topic moves to the one Alanna was avoiding. 'You know Simon's sister is not looking good,' Mairead says.

Alanna goes silent trying to block the feelings that this evokes 'OK, that's very sad, but can we let it go?

Simon and I are not together anymore,' she reminds them.

'OK, chica, chill… So, tell us about this Carlton lad. He's so handsome. Is he mixed-raced, as they say in London?' Liz asks.

'He looks a bit Spanish but also he is dark. Very unusual but in a lovely way,' Mairead continues.

'Yes, ladies, his mam is from Brooklyn and his dad was black from South Africa, and he lived in NYC and LA so he is very interesting. He is very handsome, but he is not free to date. In fact he is in Mexico with someone else.'

'OK, Lani, that's a pity,' Liz says.

'Well sure, we'll see him at the show,' Mairead says excitedly.

'Give the lad a good feedin',' Liz says, laughing.

Alanna smiles. 'Once ye see him on stage it will all make sense,' she says, laughing.

***

Fewer than twenty minutes later, having covered talk of all female kinds including love, loafers in London and even the local priest, Alanna cuts in, 'Well, sorry to be rude, ladies, but I have to go. I have to get to a casting and I am already late.'

'Oh, of course, go. Best of luck and sure call us when ye get a chance.'

'I will buzz ye all over the next day or so,' she says.

'Same for ye, Liz. Best of luck with everything.'

Liz assures her, 'Sure I'm yer biggest fan on yer blogs, and the videos look bleedin'. I'll sort the flights and we will have a great time when I'm over for the show.'

'Jaysus, we'll be all glammed up!'

'Love ya, Lani.' Liz ends.

'Love to ye all.'

As the Skype call quits, tears surface and Alanna wipes them off her face. Looking around with despair, she leaves and moves, upset, out into the crowds.

As if she knew her thoughts, a text pops up:

Liz: Love ya always, like a sister.
Chin up love.
You'll be home soon.
Liz, x

***

Essex-to-London Train
Alanna, with tears in her eyes, looks out of the window and writes:

Dear Sally,

Houses passing all colours blue, blue as I feel each time I miss you,
Fast and slow emotions too.
Leaving them, all happy at home,
Sorrow comes first as my joy is overthrown.

Buildings of beauty and history fleeting,
Too busy I am to focus on.
Scared too if I turn in too far,
Will I cope when they find out my truth and see my sad scar?

Through streets and lanes the noises rhyme,

Yet, I move on glancing by every time.

Feeling alone and yet safe for now,

One day I will know to be happy here, to know how...

Yet, for now, it's twilight time and once again,
I sit in on this lone train, tears overflowing.
People, life and love moves by my side,
While I can't reach this tonight,
The journey, it begins, it is in sight.

xx

Chapter 9

Tweet: *@CStar I'm Beautiful @ Christina Aguilera*

Marks Bar, London
Alanna staggers out of *Marks Bar* leaning on her date Josh, trying to keep herself up.

'Do ye want to come back for a nightcap?' she says while stumbling.

'Damn, gurl, you can't cope with much drink. Let's get ye to bed,' he says.

'Sure, let's do it!

'Let's do it. Let's go to BED!'

Josh agrees, 'You are made for LA.'

Alanna, having no clue what that means, just screams hers and Carlton's song – 'Yay, I am so LA! Yay, yay, LA all night' – which, despite her remarkable voice, is annoying everyone, especially the cab driver, on the way home. So much so that he blares up the music in the hope of drowning out her screams.

***

Alanna and Carlton's apartment, Earls Court, London
Alanna, struggling to get the key into the door while Josh wraps his arms around her, looks surprised as she sees Carlton open it, looking upset.

'Mexico… you are in Mexico? What happened?' She hiccups while reaching out to hold Carlton's hand.

Josh looks around and follows them into the living room, now filled with take-away cartons, wine and Christina Aguilera's *Beautiful* blaring out on Wii Karaoke.

'Carlton, when did ye get back? How was Mexico? I missed you so much!' she says while she kisses him on the lips.

'What's with Aguilera?' Josh asks.

Josh makes an imprint on the couch, clearly not noticing the mess, as he watches his date kissing someone in front of him.

'Earlier today,' Carlton says quietly.

'Anyway, who is this?' Josh asks excitedly as they turn from kissing.

'Hello, more like, who are you?' Carlton bites back.

'Carlton, this is Josh. Josh, this is Carlton. Carlton is my roommate and dance partner, and Josh I met at an event.'

'Hi.'

'Hi.'

'Would you like a drink, lads?' Alanna offers, trying to pacify the tension growing between them.

'Sure, something strong, please,' Josh says.

'OK, I am going to switch this up first,' and she flicks to Aguilera's *Stronger*. 'That's more like it!' she screams.

As Alanna moves into the kitchen, which barely fits two people, she winks at Carlton to call him in. 'What's up? Where is Marcello?' she asks.

'He went home from the airport and never came with me. I tried to call him many times… Then, OMG, I went online to check his Facebook and Instagram and he was out, uploading photos with a hot Mexican guy we met on holidays. So, I decided to erase his number. And I did a rage page on him. Loser! Anyway, I got take-away, joined an online dating forum and lay in misery waiting for my wife to return. Oh, and I never told you but… worst of all...'

'What?' she asks.

'Well, he says he was taking me away to do our shoot and then we'd stay on in Mexico for a romantic trip. We did a great shoot. He paid for everything. I thought it was love. Well, I called around, as you do. My friend Ben, well, his friend's cousin's wife's best friend's sister's daughter told me he was in a relationship with another model. A lady. They have a kid.'

'Are ye fecking kidding me?' she screams in shock.

'He wouldn't let me take any photos... So I knew there was something up. I just ate my feelings down. Anything with carbohydrate, I ate.'

'What a fecking bastard! Jaysus, I've never heard the likes, Carlton. Ye must be hurt,' she hugs him. 'Ye poor lad.'

'I don't know what I feel, but I am such a FM!'

She looks at him with confusion.

'Fat mess.'

'Ah... Carlton, that's nearly worse than the guy who took you to Thailand and sent ye a spreadsheet of the costs,' she says, looking at the tears in his eyes, which quickly turn to laughter.

As she sees the tears streaming down his face now turn to tears of laughter. 'Anyway, you are so late! I was worrying about you! I have never seen you this drunk. You are a mess too,' he laughs while wiping away his tears.

She hugs him. 'Oh, I was playing around with your cameras. I kept one on. I may do reality TV one day, so I was testing it out,' he admits.

'Ye mad thing! I hope you turned it off...'

'We are both a mess, but at least we are not fecking tight-arse spreadsheet Sams,' she says, slurring.

'Hahaha, fo sho!'

'May I use the bathroom?' Josh calls out to Alanna, who was hugging Carlton in the kitchen.

61

'Sure, there are only three doors. Guess which one?' she jokes.

***

Back on the couch, Carlton asks curiously, 'Oh Lani, what's with his man-bag? Does he have PJs?'

'I don't know. I thought about that earlier, but I was too busy having fun so I let it go. If he wants, he can sleep on the couch or my wonderful Murphy bed.'

'What an offer you give a man!'

They both laugh together hysterically.

'He is pretty fine-ass. Is he a keeper?' Carlton asks.

'No, he drinks way too much and is not my type but it has been fun,' she hiccups. 'Oh, I kissed a girl, I didn't mean to but it was a dare. Either that or I had to take off my top. At least I could deny the kiss!'

'I am shocked, sista. What has gotten into you?' he says, smiling, seeing her struggle to keep her eyes open and stuffing Chinese in her mouth with chopsticks. 'I think you're just about ready for LA. One more year in "The Industry" and you'll be ready for New York.'

As she lays across him, forgetting the camera and her date, she stuffs her face with chocolate that has miraculously ended up in her hand. She tells him about the night, every detail of the dinner in *Gaucho*, how they met up with Josh's actor and model friends, and how they got invited to a VIP poker game. 'The rest is history,' she slurs.

***

'Where is that dude and what is he doin' in there? He has been in there for over twenty minutes,' Carlton wonders.

As if he can hear them, Josh calls out from the bedroom at that exact moment.

'Alanna, come here. I have something to show you!'

'That sounds creepy, Alanna. Sounds like something I would say. You stay here. I am going in to check on this.'

Struggling to keep her eyes open, Alanna falls back asleep on the couch.

'Surprise!' Josh screams out so loudly that it even startles Alanna as she jumps up but falls back down to rest. Seconds later she is disturbed by an even louder roar.

'Aaaahhhhh! LANI!' Carlton screams. 'Get your ass in here!'

She jumps up and fumbles over to Carlton's room, curious to see what is happening.

Most importantly, why is everyone disturbing my wonderful nap?

Entering Carlton's bedroom, her eyes open to see Josh naked apart from a bizarre PVC harness around his waist, a video camera set-up, whips, oils, candles and some other instruments that Alanna is too drunk or Catholic to understand.

'What the fuck?' She looks around, investigating the situation further, and repeats, 'What. The. Fuck. Is. this?'

'It was playtime. You say you like to have fun. I brought it with me so we could play. All three, if you want,' Josh says while lying with 'Alexander the Great' arrogance across Carlton's bed.

Carlton says, in a state of hysteria, 'OMG, this is the funniest thing I could ever imagine, particularly to Lani!'

Alanna, on the other hand, is in shock as the man spreads himself across the beautiful new John Lewis

Egyptian cotton sheets she'd given Carlton for his birthday.

Despite the fact that he was positively *edible,* it is crazy of him to assume she would hang him from the ceiling and literally eat him. Or vice versa.

Realising this wasn't going to end up in a fun trapeze event, Josh unstraps himself and starts to dress.

'What is this, Josh? I thought you were a normal guy. Just a fun, happy-go-lucky actor from LA?' Alanna asks.

'I *am* an actor. I am a *porn* actor. You never asked me what kind of acting. Plus, what's wrong with it?' Hugely defensive he continues to dress himself. 'I mean, you are the one who asked me out. We met speed-dating in a bar in London. What did you expect? That we would get married? And have babies? I mean, you kiss my best friend Sandy in front of a whole bar – she's a woman, remember – then you ask me back. Kiss this dude in front of me. Nice girls don't do this stuff. I thought you were up for it!' he shouts out sternly as he puts his shirt over his head.

***

Alanna is in shock. 'So, it's my fault for not dangling off a ceiling like a gimp with Mr Magician here? Oh and excuse me! Ye pervert! I kissed her for like five seconds, while you were carrying a box of yer *pervert* tools around in yer *pervert* bag all night. Then ye attack me for not letting ye hang me from the roof on our first date. Ye are nothing but a pervert.' She is slurring slightly as she speaks, but her strength is very clear in her tone.

'It is actually our second date, ma'am,' he cheekily remarks.

'Oh, ye have some nerve. Get your stuff and get out, ye bleedin' pervert!' Carlton holds her back from dragging him out by her hands.

'Yeah, yeah, get your things and get out or I am callin' the cops,' Carlton agrees, protectively pushing Alanna into the living room.

'I feel like killin' the prick!' she screams.

'Sista, I gotta warn ya, men are from Mars, women are from Venus. If you even sniff a look at a man, he thinks you want sex. The one-eyed snake takes over. You gotta be more careful. You ain't dealing with the farmers now. It's London and you could get your white ass taken out big time if you ain't more careful.'

Angry but half laughing, she pulls him onto the couch, knowing he is right. After a few minutes, they hear a shout from the other room, 'You're such a cock-tease!', followed by the front door slamming.

Looking at each other, they both laugh at the evening's events.

'Only us,' Alanna says,

'Only us,' Carlton affirms as they both fall asleep holding hands on the couch.

Chapter 10

Sketch Bar, London

Hours of training in the studio leave Alanna with only thirty minutes to prepare, yet, looking like a model in a blue dress and impressive heels with straps driving up her legs, she arrives at the infamous *Sketch Bar*. Dennis is suited up and tanned, with black hair and hazel eyes, standing beside the bouncer as he awaits her arrival. As usual, he skips her through the queue, double-kisses her and directs her inside.

'Nice dress,' he says as he looks her up and down and leads her into the gallery-like bar with a DJ in the corner. She is led in to meet a table of young, retro-looking men, all of whom fit in with the slick décor and tunes of the bar.

'This is Alanna,' says Dennis smugly, as if he is showing off a toy he has bought that day. 'This is Ed, Oliver and Example.' He points to the three guys sitting at the sleek table.

'Alright, Alanna,' says Example, the dark man with green eyes who looks really familiar.

'Nice to meet you,' says the skinnier blond guy, Oliver, with blue Ray Bans and matching jeans on.

Smiling and shaking hands, Alanna says 'Hi' to each one.

'All good with you, Alanna?' says the other guy Ed, with red hair and a normal build.

'Don't you know me, babe? I am sure you have read about me on Wikipedia,' says Oliver.

Although they look very familiar, as if she hass seen them on *YouTube* or something, she responds, 'No.'

Dennis, noticing this whispers in her ear, 'He's a stylist and knows some of the guys from *Made in Chelsea*. He may be your stylist one day, so keep him sweet.'

'*Made in What*? State of him, as if I give a shit... Let me work them out myself,' she says.

The guys clearly hearing her laugh, aside from Oliver who blushes, while the conversation moves on.

***

Leading Alanna to the bar, Dennis says, 'DJ Pronto is over from LA to do a set in a private party in Shoreditch, so we're going after this round.

'What would you like to drink?

'Mojito, please,' she says, while quickly glancing through the array of eclectic cocktails. As she looks up, she realises his eyes are staring at her.

'You look good, Alanna.

'Even better is that the show is good, Alanna. You're a pro. When this hits the stations and goes viral, you're going to be the next big thing,' Dennis announces.

'Sure, I've only done a few hours' filming... there's not enough footage for a show.'

'Oh yeah, sure, sure. You enjoy being Alanna, as you're going to be A Star very soon'. He looks intensely into her eyes. 'My A Star.'

'You know the camera is on; I will hold you to that,' she winks and seductively slides her curves back to the table, drink in hand.

***

They continue to talk music, clubs, pubs and London life. She makes small talk with each of the guys, cracking her self-deprecating Irish jokes, which go down a treat with her crowd of men.

'Ah!'

Alanna looks at Dennis. 'Shit, Dennis, what the feck? You're having a major nosebleed. Let me bring you to the toilet.'

'No, no, I'm fine.'

'You're clearly not, look. Let me help you. Excuse us, lads, my sister was a doctor and if…'

'No. Back off!' Dennis storms off out of the door.

'Don't ye ever speak to me like that, ye prick!' she whispers under her breath.

The conversation progresses without Dennis. They talk of music, and Alanna impresses them all with her knowledge.

At one point, 'Example' starts to beat-box, 'You need me…', and Alanna joins in:

This girl is on fire…
This girl is on fire…
This Irish girl ain't no liar,
She is the one who is gonna show you how it's done…
Getting to the top,
She ain't stopping until she is number one!

The guys' jaws drop. 'Sista, you sing like a home girl. There ain't no white girl in there,' Ed announces.

'Your voice is… Like it's a cross between Joss Stone, Amy Winehouse and Alicia Keys, with a unique slant of old school jazz. Off the charts!' Ed states.

'Back up. What the hell happened there?' Example says.

'You have some voice, Alanna. Wow, do you sing professionally?'

'Yes. I write too. And I'm a dancer, training in LUCE Studios,' she says, blushing.

They all high-five as if to say they have appreciated her talent. They start talking about their new album and recording together.

Dennis arriving back in sees the group of men smiling.

'Den, why didn't you tell us she could sing?'

For the first time ever seeing Dennis vulnerable, Alanna cuts in, 'He was saving it until now, weren't you, Dennis?'

'Yes, she's right,' he agrees.

As Alanna stands up, all eyes follow her. 'Anyway, boys, speaking of diamonds, I must go touch these diamond-encrusted toilets. Please excuse me.'

Stopping outside the door to check her phone, she overhears, 'Den, she's fitness! And her voice… it is off the mark. Where did you get her?'

'Smokin', man. Smokin' voice and looks,' Ed says.

'She is G Man!' Example adds.

'G?' Dennis asks.

'Gangsta man, if you 'G' you is da bomb' he assures him.

'Alanna Star indeed. We need her on the track,' the quiet dark-haired guy calls out.

'Hands off, boys. Leave her to the big man. She's mine. Any deals or dates come through me,' Dennis says defensively. 'She's mine…'

Alanna returns and ignores the quiet.

'Shall we head, lads? The night has, only begun!' she says as if she is on her own mission.

Chapter 11

Hoxton Square, Shoreditch, London
As they pull up in Hoxton Square, they move past a *Rocky*-like bodyguard wearing black shades and with a face that embodies a don't-fuck-with-me-or-you-will-die attitude. Enough to keep trouble at bay. Within seconds of hearing instructions in his head-set, the same man smiles, gesturing to let them in.

Moving up in the lift, they reach a glass-filled penthouse, filling up with music, food and people.

'Jaysus, what a remarkable view over London!' Alanna exclaims. At a further glance, she sees the DJ and many well-known models, musicians, actors and designers floating around, happily smiling. She looks down to her phone to dial Carlton's number.

'Wazzup, sista? I'm so bored, I miss you. I'm watching repeats of Kim and her sisters and *Made in Chelsea*. Where you at?' Carlton asks.

'Carlton, you know I have no idea what these shows are about. If you want to know, I am in a celeb party in Shoreditch. Ye gotta get down here.'

'CELEB!' he screams. 'Like A or Z?'

'I would say A to C,' she says.

'OMG, on my way. Got new leathers on a shoot. I am getting dressed as we speak.'

'Do come looking fierce. Don't bring a gay parade. Enough delicious men for you here,' she assures him.

'Literally speed-dialling cab now... can't breathe! Laters.' He hangs up.

Alanna quickly fires off a text:

57 Hoxton Square.
This place is very cool.
Get your fine ass here.
x A x

Within seconds she looks down.

Carlton: On the way.
Looking fierce.
Can't miss a celeb party
Love you.
You da bomb.
x C x

***

The people, music, food and view are all very chic. As a new performer, Alanna continues smiling to all as Dennis ushers her around the room. Meeting women and men of all shapes, sizes, races and styles, she realises how far away she is from home.

Not long after, but three glasses of champagne later, the DJ winks at her. Staying on her alcohol-fuelled wild streak, she moves straight towards him. Without stopping, she goes to kiss him on the lips and then moves to his cheek and whispers in his ear, 'You rock.'

As if nothing had happened, she turns around and moves to the dance floor, just as before. Yet, it was on the dance floor, her stage, that she truly stands out.

Everyone except for Dennis, who is crowding a group of blondes, are watching her moves, knowing that there is something magical about her. She is a true star.

'Alanna do you know a guy called Carlton?' Ed calls in her ear to ensure she hears over the music.

'Yes!'

'He is screaming at security.'

'Well, then let him in, for crying out loud!' she commands.

Going down in the lift, she hears huge screams of, 'Don't y'all know who I am? I am here with A Star. There she is, that's Alanna!' Carlton points her out…

She runs over to him. 'Oh, he is with me!' she gushes. 'Darling, mwah, mwah. So happy to see you!'

'Some people here clearly need to get *laid!*' he screams.

'Hahaha, OK, let's get upstairs.' She grabs his hand and leads the way. Turning around, she mouths 'Thanks' to the bouncer, who smiles back.

Best to keep enemies close in this business.

***

As always, Alanna and Carlton rock the dance floor, impressing everyone, but most of all enjoying themselves.

Speechless at Alanna's innate confidence, the DJ calls Dennis over. 'Who is that?'

'Alanna. Alanna Star, and she's mine. I mean, she's on my books. Irish singer and dancer. She has a show coming out. You gotta check her out before someone else does.'

'Let me see for myself… Attention, ladies and gentleman! For my last mix, tonight we are going to mix it up. I have new act, Alanna Star, who is going to join me. Come on over.' He beckons her over.

She walks over.

He plays a beat to sound her in, while everyone starts to cheer. 'Hit it.'

Alanna starts:

Ready or not, here I come,

You can't hide…

Then she moves into beatboxing:

Ready or not, here I come, I'm gonna find you,

Find you…

Now I'm in town, break it down, thinking of making a new sound.

You need me, man, I don't need you, at all.

You need me, man, I don't need you.

She hands back the mic, moves back to the dance floor and continues dancing. With everyone cheering her on, she smiles.

'You nailed it, sista! You nailed it!' Carlton calls out.

'Impressive. *She is G*! Finishing up here then heading to Shoreditch House. I want her there with me. Sort it out, man,' DJ Pronto requests.

Dennis walks over and whispers to Alanna, 'You and DJ Pronto are heading to a party in Shoreditch House soon.'

'Shoreditch House? Is that not some VIP place?' she says innocently.

'Yes. Keep doing what you're doing, lovely, and you'll be a member there and LuLus and anywhere you want soon.'

'Sure, Den, sure,' she responds and continues dancing.

Dennis moves into the bathroom and onto his phone. 'DJ Pronto and Irish presenter Alanna Star are on their way to Shoreditch House. They are the newest couple on the scene. Get your men there.' He cuts the call and waves to Mark and Alanna.

A few sets and shots later, DJ Pronto closes up and another girl with the cutest face, white hair and tattoos all over takes over his decks. Mark says a few *hellos,* but moves immediately over to Alanna. 'Let's go,' he says, taking her by the arm.

Like a pro, Alanna follows suit, walks out holding his hand without saying goodbye or asking anyone to join them.

***

Arriving at Shoreditch House via chauffeured car with DJ Pronto, laughing most of the five-minute journey, *This is fab. I have a feeling this is going to be a special night.*

Stepping outside of the car, she is unexpectedly met with twenty paparazzi snapping their lights, blinding her, along with loud screams.

'Alanna, Alanna! Look here, look here! And smile for the camera.'

'Good woman, Alanna. Keep smiling.'

'Over here, look here!'

Mark, proud of this moment, grabs her and wraps his hand around her curves as they both smile.

'A beautiful couple!' voices from the paparazzi crowd call out.

'Fierce!'

After a few moments, Mark announces, 'OK, lads, I think you've had enough. Myself and my lady need to go inside.'

'Pronto, man, what's her full name?'

'Alanna.'

'Alanna what?' they ask in unison in their cockney and international accents.

'Alanna Star. She's A Star.'

She turns back and smiles, blowing a kiss at one of the paps as if to prove to the world or herself that she is destined for this.

Travelling up in the wooden lifts, they move out an array of 'funky people' crowding around in huddles.

DJ Pronto introduces her to everyone.

Alanna is unimpressed by the people, but likes the décor. She walks towards the rooftop pool, drawn to the water. Without any time to talk, Mark watches as she throws off her shoes and bombs the pool like a child in a water park. In awe of her fearlessness, he laughs hysterically, especially at the screams from all the models and crowds of gay men she is splashing at the edge of the pool.

'Get over yourselves! It's a pool for swimming, not posing,' she reacts.

Looking at Mark with fearlessness, she exclaims, 'I love London!' as she disappears underneath the water, enticing him in.

***

Mark catches on and, in a cooler fashion, takes off his top, pants and Teds and joins her, entering the pool with a slick dive. Like a shark hunting his predator he approaches her, grabbing her from behind. Removing her dress, he throws it out onto the edge, leaving her bare apart from her sexy black lace underwear. His hands wrap around her like she is his gift. 'My Alanna Star,' he says, then whispers to her from behind, 'Sing for me again, sexy.'

Turning around to face him, she looks up into his blue eyes and she starts to sing a song she wrote about London. 'Wow!' His eyes look at her with amazement. 'You are talented. Let's join forces. Start it from the top.' She follows suit;

London, London, like you, I was so lost and yet now I am found. It's a place where the beat remains underground...'

Alanna cuts in with a rap, *'New York, London, Dublin, she's Alanna Star and Pronto, they're makin' it large...'* She smiles back, equally impressed with his beats.

The crowds hear this and start to look over to see what is happening. After the initial shock of having their loafers dampened, the crowd screams out loud when they realise who it is. 'Ah, it's him!' they holler out. Mark ignores them and kisses Alanna. As the roars increase, they hear nothing else. They are in their own moment, music playing, close together, ignoring the shrieks, kissing like lovers who have been separated and reunited, filled with passion and immediacy.

She is number one. He is number one. They are number one. They kiss again.

'All that matters is here and now,' she murmurs as she slips back underneath the water.

Chapter 12

Tweet: *@AStar Who knew that you'd be up here,*
Lookin' like you do I wanna take you away,
Let's escape into the music
Please don't stop the music @DJPronto
@JamieCullum

Alanna and Carlton's apartment, Earls Court, London
Carlton runs into Alanna's bedroom and screams loudly, 'OMG, darling, you are *fierce! Naked Alanna*, I didn't think you had it in you!'

'Are ye hyperventilating? Take a breath, Carlton.' It is as if he has so much to get out that he is finding it difficult to breathe, never mind speak.

'Is you, like, dating, like, this Pronto dude?' His Brooklyn accent and gay undertone is even stronger and louder when excited. He answers his own question, 'Like, that's so cool. My Alanna is on fire. Ah. You is now famous. Sista, you are a diva!'

Half asleep, Alanna looks up from under her covers. 'Morning, Carlton. What are you talking about?'

'Sista, you need to check the press! You is all over it! You now a star, Alanna Star. FYI. Lovin' the name. Lovin'. The. Name!' he repeats.

He places around six national newspapers and four well-known magazines on her bed.

'How did you get these so early?' she asks.

'Darling, it's 1pm, only early in Brooklyn,' he laughs. 'Must roll, agent calls, have a casting for some cheese ad. Dread! You're so lucky you got to miss this morning's class! Everyone was talking about you. Especially the green-eyed monsters like Nina, *hahaha*. Remember, your class is at like three to six, so get your naked ass ready, sista, or Fran will kill you!'

'My Lord, I have never in my life slept this late.'

'Later we will celebrate.'

Shit, shit, shit… naked! Oh, Mam will kill me.

'Alanna Star. My Alanna Star,' she hears him repeating over and over while moving out of her room smiling.

***

She picks up her phone to see Whats'App message from Jack:

Jack: Hey Alanna, ye mad cow!
Alanna: Who's this?
Jack: It's Jack! Saw ye in de papers. I didn't know ye knew DJ Pronto.
Alanna: Well, we just met.
Jack: Wow, doesn't seem that way.
Do ye want to get some food later?
Alanna: I'd love to go out!'
Well, mmm. Sure. I'll call ye after my class.
Jack: Sounds great darling.

As she looks down at her phone, she sees a text from Harry:

Not to sound too presumptuous, but are you in fact dating some DJ called Pronto while we are dating? Or are we actually dating?

I am a little perplexed as you keep cancelling. Clarification would be great. Look forward to meeting you tomorrow.

See you at the location, as per our call. Also, I would still much prefer to pick you up, so do please let me know your arrangements? I have a car available.

Regards. Harry

'Carlton! Carlton! I am *dying*.' Alanna is just realising what a hangover means for the first time. 'I want to crawl under the covers and hide away from light and day.'

'Sista, you have "The Fear", but you have a class of young vibrant dance students gunning for you, and no time or energy to waste. This job aint as easy as it looks. We gotta get up and look fine and back out. That's why so many crash and get help by their crew.' He winks.

'Give me some help!' she screams.

Alanna responds to Harry's message:

Sounds great, Harry. Let's talk face to face. I will come from studio so I'll meet you there. Thank you for the offer, though – too kind. See you soon.'

Close to signing off as Alanna Star, she leaves it at Alanna:

Regards, Alanna.

***

Alanna moves in and out of the shower in a flash, knowing she has to arrive on time at the studio. A few minutes later, she looks at her phone and sees a text from DJ Pronto.

DJ Pronto (Mark): Pronto here. Nice to meet you last night. You're A star. I wanna record something for the album before I hit the States.
Gonna hook it up with Dennis.
We will see ya in the studio soon.
Kiss, Mark.

This is followed immediately by a call from Dennis.

'Have you seen it? You and Pronto? The new couple! The Record! The Press. The Fans. Soon the money! You can thank me! Meet you later to talk business.'

He hangs up.

***

What does he mean. thank him? Thank my parents for my genes, my voice or my chest perhaps, what has Dennis got to do with anything?

Before she has time to consider any responses, Dennis, as if he could hear, calls again.

'*You* can thank *me*. I mean, I'm the star here....' she reminds him.

'Before you get all confident, you need to know I set it up. I set up the photographers. This is how it works. This is showbusiness, Alanna.'

'What do you mean, you set them up?' she responds defensively.

'Darling, Google Guerilla press. For now, don't worry your pretty little face, just get dressed as we're going for lunch to celebrate Alanna Star's first pap moment and record. Mark is booking a studio sometime this month for you to mix it up. He says you've written a tune about London and your voice is impressive. Lots of money involved.'

Alanna is speechless.

Since day one, Dennis has had a profound effect on Alanna. It is a hypnotic effect, and she is under his spell. When apart, she realises this control he has over her, but when they meet she moves under his spell again.

He is the only one who know hows desperately she needs money.

He is the only person who can push her buttons.

He is the best at it.

'Moving forward, looks-wise you are pretty-ish and you are lucky: curves are in. Yet we are getting you a stylist and the apartment situation has got to change. I have discussed it with the producers and to add to the show's glamour it has to be fab. It doesn't cut it to have a small one. From what I've seen on Skype, yours is Chav Central. You will move in the next week or two, so get your stuff together.'

'Look, Dennis, ye can really go fuck yerself, judging me! Who the hell are ye to judge me? I am sick of bein' broke. All you do is talk shite. So many people want to work with me and date me, and I am wasting my time talking shite back to ye. I am sick of it. I should go to X-Factor... Or get a real agent. I need money! I'm sick of all the feckin' castings and getting nowhere, borrowing off Carlton for rent. It's been a year now, and nothing has come up other than porn shoots and shite. There's a big show and I am startin' to think ye're really full of shite. I haven't got a penny to show for it other than people following me. Not even a few free outfits. I can barely eat or make my rent, and if it weren't for Carlton I'm sure I'd be out on the street. So sort out my cash and if ye don't ye can stick yer camera and yer contract.

'I have talent and I will make it on my own. I need to see cash soon or I'm out. Ye can start by getting me a place. Ye better know I won't go without Carlton so make sure there is a room for him too. Sort this out or I'm cutting this contract today.'

She cuts him off and screams out loud, 'Ahhhhhhhhh!'

***

Twenty minutes later, Dennis calls her back, this time with fear in his voice.

'So, Pronto is ready to record this month…'

They talk recordings, contracts, his fees and her future.

Finally I can call home with positive news.

'You now have a Soho House Global Membership. With the show itself, the producers love you but want to meet you in person. After some more footage we are heading to LA. After your trip to Ireland you can move to LA and sign this off. They are talking 250K, with 50K up-front. I will send some money to your parents and sort flights.' He says this as if reading out a shopping list, with no emotion given the significance of what he has just shared with her. 'See you in sixty minutes in Soho House. We have lots of plans to make.'

'This all sounds fantastic, Dennis. Unfortunately, I have classes to teach and it is agreed that I will never compromise my rehearsal times. Yet you'll be pleased to hear I have another date with Harry Mac tomorrow. I know you want me to film this too, so it's all lookin' good. Let's meet after this.' She knows how to get the reins of power back: studio is always the way out.

'Yes, sure,' he responds.

A silence follows… then…

'Moving forward, at all times with Harry you wear that camera. Ask as many questions about the family as possible and don't sleep with him. Well, not just yet. Anyway, I'll see you soon.'

'Sleep with him? Who do you think I…?' she reacts.

Midway through speaking, the phone cuts.

She looks at the phone, enraged. It's as if he is renting her out and she has no say.

***

Too tired to argue, she lets it go. She gazes through her window at the crowds entering Earls Court station, avoiding the droplets of rain. She feels part of London rush hour as each person dashes from one thing to the next with no time to breathe.

With so much happening in such a short space of time, she knows she has to slow it down otherwise her rehearsals will suffer. Like a drug, what is happening with Dennis may not be good for her, but she isn't ready or willing to let it go.

Brendan needs me.

Mam and Dad need me.

Be strong, Alanna.

She grabs her bags, knowing she needs him as much as he needs her – for now. Shutting the door behind her, she leaves her feelings behind and, like one of the crowd, she follows them at full pace.

Chapter 13

Tweet: *@AStar You don't know you're beautiful,*
If only you saw what I can see,
You'll understand why I want you so desperately,
You don't know you're beautiful
@One Direction

LUCE Studios, London

Alanna moves through another day in rehearsals. Each day is a strict routine of voice coaching, stretching, dancing and finalising her end of year performance.

Nic announces, 'Every casting director, press agent and peer will be here for our show. It will be the highlight of your career.'

For Alanna, the youngest person in the college and on scholarship, the pressure is on. Francesca stands as still as a statue, her sharp voice ringing out, 'The year has led up to this point. For most of you, your entire life has led to this point. Every movement, every note, every ounce of energy is needed. This performance will make or break or you. Some of you will go on to become big stars.'

Everyone looks at Alanna and Carlton as if this is inevitable.

'And some of you won't. This is showbusiness. So, start as you mean to finish. Shine, my little lamps! It is up to you how long your light lasts. Be smart. Be brave. But most of all, be a star.'

Alanna moves into the recording to prepare her jazz song;

My love, my soul, mmm, mmm, mmm…
My soul, mmm, mmm, mmm….
Oh baby, baby, baby,

Why can't you come home?
I need you in my arms,
It breaks my heart being all alone.
Mmm, mmm, mmm.

OK, let's take a break, Lani,' the voice coach Sam calls out.

As Alanna takes a drink, she looks at her phone and sees a text:

Jack: Just out of training,
I'll pick you up from studio.
See ya soon, darling
X

***

Alanna walking out of studio turns as she hears ' Damn, sista, you are getting finer day by day. You too damn hot to be alone! Let me walk ye out to the car,' Carlton demands.

Seeing paparazzi flashes, Alanna keeps her head down as she makes her way towards the Lamborghini with Jack inside. She feels anxious with this attention outside her studio, and it shows in the way she moves.

Carlton struts with his head high, acting like her bodyguard. 'Pleased to meet you. Treat her well. She's my queen,' he says to Jack.

'I promise.'

'Have fun, kids… don't be out too late.' He double-kisses to the air. 'And if you are, then call me to join, *hahaha*!' He turns around and struts back towards the studio in slow motion, ensuring the flashes are hitting him too.

***

Bluebird Café, King's Road, London

As Jack pulls his jeep up outside *Bluebird*, he looks over to Alanna. 'I thought we could go for some coffee with one of or two of the lads. They would really like to meet ye. Is that OK?'

'Sure, why not?' she smiles back.

Moving around the front of the car, he opens the door and helps her manoeuvre out of the jeep in her short dress and wedged heels.

'Are ye alright?' he asks, moving her hair off her face.

'Great, thanks,' she responds

Ignoring the photographers who flash their cameras in both of their faces, he leads her up the stairs and through the doors into the main café.

'Alright, man!' they immediately hear one of the guys screaming from a group sitting at a large table in the centre of the room.

Jack holds her hand and brings her towards the table of young guys.

***

'Alright, lads. This is Alanna.'

'Nice to meet you all,' she says with a smile, standing over them.

Jack continues and introduces them one by one. 'This is Spence, Ollie, Hugo, Francis and Joe.'

'Nice to meet you,' they all say in unison with posh London accents, mirroring the style of their smart shirts and trousers.

'We've heard a lot about you,' Spence remarks.

'Really?' she says in surprise, blushing the same colour as her red hair.

'Honestly, he never shuts up about you, but in fairness now we know why,' Spence states, looking her up and down.

Unsure of how to react to their comments, she looks at the floor.

'Please, sit down,' Jack says as he pulls out a chair for her. 'Darling, what do ya want to drink? Anything to eat?'

'Can I have a cappuccino, and whatever you're having to eat, I'll have.'

'OK, great. Lads, what do ye's want?' he offers.

'No, we are good, man. Trying to get through these,' Hugo says, pointing at beers and sandwiches filling the glass table.

'OK, back in a sec,' Jack says, moving towards the island to place his order.

'Well, you must trust him if you're letting him order for you,' Joe remarks.

'Who knows?

'You look familiar,' she says to the brown fluffy-haired guy, looking notably casual in comparison to the rest.

'Ollie. I met you out last week with Dennis and the guys. Don't you remember?' he says with a negative implication.

She smiles back, blushing, 'Sure, of course I do.'

'So, what's your story, Alanna? You're a singer? And a dancer? You've come out of nowhere and now you know everyone. *Très intéressant*,' he remarks sharply.

'Yes, well, clearly you know enough. Anymore about my story will cost ya! And you? What's your story? Maybe not so great if you know so much about mine?' she reminds him.

'Ouch, she's fiery. I like it. I'm a DJ and designer. I create and sell my designs by day, then at night I hit the decks. Non-stop work. It's a tough life,' Ollie says.

'Tough. Tough. *Hahaha*. Your family owns a share of every top company in London, if not the world; there's nothing tough about your life,' Joe argues.

Jack moves back from the bar to the seat beside her and puts his hand on her leg. 'I got ye a nice surprise. I think you'll like it,' he says confidently.

'Thanks,' she responds.

'So, A, the big question is: which football team do you support?'

'Manchester United,' she responds immediately.

'You have to say that, don't you?' one of the guys shouts out.

'No, I don't, sure. If I thought they were crap, sure, I wouldn't lie. Everyone including me knows that they are the best. I like being around the best,' she says, looking away from Jack.

At this point, all the guys wink and gesture to Jack, who is blushing and smiling over at her.

'Apart from Mr. Cool Decks, are ye's not all on Jack's team?' Alanna asks.

They all laugh loudly, which leaves her face showing confusion.

'No, no, we are not footballers. Other than getting corporate seats to the games, like yourself, we are more into music, dancing and partying. That's our sport,' Hugo confirms.

They all smile in agreement.

'So, if music is your thing, then who do you like? All the girl bands? Lady Gaga? Beyoncé? The Saturdays?' Francis asks.

'No, not really. Well, they are all great. What I love is jazz. Jazz, R 'n' B. Oh, and rapping, but jazz, R 'n' B and soul are my favourites.'

'Oh really? Jazz artists like who?' Spence asks inquisitively.

'Diana Ross, Frank Sinatra, Jamie Cullum, Stevie Wonder, Nina Simone, Melody Gardot... I could go on forever. I also like the new genre of free-styling like Macklemore, Nicky Minaj and Lily Allen. I've written some of that stuff into my lyrics too.'

'Gosh, a glamorous Irish lady who sings, dances, writes and also can free-style. Well, I must say you are an interesting one! Where did you get this one, Jack?' Spencer remarks.

'Her name is Alanna. Please stop giving her the third-degree, lads. She came here to chill out, not be grilled.'

Appreciating his support, she puts her hand on his leg then quickly moves it back, hoping that no one else notices.

***

After idle chat, the coffee and plates of sandwiches and desserts arrive, carefully laid on the table by the blonde waitress.

'Just for you darlin',' Jack says, handing her a plate with slices of four different cupcakes and finger sandwiches to choose from.

'Thanks so much,' she says, looking into his green eyes and back to her plate again, avoiding too much eye contact at all costs.

Over the next hour, while enjoying the treats, their conversation moves through sport, London life and the role shifts between men and women.

Jack's eyes remain on her throughout.

***

'The girls shall be here soon...'

'Speak of the devil. Here they are,' Ed points.

Three young ladies wave over – two blondes and a brunette with some paparazzi flashes going off behind them. Groomed to perfection, each makes their way towards the table.

Alanna smiles faintly while the girls sit down, making their mark on their men. 'This is Millie, Andie and Phoebe.'

'Nice to meet ye's,' Alanna says.

'Pleasure is ours,' Andie says.

They all double-kiss her and sit down.

For ten more minutes they talk about the number-one player of the football season, top fashion lines and must-visit events. Each minute Alanna watches Jack interacting with his friends. He notices her interest and Alanna, blushing, interrupts, 'Please excuse me. I need the ladies' room,' she says while jumping up and moving towards the bathroom.

'She is some woman.'

'Yes, she is, lads. If I ever get married, she'll be the lady.'

'Go on, Jack!' they all scream.

'We shall see,' Phoebe says as she places her hand on his leg.

Jack removing her hand joins as the entire bars' eyes follow Alanna's curves at every step as she walks away.

***

'Are ye having a good time?' he asks.

'Yes, I am. Your friends are fun,' she responds.

'I'm glad. Look, I thought… well, I was hoping… only if you wanted… well, that we could head out, just us, and catch up alone. Only if you want. You may have other plans, given it's Saturday night, but I thought I better ask,' he says nervously.

'That sounds great,' she says, smiling, with an expression showing it is the best news she has heard all day.

As she moves back towards the table to say goodbye, he quickly takes her hand. 'Let's leave the goodbyes. I have somewhere special I want to take you. We have to leave now if we want to make it.'

'OK, sure, let's go,' she says as he leads her towards the lift, holding her hand tight.

***

Open Air Cinema, Battersea Park
'This is class. Honestly, I never thought these places would be around still, especially in London,' she says.

'I'm glad it's just us,' he says, smiling. 'Do you know what I love most about you? You say it like it is. Everyone talks shit, yet you never do.'

'I have something to tell you: I'm doing a show. It's a secret camera show,' she says.

'Like the *Made in Chelsea* lads? Sure, the more cameras the better. Do ye have them at home, ye kinky lady…?' Seeing the fear in her face, he puts his arm around her.

'No, it's not like that. I am not sure how it's going to work out. The only person who knows is Carlton.'

'Are you safe, Alanna? Are you trying to tell me you need help?'

'I don't think so…' she says despondently.

'Well, if anyone is hurting ye, you tell me and I will sort it for ye. No one will ever hurt you, Alanna. When I'm around, nothing will harm you,' he says, giving her a hug. 'I am always here for you,' he adds, looking into her eyes.

'Thank you.'

He kisses her forehead protectively. 'I mean that. You are my queen.'

At that moment both see a series of flashes and notice the paparazzi beside them.

'Jaysus, those lads have too much time on their hands… lay back, darling. Chill. Don't let them ruin our night.'

***

'So, what's your story?' he asks.

'What do ye mean?' she reacts.

'Your family. Don't ye have brothers and sisters?'

'Yes, a sister and a brother. Well, I had a sister. We lost her.'

'What de ye mean, lost her?' he asks.

'She was killed. She was my twin.'

'Jaysus, love, that's awful. Ye poor thing. How long ago?'

'On our eighteenth birthday, so nearly two years ago.'

'Ah, Lani, ye poor thing. I can't believe ye had to deal with that,' he holds her tightly. 'So, what brought ye to London? Why did ye leave yer family? Didn't ye have a fella to take care of ye?'

'Well, I was with a guy, Simon, but I needed to get away and he stayed there.'

'What a bleedin' wimp leavin' ye to come here on yer own. Jaysus, if my da heard that, he'd bleedin' go mental.' He hugs her tightly. 'So, how do you take care of yerself? With money? Well, ye're not working so how do you get by?' he asks.

'Well, I'm doing a show… It's going to make it big.'

'That's a lot of pressure for ye. Look, Alanna, ye're never alone, so if ye need any help with anything you let me know, OK?'

'Will do…' she says while looking back at the movie.

'You are Irish so ye're better off dating me rather than some muppet, especially one that lets ye go,' he reminds her. 'I like ye, Alanna… Ye're really different. I never talk about this mushy stuff. Sure ye're bleedin' deadly on stage, but ye're a softie behind it all. A bit like meself.'

He looks back up to the movie while moving in closer to her.

'No reality TV cameras with me, OK? Jaysus, ye're probably wearing one now. God, Alanna, be careful or they'll be filmin' ye on the toilet and all. I'm sure ye're da would be scarlet.'

'*Hahaha*,' she laughs out loud. He moves in to kiss her.

'Ye know I get what I want,' he confirms, looking into her eyes. 'I never give up.'

'Really?'

'Yes, really. I play to win,' he says, looking deep into her eyes.

***

Passing through the crowds leaving the park.

'Do ye believe in soulmates? Like Plato the play?' Alanna asks.

'Plato – is he not dat Disney character?' he questions.

'Ye're such a laugh,' she says. 'Can't ye see the paps everywhere?'

'Fuck them.'

'Look, I don't know what ye want, but I only do dating.'

'I am training like a mad thing, so I need a proper lady. Someone like you. Can we hang out more and see how this goes?' he holds out his hand to see her reaction.

'Sure… why not?' she replies, taking his hand while driving out faster.

He stops the car in between all the flashes and kisses her. 'Ye're bleedin' deadly. My ma would love you, ye know that. Ye're a proper star. My star,' he says proudly, moving past the flashing lights.

Chapter 14

Tweet: @ AStar @ CStar Girl let me love you
And I will love you
Until you learn to love yourself @Neyo

Bread Boutique, Sloane Square, London
On the Tube and off the Tube, another casting, another rejection, another high, another low. Following another delay, another layer of people's sweat on Alanna's skin, another tighly wedged transit, another fast entrance and exit, eventually all blurring into one. Moving out of studio, leaving back-to-back classes of dancing, singing and piano, she makes her journey onward.

Running out onto Sloane Square, framed with stunning cafés and shops, Alanna agrees with the compliments people pay it. Meanwhile, she sees if everything is still in check. *No shoes lost on the Tube – check. Skirt adjustment – check.* She glances at her reflection in a shop window. *No make-up smudges – check.*

Looking up at the sign for *'Bread Boutique',* she rushes in through the crowded café. Her face looks all around, hearing various accents bouncing off the walls, and eventually she sees Harry.

Tall, dark and handsome with…

…With a feckin' major swollen face. Not as handsome as I remember. Better not drink any more. Foolish lady!

She sees him waving in her direction, and she moves over to him.

'Darling, you look beautiful,' he announces, while double-kissing her.

'Thank you.'

'Please take a seat,' he gestures at her to sit down on the leather couch opposite him. 'How was your day? More importantly, your weekend?'

'Today was hectic, lots of training and two castings. The weekend... well, it was fab, a lot going on...'

'So, I see you're dating DJ Pronto and hanging out in members' clubs. Gosh, that must be fun?' He cuts her off, showing a slight angst in his voice while scratching at his eyes. 'Also, driving around with footballers...' he adds with a rash appearing all over his face.

Alanna is unsure how to react. 'You should never ask a lady her secrets,' she says while blushing.

'Alanna, I am not one of these cool guys. I am running a company and I have huge responsibilities to my company and my family to keep my life grounded. If you want that lifestyle, that is fine, but if so then we are different people and best to not start this.'

She looks around, blushing and avoiding eye contact, then when she looks up she realises he can't see her through his swollen eyes. 'Are ye OK, Harry? You look a bit flushed!' she states.

'I'm fine. I have allergies. Anyway, I got the impression that you're a classy singer, and then I hear from friends that you're painted all over the Press. I mean, this is not a ladylike way to live,' he says matter-of-factly while struggling to open his eyes, which have now swollen up.

'Wow, Harry. Wowee. We just met, man. Cool the jets,' she reacts.

Despite the obvious look of pain, his face is serious, as if he is awaiting something profound.

'I really need some water. Yes, I think we could both do with water. Waitress, could we order some water?' she announces nervously, causing the people sitting next to them to look over.

Without hesitation Harry signals to a waiter to order the water, along with various breaded treats. 'Trust me, you will feel better when you eat. This place does the best cakes.'

'Thanks. Look, you're right. I don't normally party or drink, and no, I'm not feeling great today, Harry. So this talk is quite serious, even *too* serious, and I am not sure I am able to deal with it,' she says, fanning a tissue at her face, then moving on to his.

He waits quietly for her to elaborate.

'Since I was a kid, I have always been on such a strict diet and routine with school, rehearsals… Now I have freedom for the first time in my life, and although I may not be feeling great, I can't let anyone stop me having some fun. I don't need any more pressure on me.'

As the cakes and water arrive from the Vietnamese waitress, she comments, 'Plus, not to be rude, but I have just met ye, so I don't believe it is any of your business if I am.' While tucking into one cake after another, she continues, 'Anyway, I am not dating DJ Pronto.'

Well, not dating – just kissing in front of large crowds and maybe recording a live album, but not dating. Not yet, at least.

'Nor do I hang out in members' clubs.'

Yet, membership card may be in the post.

'And I am not with anyone else.'

Particularly not a DJ, nor a footballer. Given the circumstances, it is probably best not to mention these instances. Back to the carbohydrates!

'All I do know is that I am single and living in London and work really hard. If men like me, I should enjoy dating until I am settled. Until then, I will be free to date as I please. Do you disagree?'

'No, no, Alanna, I don't. Well, yes, I do. It's just…

well, I think… no, it's just I do like you.' His face is now moving from red to very pale. 'I know we met at the most bizarre and untraditional event, yet I am a true romantic. I understand that men will like you and the media will want to write about you, but I want this to be special. If I was with you, or any lady, I want to treat them better than they have ever have been treated. To make sure people respect them. Yet, I need to know that you want to be with just one man, and maybe one day that would be me. That's all.'

Smiling back, she kisses him on the cheek. 'Oh, you're so sweet.'

'Alanna, you must know you have this magical quality. You have hope in your eyes. You have talent, and I know that you need someone who can help you manage that.'

Nice thought, but how can ye even see out of those eyes?

'All I want is to be part of your dream,' he says, looking into her eyes.

'That is so sweet, Harry. I like you too. Equally, I want to be in your life and I assure you that we can be friends and see how that goes. I will always respect you, no matter what happens.'

His eyes glisten. 'Alanna, that is great news. Such great news and really all I wanted to hear,' he says, squinting his eyes, which are swelling up more and more.

***

As the date moves on, Harry pulls something out from under the table. 'I have brought you a small gift.' He hands her a Hermès bag. 'I know you have just moved, so it's a "welcome to London" gift. Only a small thought.'

She opens the impeccable bag to find another gift inside. Peeling open the beautifully crafted wrapping to find a Hermès scarf in the traditional colourful Hermès print, her eyes glisten.

If this is a just a small thought, I would love to see what a major thought would be!

'Harry, I don't know what to say. You are too kind.'

'Do you like it? Perhaps the colour is wrong? I have a gift receipt and you can exchange it if you want to. There is no problem, but I thought you didn't have a scarf and it's moving into winter so I don't wish for you to be cold.'

'Harry, thank you. You are so thoughtful. I will cherish it.' As she moves over, she kisses his cheek.

***

'Is it possible to have such a classy, decent and wonderful man seated opposite me?' she whispers.

I am so lucky.

'So how is your career?'

'It's a tough business, Harry. I'm doing all I can,' she assures him.

'Nothing can harm you, not while I'm around,' Harry says.

***

Meanwhile, Dennis is at home watching with jealousy, yet smiling happily.

'Enjoy the moment, darling, as very soon I will release your tapes and destroy your wonderful reputation. Then 'Alanna Star' will lose any chance of meeting men like Mark, Jack or Harry, and you will be mine – shamed and stuck out in LA far, far away from everyone you know,' Dennis says as he sits in silence, watching her with Harry.

***

Dear Sally,

I am now ignoring the fact that I am wearing a camera on all my dates. I felt as if it was real but also all a joke. As if I had been cast in Big Brother *and waiting for the directors to say 'cut', back to Killarney and reality. Within weeks I have been on more dates than the entire single male population in Killarney and perhaps the county of Kerry. I have also kissed the best Irish footballer, the biggest DJ around, been papped, soon to be getting a new apartment, flights to LA coming up, Soho House memberships, rooftop parties, pools and remarkable men – not losers – falling at my feet.*

Every time I think about this, I take a deep breath and realise I am one of the small percentile who love my job, meet nice men, am happy with my figure, love and eat food and have great family and friends.

Money isn't great but life is good, sister.

You're with me every bit of the way.

x

Chapter 15

Tweet: @CStar Music, I'm so in love with my music @JossStone

Polydor Studios, London

After a morning of vocal exams in class, Alanna feels more nervous than before, knowing that she is going from class into a recording studio.

Alanna's cab pulls up at Polydor Studios. She steps out wearing the 'coolest outfit fo sho', as Carlton assured her.

Her palms are wet and slightly shaking. She's never had this feeling before, other than during her casting to LUCE Studios.

Yet, this is different. She has so many questions: *What will it be like? When will my music be released? Many more.*

As soon as she enters, she is met by Dennis, who has his usual nonchalant smile and suit.

Moving straight into studio, Dennis does a brief meet-and-greet to the two sound engineers and a mixer.

'Do you have any more questions, or are you ready to go?' the burly man named Jim asks.

'Is DJ Pronto due to arrive soon?' she says with a face of confusion.

'Oh, he's already out in LA.'

'We are going to mix you over him, didn't you know that?' they ask with faces of confusion.

'Yes, she did. She's just overwhelmed with what's going on,' Dennis answers.

'Don't speak for me, Dennis. I am the one with the voice, after all. No, lads, I had no idea he wouldn't be here. It's my first track, so it's all new to me.'

'Oh, OK, Alanna. No worries. You're with a great team. We have produced many upcoming stars... not mentioning any names. You just go into studio and have fun. We will play Pronto's version and let you know if there is anything you need to change.'

'Sure... Thanks, guys.'

***

She walks into the recording booth.

After a few minutes of vocal warm-ups, they play a background beat and she begins singing. The music plays like a dance track, full of energy and beats.

'Three, two, one... go!' they call out.

Ready or not, here I come, you can't hide, gonna find you and make you want me...
Ready or not...

Following a few takes, the guys call 'cut'.

'Alanna, you're a natural at this. We will be finishing up in no time.' 'OK, let's try your other piece...'

I'm A, I rhyme, in London to have a good time,
With my crew, Pronto, me and you...
Finding you, finding me,
A new space perhaps an affinity.
For people meet at that special time,
I never thought I would find someone that is only mine.
Finding you, finding me,
Waves of deep insecurities.
And passions of a life craving inside,
Now I am letting this out, with no fear of losing my pride.

Finding you, finding me,
The fears are potent ones and truly see.
Yet, now it's the moment I must face,
Looking for love inside, our special space.
Finding you, means I found me and now,
Part of me I cannot still express.
What you mean to me is I can't speak without a
mess,
Yet, in word, in truth this is live, finding you, I found
me, you've set me free.

The dance music gets heavier while Pronto's rap comes in and the editors sync the two.

***

Smiling while walking out, she shakes hands with all of the crew.

'Here's my card,' says the producer. ' If you need anything let me know.'

'I hear you're coming out to LA with us?' Jim says.

'Yes, I hear I am too…' she replies.

'So, let's hang out over there. Sort out a few more tracks.'

'Sounds like a plan,' she says.

'See ya then Alanna, Star!' they call out.

'She's got a beautiful voice,

'Well done, you did great.' Dennis remarks.

'Wow, that's like the first time ever you've complimented me about my voice,' she says to Dennis.

'I say it when it's due. I'll grab you a cab, Alanna Star.' He dismisses her.

'So, where's the after-party?' she jokes as the cab pulls up.

'You get home and get rest. You will need it for what's ahead,' he says.

Driving away, she feels beyond excited, but also suspicious as there is no guarantee where this will go and that she will have any control over her music.

Dear Sally,

So, I am now officially a 'star'.

I can't make my bleedin' rent payments, but I'm a star.

I've reads Carlton's Cosmo *magazines and think I wrote down my checklist of a star.*

Love life:

My love life is booming, but a recent date was with a man who hung from the ceilings, so not sure how that will go down with the folks or status.

Oh, and let's not forget I did meet him speed-dating.

The other lads... well, I suppose I met them fair and square.

Love life: check.

Figure:

Thankfully with all the training, I keep in shape. Well, in the sense that at least I'm making the classes, but sure after all this Press they may have me out on the street.

Jaysus, I hope not.

Figure: check (for now).

Money:

With work, or lack of it, I haven't earned a bean. Ironically I'm bleedin' living off them.

I have done at least 50 castings and each one is worse than the last. Some include dance-off, cheese campaigns, or else strutting like a model (when was I ever a model?) and sure let's not forget Babe Station.

I feel like I'm a seal on show that has to jump through hoops. I thought this was professional.

Yet, I'm so desperate at this stage, if they say jump it will only be how high!

Work:

Track coming soon...

Agent:

I have an agent, but don't we all? I hear it's easier to get an agent than it is to get a date, and that's pretty easy in a city like London.

Check.

Fame:

Everyone back home thinks I've made it big, but sure I couldn't care less about this. Yet I am in all the papers and Liz says everyone in 'the village' is talking about me.

Check.

Overall health:

I haven't slept in days, other than the odd hour here and there. Sure, I've never drunk in my life and the last few weeks are a blur. I wouldn't even know where my head is from my arse.

As far as everyone knows I'm doing great and that's all they need to know.

Check.

Summary of Alanna Star:

So, being a star isn't what I thought it would be. I am broke, dating people but not even sure we're dating.

I am bleedin' dying to make it big, to help dad and mam and of course Brendan, to get me own place, to have a bit of cash to roam the shops and sure live it big.

At the moment, I have a camera strapped to my left boob. Can't go back to Killarney broke so I may have to go the typical route of being an escort to get these payments... wonder if I can call yer man in Babe Station back?

Oh, I dunno. Mam would kill me.

Star status: check!

More like, cheque please!

Miss you, sister,
Love ya
x

Chapter 16

Tweet: *@Jack @AStar I've got to see you again*
Just to live in a dream @NorahJones

Alanna and Carlton's apartment, Earls Court, London
In her bedroom changing from studio, Alanna answers
her phone.

'How are ya Lani, how are ye? So funny, ye keep
missing my calls then I miss yers. Anyway, me and de
lads have training for the big game but are goin' out
next week. I really would love to take ya out. Bring one
of your friends if ye want?'

'Oh, hey, all good with me. That sounds great, Jack.
I hope ye're kicking ass on the team. Sure, love to go
out. Why don't ye give me a call next week and I'll
come with a friend?'

'Great, Alanna. That's great.'

'Talk to ye soon.'

'OK, sure I'll probably see ya before.'

'Sure, keep in touch,' she says.

'Will do.

'Speak soon.'

Phone cuts.

Just then she looks down to see a text.

Dennis:
Well done in studio, everyone was impressed.
We will try and get this sold to the guys soon.
I will let you know as soon as we do.
Enjoy your evenings off.
You'll need the rest before the storm.
Talk soon.
D

***

Alanna walks out into the living room unsure of what to say, and looks to Carlton who is in his full-blown evening routine singing:

Sista, party people say ah it's a new day...
World is getting ready for a new day,
Celebrating, ah ha ha ha ha ha.

He screams out while doing his ritual to songs on the Wii.

His evening ritual consists of black coffee, and lots of it, along with a stretch or dance-off, and if Alanna is present he's like a moth to a flame. Her being the flame. Like a child craving attention, he dances around her, even on her, or over her at times, given the lack of space in their humble home.

She can't help but smile.

He has that talent to always make her smile.

He has the talent to always make everyone smile.

***

While sitting on the couch watching Carlton, she reads through *Evernote* diary on past entries about Carlton.

Dear Sally,

Until seeing him rehearse I had not seen many men, especially in Kerry, reach those positions, in public at least! Perhaps they were too fearful of what their mammiess, or worst of all daddies, would think.

From day one at LUCE, we all knew he had a gift. Not because he was older, more experienced, etc. He was just a star. It was only a matter of time before the world would agree.

Yet, there was something sad in his eyes that said otherwise.

I only hoped he could let it go.

Inside and outside studio he was magical. He had a special energy that was utterly unique – likeable, but not out to please anyone but himself. Being housed with someone, I wasn't sure how it would work out. I couldn't have been luckier. I feel like I've known him all my life.

Carlton knew about our family, but with his, he only scraped the surface. Yet, I knew enough to match up the pieces, that his father ran out on him and his sister, and there was some connection to drugs. Everyone and anyone would know due to the rage he showed at each movie or association to men who are that way inclined. Phrases such as, 'That mo fo', 'No, he didn't... oh, he just did', 'Hell, no, he should be locked up and have his ass whipped'. Along with his hatred for drugs, his icons were Diana Ross, Tina Turner, Britney all extremely talented women but all had suffered in love.

We both had pain from loss. As a result;

He loved too much.

I loved too little.

We had so much in common.

It was destined that we would be friends.

I wish you could have met him.

x

***

'What you looking at, sista? You is staring at me like a mad woman for like five whole minutes.'

'Sorry. I was writing and in a world of my own,' she responds.

'Anyway, I have something to tell you. Well, three things to tell you. You may need to sit down, Carlton… these are big,' she states.

'Sista, I can't take much more excitement today. I just has had my heart broken. Again. You know I can't help that I love too much. I am hooked. I am a love addict. You know the guys in studio say I need my own helpline – how dare they!' he shouts.

Sprawling across the couch like a princess, hand on his head, he looks at her to ensure she is focused on him. 'Continue…' he says.

Hearing a loud scream from behind the wall, he moves from his beautiful pose, turning into a man on a mission and starts the ritual banging of the sweeping brush on the loud neighbour's wall.'C.D. Sista. C. F. D. Take it from a ten to a two in there, you crazy biatch!' he screams. 'She is *so* loud. What a ho! I swear, she has more men than Madonna has eras.'

Screams come back to him through the wall.

'What you say, sista? You dirty biatch! You come in and say that to my face or else get back to work, you ho,' he reacts.

Taking a deep breath, he turns back to Alanna as if nothing had happened.

'Now, what you say, Alanna?' he says, sweetly.

'C.F.D.?' she asks curiously.

'Calm the Funk Down' he says smiling.

***

Alanna takes a deep breath, realising that this is a special moment – a crazy yet equally special moment. She finally feels at home, in London with Carlton and herself. Everything is in chaos but also part of city life.

'You've changed my life. If I'd stayed in Kerry, I never would have met you, Carlton, and all the guys like Harry, Dennis, DJ Pronto, Jack and many others. I never would have taught or learned dancing in a successful studio, never would have experienced this side to life. Never would have found a way to make money to help Brendan and my family.

'Everything is as it should be. Thank you for being part of this. Number one, I know you're suffering in love, but I just want to know if you wanted to have a diva dinner tonight, just us? I thought I could cook, we could watch Beyoncé's videos, choose our songs and prepare for the show.'

'Yes. Yes. I'd love it, Alanna! Let's pray that the diva next door calms down her act first.' He smiles and pulls her onto the couch to hug her.

***

'What's the second part?'

'I have recorded my first track with that guy Mark Pronto and his crew.'

'OMG, OMG, OMG! Sista, I can't believe it! Please can you sing for me?'

'We are covering a song I wrote with some of his beats.'

'OMG,' he says as he looks down at his phone. 'I am teary, can't talk, gotta text Momma and Mel to tell them about this.'

Meanwhile, she prepares her song and after a few moments he looks up to her.

'Are you OK? Are you sure you want to see me?' she says, while seductively picking up the mic from the Wii and setting the song ready to go.

'Yes, yes, yes!' he screams, like an adoring fan.

She hits play, spins around and transforms from Alanna to Alanna Star as she sings her song with a mini-rap midway, half-joking but mostly serious.

Her body and voice hit every note, dancing around the living room as if she was heading a show.

Speechless, Carlton responds, 'Sista, ye're fab in studio but you is holdin' back. Where did this voice come out of? You sing like a black woman. OMG! You are *fierce*! You are gonna be a star. Hell, what am I saying? You is already a star!' he laughs and high-fives her.

'Just like you, Carlton. We will both be stars,' she says, as if it is destined.

***

Over an hour later, Alanna walks from the adjoining room to bring in food that she has prepared for them. They take turns using the kitchen.

'Diva dinner, like a husband and wife,' she jokes. 'An Irish roast for my man is served,' she laughs at her traditional ways.

'Wow, this is amaze! Thanks, Alanna,' he says as he starts to shovel in his food.

Both eating on the couch – given the lack of dining facilities, it is their only option.

In between the sound of munching, the Beyoncé track list playing and the neighbour next door, he remembers, 'Oh, what is part three? You only told me two things. It can't get any better.'

'Oh yeah, remember that Irish footballer, Jack? He called. I have been asked out by the Manchester United football team on one of their big nights out. Well, I need someone to come along and thought you may want to. Only if you're not too busy?'

'Yes, yes, *yes*!' He jumps onto her, his glistening eyes suddenly lit up. 'Oh, Alanna, if you were a man I'd marry you now! Count me in.'

Just then, the neighbour hollers so loud that the vibrations of her voice and bed against their wall pass through– so much so that the couch shakes and shifts forward slightly. With nothing else to say, they both look to each other and erupt into hysterical laughter.

Chapter 17

Oblix, The Shard, London

'Thanks for dinner. The views are amazing!' she says as they move down in the lift, out of the restaurant, and to Harry's apartment

'You're most welcome, Alanna. Let's get a drink in mine and I have the car lined up for you straight after,' he assures her.

'Sounds great. I have some news,' Alanna says, looking excitedly at Harry. 'I didn't want to tell you, but I just recorded my first single. It was with Mark, DJ Pronto. That's why we were in the newspapers.'

'The guy you were naked with?'

'We weren't naked. It was just the Press exaggerating!' she explains. 'Anyway, it's being released in the next few weeks worldwide. So I will have to make a trip to LA in the new year to launch it. I am just a backing track beat, so nothing big, but still not bad for an Irish lass,' she says self-deprecatingly.

'Wow, Alanna, that's great news! I was wondering why you were so distant this week. You should have told me.'

'I was nervous. I only just told my parents too. My parents are both such talented musicians and some of my relatives too, so I didn't want any pressure.'

'Wow, tell me about your parents?' he asks.

'Mam and Dad met in a local band years back. He would play piano and she would sing. They did the odd gig around Ireland, some jazz and folk. They're both great dancers too – won some competitions back in their day. They fell in love through their love of music,' she says, smiling.

'It's innate then, Alanna. So lovely to hear that you're carrying on the flame,' he states.

'Yes, growing up, Sally and myself were in classes from a young age. I grew up having singsongs in the house. Music is in my blood. Dancing is my way of expressing it. I don't know what I'd do without it. Well, that and church,' she laughs in the sweetest way, reminding Harry of her innocence.

'I am so proud of you, Alanna. I am sure they are too. You're a wonderful, wonderful lady, don't you ever forget that. So, did you create a video for this song?'

'Yes, we worked with Polydor and they took some photos. As it's a dance song, they are going to do a 3D cartoon-like version,' she explains.

'That sounds exciting! Polydor are great, Alanna. I'm glad you worked with them.'

'Oh, do you know them?' she asks.

'Well, yes. I own them... well, shares and some other similar companies.'

'Oh! Oh, I didn't know that,' she says, in shock.

'I thought as much. You're the only woman who hasn't researched me, and you like me as I am. As I do for you. That is why you're here.'

'Thank you, Harry,' she says, blushing.

'One last thing, who is Sally?'

Building up a sweat, she reacts, 'Oh, she's... well, she's my best friend.'

'Oh, I hope I meet her one day.'

Alanna smiles back, nodding with a tear in her eye, doing her best to hold it together.

***

'Anyway, can I ask you to sing for me?'

'Well, only if you join in,' she says jokingly.

'Sure, let me get the music on.' He claps his hand and immediately jazz music comes on.

Moments later she lifts the lid of the small but rather grand piano taking up the top of the loft. She sits down and begins playing, starting with her own song.

Every note she strikes echoes with her voice and around the room. Closing her eyes, she sings from her heart until the end. Without asking she continues with a song she wrote for Sally. Tears welling up, he realises exactly what she means when people are natural musicians. She is one of them.

It is so intimate. She is destined to sing, to play, and to move. Until the end he watches in amazement. His lady bringing music to life in his home. It is a dream come true.

Walking over and saying nothing, he sits down on the chair beside her. 'Alanna, you're a star, you really are. I know we just met and it may sound strange but I feel like I've known you all my life. If I ever get married, it will be to you,' he says, and kisses her.

'Thanks. I don't know what to say.' She keeps kissing him passionately.

Pulling away, he looks at her as he moves a strand of her hair from her eyes. 'I love you, Alanna. I don't know how I can this early on, but I do.'

'I think I love you too,' she says immediately, with a face that looks surprised at the words coming out of her own mouth.

***

Next morning, Harry's apartment, The Shard, London
Alanna, peeping out of the cream-scented sheets, smiles at Harry, who is sitting at the end of the bed.

'Morning, darling,' he smiles back.

'Morning. What is that wonderful smell?'

'Lavender, your favourite. You mentioned it when we were at Sloane Square'

'Thank you, Harry. You're so sweet,' she states.

As she pulls back the sheets, she winks at him. 'Harry, where are my clothes?'

He laughs and points towards the satin black dress carefully placed on the bright red dress on the floor.

Sitting up, her red hair is met with a ray of light coming through the bright apartment, leading her to the view outside. 'Harry, the Shard is stunning. Everything here is stunning!'

His eyes focusing on her, he closes his black shirt and places a kiss on her forehead. '*You* are stunning.' His big arms wrap around her like another layer of blankets. As they kiss, she wraps her legs around him while he lifts her off the bed and onto the floor.

She looks around. 'Your house is stunning too. I love the lighting, the colours and the family photos, especially you and your father.'

I wonder what he was like.

'Thanks. He was a great man. I chose the art, but the rest I credit to a very talented designer. I'm just glad you like it.'

'It's fantastic. You're so talented, Harry. I love your modern, authentic style.'

'Speaking of style, let's not forget the view. I may be good, but I can't take credit for the city of London, *hahaha.*'

'*Hahaha, are ye sure, Harry?*'

Minutes later, while checking his iPhone, she is doing her best to slip away. Alanna carefully takes her *La Perla* bags into the bathroom.

'Take your time getting ready. I will head to the kitchen to prepare some food, so meet me there,' he explains.

'Sure, see you in five.'

'Ah, the state of me!' she screams out, seeing herself and the wreckage of her make-up in the mirror.

Within minutes she slips on her newly gifted underwear, including suspenders, some red lipstick, perfume and stiletto heels. 'Good to go,' she says, winking at herself in the mirror. 'OK, what will I wear to disguise it? A shirt, another shirt? Which colour will I choose?' she says looking through Harry's wardrobe.

Choosing black, she leaves the top buttons undone and moves down the spiral glass staircase. Step by step moving closer towards the kitchen, she smiles to the blaring sound of Marvin Gaye's *Let's Get It On.*

'Oh, Marvin is on. Harry, you know my plan. *Let's get it on... Let's get it on*,' she sings, reaching the kitchen and moving towards him while dancing slowly.

'Alanna, wow, wow, oh my lord! I have something to…'

'Harry, do you need any help?' a woman calls out. 'Well, hello.'

Turning around in shock, Alanna sees a *Chanel*-suited, middle-aged woman with blonde hair looking back at her with a smirk.

'Ah! Who the feck this that?'

As fast as possible in her heels she makes her way towards the bathroom and locks the door.

'Shite, shite, shite!!' Alanna calls out.

'Alanna, please come back. This is my mother. Mother, this is… or should I say, that was Alanna.'

'What a delightful young lady she is!' responds his mother sarcastically.

'Crap, crap, crap!' Alanna screams while staring in the mirror with her shirt still open.

'Alanna, please come out.'

'Yes, please do!' the woman calls out.

After a few minutes she looks down to see if her shirt buttons were closed and moves into the kitchen with her head high. 'Pleased to meet ye, Mrs Mac. What a delight it has been. Please excuse me while I go upstairs and get myself dressed,' she states.

'Yes, that's a good idea. Eggs are nearly ready. We don't want them to burn,' Mrs Mac assures her as she moves up the stairs.

Chapter 18

Tweet: *@DJPronto @AStar releases their single 'London Life'. Check it out on YouTube. Spotify, 8 Tracks etc…*

King's Road to LUCE Studios, London

Alanna and Carlton, running late, make their way down the stairs onto the Underground. Carlton rushes on the left side with his long legs, double-jumping the steps. As per usual, Alanna has every man looking as she Superwoman-dives the steps while retaining the air of a queen.

As soon as they get on to a packed train, they are wedged together. Alanna looks around to see who Carlton is screaming at.

'Who you looking at?' Carlton shouts over at a gang of guys. 'Who you looking at? Is it because I is black?'

'They better not say anything for their sake,' Alanna whispers with a smile, knowing only too well how Carlton reacts to someone arguing back with him.

'They look trash. Could be mistaken for X Factor auditionees. Look over, look over, sista.'

They look together, back and forth.

One of the guys speaks up, 'No, it's because she is fitness. I saw her in a magazine with DJ Pronto and some other celebs, so I'm wondering if I can get her autograph?'

'Get over yourself, you arsehole,' his friend screams.

Alanna protectively screams, 'Pronto and the guys may be my men, but this guy is my lover!' She grabs and kisses Carlton, pulling him close as they embrace passionately in front of the entire Tube.

They hear screams from the crowd.

'Get in there, lad!'

'Good man!' they hear the Scousers shout in their northern accents.

Each of the guys hops off at the next station and winks at Carlton in a man-to-man code translated as 'legend', leaving Carlton blushing.

Whilst Alanna realises what she has just done, she thinks to herself, *Carlton is gay, so technically it doesn't count. No paps around, so best not to tell Harry, Jack or anyone either way.*

***

Arriving in studio, everyone looks exhausted from the endless rehearsing, yet as soon as the music comes on everything else is forgotten. She explains to Carlton 'Teaching my younger students is always a pleasure – seeing them thrive is my favourite part. Now, I understand why my parents love it.'

'Today, everyone, we will continue preparing your piece for your show.'

She yawns, appearing more tired than usual, but she continues, 'OK, everyone, it's time for a break. Please go take some air and a snack and come back here at 2.15,' she announces to her students. She can tell by their flushing faces that they are equally relieved to hear the word 'break'.

***

Looking around to see if anyone is looking, she is drawn to the grand piano placed beside the window. The intricacy with which she touches her fingers on the keys brings her music to life. Adding her voice to the tune is natural to her, so she lets go and sings freely. The joy of sharing her passion is clear with the light in her eyes. Once she is performing, a dormant light comes on, and it shines brightly.

Looking up, she sees the little girl Lisa, with dark hair and green eyes, staring back.

'Come here, lovely. Come sit with me.'

'Alanna, have you always wanted to be in the Industry?'

'Not sure about that, but since I was five years old I listened to the notes of my father on the piano, and it was so natural for me to repeat and understand. In the years to follow, teachers couldn't understand how I could play instruments without any training, other than Dad and Mam in the house. I can be shy, like you.'

Lisa looks surprisingly at her.

'Yet, when I give in, I let go, and this fearless streak takes over. Performance requires surrendering and trust. We will work on that with you, hun. You need to have more faith in your ability. You're the best here, yet you need the faith.'

'Thanks, Alanna. I will work hard for you,' Lisa says, hugging her.

***

'OK, girls, I want you to tell me how music affects you. I will start. Music makes me feel alive. Free. Awake. Life without music is so one-dimensional, so fake. So disengaged from the truth, my truth. Dancing for the love of the movement of music was something that I have an ongoing love affair with. Now, I want you to share your inspiration. Lisa you start,' she says smiling at her.

Meanwhile, Alanna looks out of the window and sees families walking past.

All I know for certain is that I have here and now.

I have no time to complain. Mam and everyone need me to keep my head down and get paid, get through this course, all of which will open so many doors.

I need to support myself and them long-term. Creating my first record is a dream, but thinking about anything further along than a backing track to a record... that is foolish.

***

Alanna does not realise that her phone is ringing off the hook. Pronto's famous LA Industry friends have Tweeted it, along with bloggers and already it has gone viral. Everyone is calling to congratulate as her, and DJ Pronto's single. So far, just got one of the highest hits this week on *YouTube*, *Spotify* and *iTunes*. While playing the piano, she joins the routine of her students. For the remainder of the class, oblivious to everything outside of the studio walls, she is an Industry success. She is already living the dream and doesn't even know.

On the other side of the wall, Francesca hears the music coming from the studio.

'Did you hear her song on the radio?' Nic asks.

'I know that we have made the right choice with Alanna. She is the most talented in her class, but like all stars they burn out. That's the last thing I want for her.'

'But, Nic, I want Alanna to know how to be professional and sustain a career, not just a quick-fix dance track.'

Did you see the video the used with the track?'

'Yes, it's a bit slutty, but that's what sells these days, I just hope she is ok' Nic reminds her where his interests are.

'Nic, most artists rise and fall, with no control of which way it goes. Alanna is determined to be famous. So, we must let her go. She will have to learn that for herself,' Francesca reminds him.

Chapter 19

Tweet: *@CStar Is your love strong enough for what's to come? @LianaLaHavas*

Alanna and Carlton's apartment, London

Francesca announces, 'Today Nina has been removed from LUCE Studios. As per rumours, it is on the basis of being found with illegal substances on her person. Nina remains in hospital under critical observation, but thankfully is expected to regain full health.'

Moving around the room, all of the class watch attentively, and she continues.

'With respect to her and her family we will not be discussing this with anyone outside the studio. Particularly on blogs. Or in the Press.' Francesca looks directly at Alanna and Carlton. 'If this is not clear enough, if this gets out of these four walls, the person or persons involved will also be removed from the college with no explanation. Do I make myself clear?'

'Yes,' says everyone in unison.

'Take it as a lesson that drugs are not the answer. Go home and get some rest. We have a busy few weeks ahead,' she tells them.

***

Alanna arrives home from studio, upset to hear that one of the girls is in hospital. Carlton calls members of the class as rumours go back and forth.

'What are ye like? The poor girl isn't well!'

'She didn't say we couldn't follow rumours within the class,' he justifies.

'Everyone knows that she had been taking lots of sleeping tablets and God knows what else.'

'Poor Nina, I hope she doesn't die!' Carlton calls out, lying across the burnt brown sofa and rubbing his eyes.

Meanwhile, Alanna answers a call to Dennis on loudspeaker. 'So let's meet. We have lots to wrap up,' he says.

'No, I'm too upset and tired. One of the girls in studio is unwell,' she replies.

'You can't afford to be tired. So, if you're too tired I can sort you out with something that would pick up your pace.'

'You're an idiot, Dennis.'

'What did you call me?'

She cuts him off.

Carlton, overhearing, screams at her, 'What the funk was he talking about "something that would pick up your pace"? Are you taking drugs like Nina? OMG. You are in on it?' he says.

'Do ye think I would be getting caught up in pills or cocaine or MDMA or NA or whatever Dennis calls that crap? Sure, I can't even say the feckin' words, so how would I ever be able to order dem for myself?' she jokes, holding Carlton's hand. As he sobs into her chest, she realises how upset he is. 'Don't worry. She will be OK. Look, Carlton... I... I mean we... we are good people and we don't need those bleedin' pills, powders or potions to be stars. We will rise to the top on talent alone and prove them all wrong.'

***

Alanna barely touches her dinner, prompting Carlton to say anxiously, 'Sista, your face is so pale and you look so sad. Your record is doing amaze-balls. We gotta be positive.'

'It's just the lack of sleep from rehearsals, castings and stuff... I need to lie down.'

'Sure, honey. Do you need anything? Anything legal, I mean?'

'No, Carlton, just sleep.'

She kisses him and moves into her room. Her eyes close as she falls asleep while hitting the pillow, but waking up shortly after, she has tears in her eyes.

'Simon,' she says out loud.

Suddenly she grabs her iPad and reads over her Evernote diary entries from the last two years;

Email; SimonF@gmail.com
Dear Alanna,

I am writing to you to tell you that I love you with all my heart. I know you feel the same but I feel like we are drifting apart. Since Sally died I feel like you're running away from your feelings. Since when did you want to be a big star in London?

Or the world?

We need you back here.

I need you.

Love you always.

Simon

Email; AStar@gmail.com
Dear Simon,

It isn't that simple. Things have changed. I have responsibilities to my family, to work and take care of them. Brendan's school and care cost them a lot and so I need to be here now. I love you, but I think you should forget about me right now. It hurts us both too much.

Love, Alanna

Dear Sally,

I miss everyone a lot.

Yet how could they fit in to this life?

Simon was too real for this. I knew I had to do this alone. I had to get money to support them or else move back and that wasn't an option for now. I loved them all and him so much. I knew that Simon was the one, but you don't always get that in life. I imagined the white dress, walking up the aisle to meet him. I knew he would never hurt me. He didn't care what I did or how I looked, and he loved me unconditionally.

But family first, sister.

Love you.

X

***

Hours later she escapes from her room and announces to Carlton, 'Listen, I have something to tell you.'

He moves his head up on the couch, and Alanna notices the tissues and wrappers all around him.

'I'm moving out. In fact, I'm moving out in the next week. Dennis has arranged a new place in King's Road. I know it's short notice, but…'

Cutting her off, Carlton reacts, 'Gurlfriend, the only ones that make it big are the ones that do it and keep it real. They are the ones who love the man who loved them before they were R and F.'

Her eyes look up in confusion.

'*Rich and famous*!' he hollers. 'Anyway, I can't believe you're abandoning me like this! I mean, who am I gonna live with? Playboy Bunny next door? Or worst of all, alone? *Alone…*'

He continues to scream 'Alone', crying into a pillow. 'I am all alone,' sobs into the pillow.

***

Ignoring his attempt to throw a fit, she lets him squirm before revealing, 'First of all, you barely spoke two words to Nina. She wasn't in your classes, so quit that drama. The poor girl is in hospital, so the least you can do is show her some respect.'

He looks up, his face embarrassingly red. 'OK, Mariah, go easy on me,' he says.

'C.D... C.F.D Carlton, I haven't finished yet! Dennis has agreed to allow you to move with me. It was my only condition for moving. I owe you so much rent, it's the least I can do. The only thing I ask is that you join me on a trip to Ireland. It won't be until this Christmas, and it's my first time back since... well, I just need your help and support.'

Looking up, she sees his face light up like a child receiving gifts on Christmas Day. Seeing him so happy makes her heart melt.

'You're the best friend I have ever had,' he says, hugging her tightly.

A wave of emotions comes over her, along with an unexpected flood of tears. *My sadness is uncontrollable. My pain is uncontrollable. My tears are uncontrollable.*

'Yes, yes, yes to all. Oh, Alanna, you're the best! You really are!' He hugs again, and as he pulls back he sees her implode into tears as she falls onto the couch. 'Queen A, no need to get so excited. You need to calm down.'

Knowing all she has been going through but not nearly enough of what she has already gone through in the past, he offers support. 'Darling, let it all out. You're just T and E – tired and emotional. You ain't used to drinking, the late nights, the highs and lows.'

With that he suddenly jumps up. 'The best way to deal with that is to take another drink... Martini moment, fo sho!' He runs to the kitchen and prepares their drinks.

***

All evening Carlton chats with her on in the kitchen, cooking dinner. He talks about their new place and the money she'll make from her new record and men, but none of it matters to her right now.

A few minutes later she receives texts;

Jack: Hi Lani, I tried to call. Carlton says you're upset. Please call me back. Want to help xxx

Harry: Alanna, I wanted you to know that I love you and am always here for you.

Carlton told me about Nina... he also said something about Sally.

I've lost my father and know what it's like to lose someone close.

Time is a healer, but for now please let me take care of you.

You can trust me.

Don't push me away.

Kiss, Harry

***

For the remainder of the night, she sits with Carlton as he drinks for hours, planning their colour schemes, party themes and wonderful times ahead. Yet her mind flits in and out of reality, watching him move around magazine cut-outs, internet images and drawings of their home.

'So, tell me about Sally... your momma told me it's your birthday and her anniversary soon.'

'Yes, it is. My birthday is a day I never like much,' she says. 'Like you, I'd rather not talk about Sally and the past I left behind. Now let's get to bed as we have to get packing soon.'

Holding hands, they both creep into Carlton's bed.

She closes her eyes, laying on his chest, but can't sleep. She does what is natural to her: she writes.

Dear Sally,

I don't know how everyone knows about you?

I feel as if I can't breathe; it's like a hot air balloon has been afloat and after many years, the air has been released. It was trapped in my chest and now the tears and pain are coming. I don't know how to cope.

Is this making it big?

Scholarship?

Agent?

Record contract?

Best friends?

Perfect boyfriend?

New apartment soon?

Family and Brendan finally secure?

Why didn't I feel it?

You'd know the answer.

You always know the answer.

I have to accept that the sadness is just a fleeting moment. As I'm trained to do, tomorrow I will get up, smile and get back in the show.

Love you.

Chapter 20

Tweet: *@AStar I can't get no sleep @Faithless*

Killarney, Sally and Alanna's 18TH Birthday

'Happy eighteenth birthday, princess,' Simon announces. 'This time next year we will both be in Dublin working and one step closer to our big day.' He closes his eyes. 'I can see it now. You will be the most beautiful wife.'

'I know you more than I know myself.' Alanna gazes into his blue eyes. She pushes a piece of his soft black hair out of his eye to see him more clearly. Slowly he takes her hand and puts it on his heart. 'This is yours. You are mine,' he smiles proudly.

Lying on a blanket, wrapped up tightly amidst the cold air, pink hue was shining around them.

Nothing but love shines out of their eyes.

They both lay back by Muckross Lake, Killarney, their favourite place, in complete silence other than the kiss he places on her forehead. *Forever my heart is yours*, she thinks.

***

They lay there for hours until a chill shows by the goosebumps on her skin.

'Darlin', you're cold. Let's head back towards the house before Sally and Michael get in,' Simon insists, looking into her eyes.

'Whatever you say,' she says, gazing back.

He arises, his six-foot shadow on her pale skin as he reaches down to pick her up. They kiss slowly for a moment and walk hand in hand back to her house in peace.

Five minutes later the peace turns into panic.
A panic that changes their lives forever.

***

Hearing the screams of her mother from afar, they both run to see what is happening. Reaching the house, they see Mam laying on the floor of the hallway in a heap. Running in to see what is happening, her father explains to her, 'Sally has left us.

'Left us? Sure, she is just going to Dublin to get our place for college... She'll be...' Alanna says

'She's been killed in a crash. Both her and Michael.' Her father's eyes are piercing red from tears. His lip is quivering as he clearly tries to compose himself whilst sharing the news.

It is like a movie voiceover before her eyes as she hears her father explain to the neighbours who have just arrived.

'They were in a crash, making their way back home from her move to Dublin. Michael, also pre-med, both went to look at houses to rent. She was on the phone telling us how they found a place with a room that you two may like. Ten minutes later, we got a call that a drunk driver hit her and Michael's car. They were both killed on impact,' her dad says, and at this point the dark-haired man looks like a helpless boy with tears running down his face, while the group console him.

'NOOOOOOOOO!' Alanna screams. 'NO NO NO NO NO NO NO NO NO...... NO! SALLLLLY. It can't be her! It just can't!' She collapses on the floor and into the arms of Simon, who catches her fall.

Shaking, gasping for air, a thousand thoughts, images, moments of them together and her beautiful sister rush through her head. 'This can't be happening.

She was going to be a doctor and a wife and a mother. This was not the way it was meant to be.'

The pain overcomes her as she feels her hands shake and her chest swell. The tears come rushing, so much so that it is as if she had completed a marathon and was gasping for air, fighting to breathe.

***

Alanna looks at her brother Brendan, who looks confused at what is going on. He is shaking violently.

She feels his pain, the deepest pain.

How will Brendan cope?

'Brendan was everything to her and she was everything to him. I'm the fun sister who would be there in good times; Sally was there during the hard times. When Brendan has his fits, it was Sally who would take care of him. She was the better one. She was my better half. It should have been me. I was meant to go to Dublin to sort the houses. I was meant to be there. We were meant to have dinner tonight for our eighteenth birthday. This was our big day. It should have been me... It should have been me!' she says with sincerity.

'Stop saying such things,' Dad and Simon say simultaneously.

Panic-stricken and with a cluster of thoughts filling her head, she gets up and bolts through the door. Simon and her father run to catch her and, akin to a bull run in Pamplona, both corner her until they strike her down.

In pain, she falls and lies helpless crying like a child on the frozen ground. Neighbours pass by looking at the scene. Whether they know or not, a tragedy is unfolding before their eyes. The shock in their eyes shows everything. The most beautiful house on the main road has suddenly become the most pain-filled.

Minutes later the priest arrives. He sits with the family in the kitchen, holding their hands.

'Let's say a prayer for the dead,' he intones.

'My beautiful twin sister is not part of the dead!' Alanna screams.

It can't be happening.

'Not Sally.'

***

Alanna and Carltons apartment, London, 2013

'Ah!' Alanna wakes up screaming, in a sweat, looking around her room, confused. She wonders why the worst day of her life replays over and over.

'It was a nightmare.'

After the terror passes, she goes through her usual routine: waking up and changing her clothes, washing her face and getting back into bed hoping the pain will melt away.

It never does.

As Mam says, *'Get yer sleep, dear, as everything is always better in da morning.'*

Tossing and turning, she tries everything to get some quiet in her mind. She reads a book, some magazines, plays videos, songs, even writes up some notes for her class to try and tire herself out. Eventually at about 3am her mind gives up and she falls back into a deep sleep.

***

Alanna closes her eyes and drifts back into her dreams. Recalling the days after the death, filled with tears, countless visitors and Mass cards and flowers placed all around the house. Numb from the pain she felt, she could find nowhere to breathe except the lake.

She spent most of her days there, writing songs of pain and injustice about the tragedy that had happened. The funeral came – a day they never believed would come – but it did. Showing her strength, she was determined to sing at the funeral.

Placing herself at the front of the church, she headed the choir. She knew Sally would want this send off, and her parents agreed. Grief-stricken themselves, they prayed for nothing other than some hope and that Alanna and Brendan could get through this tragic time.

'Nothing is more unjust than burying your own child or sister,' the locals would whisper.

'Nothing can ever compare to this pain,' Alanna would say to Simon. 'Nothing.'

Alanna stood at the top of the church, all eyes watching her when she opened her mouth to sing. The choir joined in.

For you there'll be no crying
For you the sun will be shining

Her voice was always remarkable, yet that day, with the echoes in the church, it was breathtaking.

***

Through the music, the pain and passion singing for her other half, she moved everyone in the church. Even the choir and priest were affected.

Other than the music, there was a silence throughout.

Teardrops fell, people's hearts opened and a special light came through the stained-glass windows, reaching each person in a different way.

She continued.

And the songbirds keep singing.

Her soulful range echoed back out of the church doors, reaching even those standing outside. Tears, total silence and shock was the common ground between the array of guests: family members, friends, school representatives and local people. It was a powerful moment for all who were there. 'Losing two young lives represents such a loss for the community,' they would say.

To you I would give the world
To you I'd never be cold
'Cause I feel that when I'm with you
It's all right, I know it's right

***

As the song ended, Alanna moved back to her seat.

'Thank you for a beautiful song by a very brave lady,' the priest called out.

The mass continued while Alanna said very little until the priest announced, 'The mass has ended. Go in peace.'

Holding Brendan's hand and Simon's in the other, she followed her parents, walking out of the church knowing she did her best.

Everyone watched her family and the Reillys family, each person with tears in their eyes, knowing or at least trying to relate to the loss of two beautiful children. Yet, unless they had lost someone themselves, they couldn't, so Alanna kept quiet. It was too hard to explain the feeling.

'How are ye love?' Simon whispered in her ear.

'I don't know. I am not sure how I am supposed to feel. I feel in agony, a deep pain, but I know Sally is

136

here. She would want me to have sung. I have to keep singing. I have to use this to get a better life for myself. Myself and Brendan.'

Walking towards the car, Simon's arms were wrapped around her. 'I will protect you. I will ensure you are safe.'

As she saw the coffin move out of the church, she grew hysterical…

'I have to get away from this place. Everything is a reminder and all I know is I need to get away.'

***

Alanna and Carltons apartment, London, 2013

'It's OK, honey. Let it all out. Your momma told me everything. We all agree it's not good to keep all of this cooped up inside. It's no wonder you ain't sleeping well.'

'I miss her. She shouldn't have gone,' Alanna says while sobbing, too tired to fight it.

'Sista, I love ya. You finally lets your guard down,' he responds. 'You just gotta stop trying to be so strong all the time. It's OK to slow down, take some time off. Maybe stop working for Dennis and just do your studio work. You have nothing to prove. We can make money other ways.' Alanna hears the sounds of her mother and father coming through Carlton. 'If you had to you could repeat the year too. Whatever you need to do, honey, but you have to take care of yourself. Like I told you with my pa, and look how he turned out,' Carlton confirms.

She continues to sob as her tears dampen her face, breathing fast as in a panic.

'I'm here, sista. I'm here, you poor thing. Look, come into my bed and we can have some more rest and freshen you up. I'll sort everything in the morning.'

She takes his hand as he leads her into his room. Within minutes, he is wiping her face and changing her into his oversized PJ's.

'We are stronger together. You ain't ever alone.' They lay closely, falling into a deep sleep side by side.

Chapter 21

Alanna and Carlton's new apartment, Chelsea, London
Alanna and Carlton both listen to *Kiss FM* while they prepare for their date with Jack and Manchester United.

'Lani, did I tell you how much I *love* our new place. Thanks for bringing me with.' Carlton walks around the sleek, modern apartment, with two floors, lacquer finishes, mirrors, white leather seats, a music studio and a gym.

'Carlton, ye're my rock. I would never leave ye. So shut up being sappy and let's get ready for our big night.'

'With our favourite men. You know Harry and Jack will never like each other. One day, you is gonna be made to choose. Until then, enjoy, enjoy enjoy!' he says to her in the mirror while watching her put on her make-up. 'Yet you must know who you like! Ya know?' he winks. 'What is with the Spanish inquisition?' she banters.

'I will tell ye, if ye tell me who were ye meeting the other night? You came in so late. Sometimes you're such a dark horse! I hope you don't have that camera on?

'I know you wouldn't mind. Don't play dumb with me, Carlton, *hahaha*,' she jokes.

He blushes, his skin going from pink to red. 'OK, I'll take it off, honey,' He says.

***

'Tell me who is your next big thing?' she asks.

'OK, well, this guy is half-Spanish, one quarter Brazilian, and one quarter French. We met at an event. Ya know, we share The Look, then he disappears and I was all heartbroken. Then later he comes up behind me, slaps me on the ass, which I felt was totally inappropriate – but then again, I loved it. He was like, 'You have an unusual look, are you a model?'. And I was like, 'no, but I am a dancer'. 'Close enough,' he responds. 'Well, let's meet. Here's my card. Next weekend I'm all yours,' he says and walks away.' Carlton speaks fast, especially when excitable.

'Back up, back up,' says Alanna. 'What did you just say about the eyes, The Look?'

'The Look! Don't ya tell me you don't know The Look? Sista, it is the modern-day live bait available on your doorstep, saving many marriages from full-blown affairs.'

'Please explain, Carlton. Once again you intrigue me with your ways.'

'OK.' He struts Prince-style out of the bathroom. 'Follow me.'

***

'You walk this way, I walk this way, look straight ahead, then when I tell you, look up at me, OK?' he choreographs her.

'OK, go.'

Alanna struts, walking in the direction of Carlton. 'Now!' he screams,

She looks up and into his eyes. Her mind is blown away. Whatever he thinks or says or whatever energy he gives off, he is on fire. He is always hot, but is gay-

Carlton-hot. With 'The Look' he is bad ass, wanna-take-ya-home Carlton.

'Wow!' she screams. 'Carlton, what the hell was that? I wanted you there. Don't tell Harry,' she laughs.

'I told you, sista! And that, my love, is what we call The Look. For that one moment in time you let go and enjoy someone else. It is innocent. No number-exchanging, no emails, just The Look, and then you are satisfied. Like a bite of a cake.'

'Yes, very innocent,' Alanna says sarcastically.

'Who is ever satisfied with a bit of a cake?'

'I'm sure that those who do this on a regular types basis are no doubt the same ones slipping their wedding rings into their pockets. Women too,' she argues.

'You're preaching to the wrong man here. I don't do no commitment. Cab is here. Let's roll.' He holds her hand and directs her out of the front door.

***

After the first time getting her make-up done by Carlton, she is never without it. Carlton taught her how to curl her hair, and add fake lashes and lipstick.

'You look fierce. Complete Tyra transformation!' he assures her.

As she gets out of the cab, she looks over to see Jack, who nearly falls to the ground.

'Jaysus, look at yer one! She's bleedin' fitness,' says the dark haired man.

'Oh, that's Alanna. Jaysus, man, she looks better every time,' Jack says.

'Fitness!' his other friend calls out.

As she reaches them, 'How are ye's boys?' she says, as she double-kisses Jack.

Moving into the VIP section, of the bar, they order drinks.

'I know you may not want to hear this, but you're fit to be a WAG. Do you know that?' Jack jokes.

'What's a WAG?'

Carlton fills her in, 'Wife and gurlfriend, sista! They are usually hot, every man wants them, and every woman wants to be them. A baller's wife is the bomb!'

'I'm looking for both, so the position is open,' Jack says to her. 'Seriously, Alanna, you have class and you're so bleedin' pretty. Plus, ye're bleedin' Irish. It's unreal,' he whispers.

'Jack, she is a WAG. You have struck gold!' Carlton shouts out.

'The only thing I would ask is if you could sing for me... well, the lads and me. Carlton told us your voice is out of this world,' says Jack.

'Carlton is my GBF. He has to say it,' she responds.

***

Although a team of men are surrounding her, Alanna feels really strange after the eye-locking moment with Carlton. It was the first time she had ever seen him in that light –

Like a straight man I could date. What the feck? I gotta stop drinking.

She was feeling something towards him and she doesn't know how to cope.

'This is Mike, Dennis, Leon...'

'The rest of the *Manchester United* guys are calling in too,' Jack confirms.

'Sure, as if we care. Let's go dancing... laters!' Carlton screams and drags her to the dance floor.

Jack looks over at them. 'Look at her. She's the one. She's perfect,' he says to his team mates.

'She is G Man.'

'Fitness!' they agree.

***

Mahiki Bar, London
The night continues with a row of cocktails, Press and lots of barhopping, ending up in *Mahiki.*

At one point Jack tries to kiss her, but Carlton cuts in. 'If ye like it you gotta put a ring on it.' He points to Alanna's wedding ring finger. He always knew what to do to make things better. 'Sista, I am not able to fight off all the potential WAGs and groupies that are lingering around. Also there are HABS hovering around… husbands and boyfriends. Let's go home.'

'If we leave can we get an Indian?' Carlton asks.

'Sure… you read my mind' Alanna says as they move out of *Mahiki* hand in hand.

***

Falling in the door at 3am with a bag of Indian food, they both fall onto the couch. Looking to her phone, Alanna screams. 'OMG, look at this!' She holds up her iPhone to Carlton.

5 missed calls from Harry.

8 from Dennis.

1 from Simon.

1 from her parents.

1 from Jack.

6 voicemails.

1 text from Jack:

Jack: I love you, Alanna.
Be my WAG.
For real.
X

143

'Those fellas are some craic. So did you like anyone out of the boys?' she asks him while eating the Indian directly out of the boxes.

'I saw some nice men. And nice women too,' Carlton adds.

'Women? Sure ye must be seriously drunk with that talk.'

'Lately I've been thinking what it would be like, to have a woman and kids and a family. You make me think about these things.'

Alanna, with a face in shock, stands up. 'Are you serious?'

'Yes, your momma and I were talking.'

'Oh no, what did she say?' Alanna asks.

'All great things. I am just considering my future and maybe I need to be more open. I have dated women. Well, one woman. If there are women like you out there, I know I could be happy. Plus, my momma and Mrs O would be so happy.'

'Wow, that's amazing, Carlton!' she hugs him. 'I think you would be an incredible boyfriend, husband, father. All of those things, but only if you want to be them.'

'I think you'd be an amazing wife and mother.'

She blushes. 'Thank you. I am curious now. So what is your type? Is she curvy? Slim? What's your thang?' she says, mimicking his accent.

'You, Alanna, you're exactly my type. I haven't been with a girl since school, but it's you. Plus, I hate seeing you go out with all these guys when I know I can take care of you better than any of them. Trust me, I've been there, done it, bought the T-shirt. I want to try. At least let me try,' he says, then leans over to kiss her.

***

On the couch, they kiss passionately as she wraps her legs around his. It isn't the first time they have been this physically close. Spending many nights in his bed, and with their dance routines, their bodies know each other's like adjacent pieces of a puzzle.

Carlton kisses her neck slowly and she feels a rush of butterflies inside. Looking up, he kisses her nose, her forehead and her lips... He does this slowly, as if every move matters.

'My Queen, Alanna. I would do anything for you.'

She stares at him. 'Kiss me,' she says.

***

Seeing her eyes close, he says, 'Let's get you some rest.'

He leads her into his room with no other intention than to be close. He respects her too much to try anything else.

As he takes off his clothes she stares at him. She'd forgotten how perfectly placed his muscles were, or maybe she had just never looked at them that way. She takes off her top as he stares, admiring her chest, her tiny waist and curves.

It is intense and intimate.

They lock eyes as they continue to kiss.

***

Lying in his bed, he turns around and kisses her neck and holds her hand. She can't breathe. She has shivers all over and tingles in her tummy.

Undressed, they lay as close as they usually do, yet tonight they are really close.

After a few minutes Carlton hears a deep breathing sound. Alanna has fallen asleep. She is an amazing person, a fighter. She is always on the go, yet she never complains or gives up.

The last one standing.

A true star.

He stares at her. 'I love you, Alanna,' he whispers. 'I love you, I just don't know what it means.'

At this point he is too scared to tell her and himself the truth.

Chapter 22

*Tweet: We used to be
Just like twins, so in sync
The same energy
Now it's a dead battery @AStar @KatyPerry*

King's Road, Chelsea, London
Alanna jumps out of bed, trying to not wake Carlton,
who is now fast asleep and facing the wall, and looks at
her phone.

> *Harry: See you at Shoreditch, darling.*
> *We can't wait to see you.*
> *Harry*
> *X*

Soon, though, they are both up and moving around
the four-bedroomed place. It was the quietest morning
they had ever spent together.

'Sista, you OK? You so quiet!' Carlton puts his
arms around her to make her laugh, and she smiles
despondently.

'All good. Hope ye're all ready for our double-date,'
she responds.

'Sure, can't wait!' he says as he pulls his arm off
her, sensing her mood.

'Let's go. We are already late,' she says while
walking towards the door.

As the lift goes down into the basement, they place
their chrome helmets on and jump on the back of
Alanna's 2013 Red Piaggio scooter – the one Harry had
bought for her as an early birthday gift when she
refused a car. Having spent many summers in Paris and

147

Milan, he thought it 'was classy for a city lady to have a city bike'. Alanna, although she had just met him, was too tired, Tube-allergic and wageless to argue, had accepted it, 'But only with the promise that I will pay ye back as soon as I get my first big gig, d'ya hear me?' she'd warned him.

***

Today Alanna is missing turns and forgetting to indicate. Carlton says nothing. Today as he holds her, it feels different.

When he is close to her neck, it feels too intimate and unnerving.

'I want to help you, be the man for you but didn't know how to tell you,'

'Yet today you are different'

'Everything is different,' he says.

Arriving, they walk past the paparazzi, who are flashing their cameras through the iron doors into the warehouse-style reception.

'Welcome to Shoreditch House. Do you have any more guests?' a pretty and retro-looking lady with tattoos, red hair and edgy clothes asks.

'Harry Mac plus one,' Alanna says as she gives her member's card to the lady and signs in.

She takes out her phone to text Harry;

Alanna; Hi H
Arrived safe. No phones allowed.
Join us on the roof,
Kiss, A

Alanna placing her phone in her bag sees an incoming call from her mam and dad, which she immediately cancels.

'Sorry, miss. Remember, no phones or photography allowed here,' the receptionist calls out.

'It's off, don't worry!,' she snaps.

Carlton reacts. 'Sista, chill. London has brushed off on you.'

'My parents, friends and Liz are giving out that I was not in contact more…and now you!'

'Sista, the Industry has changed you….' he says as they move into the lift.

'They are giving me such a hard time. Don't see them getting up and trying this out. It's so easy for everyone to give me orders while they're in their safety zone. I don't need to explain myself. Everyone needs to realise I'm not the same Alanna they once knew,' she states while storming out onto the roof.

***

Carlton and Alanna head out to the pool on the roof, lay down blankets and crash out on the pool loungers. Harry arrives within a few minutes, walking beside a perfectly petite auburn-haired lady and laughing intimately as if they are an item.

Alanna sits up to wave, when Carlton interrupts 'Who is his date?'

'I thought he was bringing a man for you. Like a double-date. A gay date for you. Harry for me.'

'She is stunning. Very easy on the eyes,' Carlton says.

'I thought you were gay. I thought you were my gay best friend!' she screams. 'If I'm honest, I am kinda getting over the shock that my gay best friend who I tell everything to and share a bed with, suddenly may be straight, likes me and also may like another woman or women. Along with the fact that the same woman my

GBF thinks is stunning is with my boyfriend or a man who may be her boyfriend.'

Alanna's instinct is already to dislike this lady, who she had never heard about, never mind met. After an especially broken sleep, this is her first day off in months. It is not working out as she had hoped.

Just as Harry and Ms Perfect draw closer, she takes in a deep breath to calm her nerves while Carlton screams, 'Oh, isn't that the pool you kissed DJ Pronto in?' while pointing at the pool.

A drop of sweat slides down her back. 'It is going to be a long day,' she whispers under her breath.

***

Shoreditch House rooftop pool, London
'Alanna, this is Emee. Emee this is Alanna and Carlton.' 'Hey,' they respond to one another.

'Nice to meet you both,

'I saw your blogs and some press... never dull with you.' Emee replies in a perfectly executed British-French accent.

'No, I don't do dull,'Alanna says, blushing.

Within minutes, a rare glimpse of 'winter sun' is out and, it being Shoreditch House, everyone is in bikinis and shorts and everything else in between, stilettoes included.

Alanna, tall and curvy but slim, with a chest and a dancer's body to die for, looks at Emee. Emee is pint-sized in her shape, but has mannerisms grander than them both and an air of arrogance about her.

'I want her out of the picture,' she whispers to Carlton.

'I must say I am really glad to be here. Most importantly to meet in person the famous lady who has got Harry out of the strip clubs and parties and thinking

150

of settling down. We didn't think anyone could,' Emee remarks.

Alanna's face drops.

Carlton protectively cuts in, 'She sure is. Why would anyone need anything to excite them when they're with Alanna Star?'

Alanna smiles out towards the pool, too proud to show any hurt.

'Oh, love your tattoo Alanna. Very classy,' Emee says sarcastically.

'Tattoo, darling? I never knew you had a tattoo,' Harry cuts in.

'It's a family thing,' says Carlton, to remind her. 'Isn't it, Alanna?'

'Yes, it is,' she says, close to tears.

'How new age. Very new age indeed,' Emee remarks.

Feckin' bitch. Who invited her anyway?

Alanna looks to Harry with disdain and excuses herself to the bathroom.

***

After crying from lack of sleep, she splashes her face with water and leaves the shower room. Harry is outside.

She smiles, but her face shows anger. Although they are 'just friends', she wanted to be his only 'friend'.

'Shall we go to the bar, darling?'

'Yes, love to,' she responds.

'Is that really your gay friend Carlton? He is awfully friendly with Emee. They would make a great couple indeed.'

She looks at him. 'Well, if he wasn't gay…'

'And course if Emee wasn't already married to my cousin,' he cuts in.

She sighs. 'Maybe in another life.'

'So what she's saying about you, about the strip clubs. Is all of that true? Am I dating a pervert?'

Harry's eyes look into Alanna's. Well, I worked in the City and I went a handful of times to those clubs with work. It was never an interest of mine. You know all about my past, but I didn't think it was important to let you know about this. As I say, it's in the past. Let's focus on now,' he requests.

'Well, you still work in the City.'

'The difference is, Alanna, since Dad died I've owned a hedge fund. In fact, I own many. I am my own boss. I have no need to go to those events. I am old-school, as I told you the first night we met.'

'OK, well, I can't be with you if you're going to these places. It's so cheap and makes me look like a bad girlfriend. I will literally walk, Harry, and you'll lose the best thing you ever had if I hear of this sleaze again.'

'That's twice you've said it.'

'What?'

'Girlfriend.'

'Oh, sorry. I'm pissed off with ye so I don't notice what I'm sayin'.'

'No, don't be sorry. I have been calling you that all along. I just know you too well that if I had said it I would have scared you off.'

'Perhaps,' she says, leaning in to kiss him...

***

'How are you, though?' He kisses her forehead as he does every time they are together.

'I know you have lots on, so thank you so much for having us.

'Plus, Emee, she's in banking so not easy for her to

get in. House rules and all that,' he states.

She smiles as Harry continues

'Two strong-minded women, I believe you two would get along so well.

'Also, I am thinking of renting out my apartment in the Shard and buying a new place off King's Road. Emee and my cousin are helping me with the deal. I know you are creative and so I thought you could design it with an artist I have in mind. I have no clue about those things.'

She kisses him – a deep and meaningful kiss as if to thank him for always getting it right. 'Yes, yes, I would love to. Thank you for asking me. I really appreciate it. Thank you for being the best man I know.'

'I think we make a great partnership, Alanna, I really do. We just need to sort your agent, etc., and get you established in the business. On the right side of it, though. Let's head back and start making our way home. I have a nice meal planned for us later.'

'Thank you,' she says.

Carlton's eyes drop to the ground as they walk back out to the pool hand in hand for the first time in public.

Alanna and Harry are officially a couple.

Shit, what will I tell Jack?

***

Dear Sally,

I have a boyfriend!

I know, can you believe it?

HE'S AMAZING!

I also kissed my gay best friend, who I am not so sure is gay anymore.

Carlton, on the other hand, my whimsical gay or not-so-gay best friend, is clearly enjoying both sides of the fence and is a loose cannon. I am so distrusting of him. Well, of everyone now. I will beat them at their games.

   Oh and I like Jack.
   It's all a bit mad!
   Miss you.
   X

Chapter 23

Tweet*: Happy Birthday, Happy Birthday @AStar my
favourite lady X @CStar @StevieWonder*

Alanna and Carlton's apartment, Chelsea, London
Alanna wakes up to a call and Stevie Wonder from
Carlton.

'*Happy birthday, happy birthday…* My Queen A.'

'Why are ye calling me? When we are…?'

She runs into his room to see him and a man pop up
from under the covers. 'Oh this, this is…' begins
Carlton.

'Clearly a model. You're very handsome,' Alanna
says.

'Hell, what's yo name again?' Carlton looks at his
bedfellow.

'Juan. I am Juan.'

'Nice to meet you, Juan…'

'Juan and I have been doing lots of photo shoots
together, and we fell in love.'

Juan's eyes look up in shock, as if he has just been
told himself, and Alanna tries not to laugh at his
reaction.

'We are so, so in love,' Carlton says.

'I'm so happy for you both. I wish you both a world
of love and happiness.'

Juan looks around as if he has woken up in a horror
movie.

'Anyway Carlton, I have great news for you. Harry
has given me a joint birthday present!'

'Sista, bring it,' he says.

'Well, after studio we have a trip,' she says.

155

'I love trips! A trip with whom? To where?' he asks, sitting up.

'It is a fashion trip, with a make-up artist and stylist,' she says.

'A stylist… *stylist!*'

'AHHHHH!'

'*Hell, yeah*!' he screams. He gets out of bed, climbing over Juan and bringing her outside the room. 'Before we go, I am not being mean, Alanna, but as much as I would love to I can't pay for this. I mean I know ye're sorting the house, but you already owe me lots of cash. I don't want anything back, but I can't afford big trips,' he says.

'You know I'll pay you back. Once the show comes out. You're going to be paid.'

'Forget it, we are evens,' he says.

'Don't worry. Harry has sorted this out. He told me that you have to get some clothes too. Then we are going for dinner later.'

'Hair, make up, dinner… Sista, you have to get your hair done before the shopping so you feel like a model,' he says.

'What if we ruin clothes?' she asks seriously.

'When you're a queen, you're too rich to care!'

'Don't worry, Christina has recommended MD from Ireland, so we have flown him in. And Lu the Mac make-up artist,' Alanna continues.

'WOW!' he screams.

'We have a driver all day, so let's get to class and get this party started!' she says, smiling.

'OK, give me ten,' he says with his face beaming.

'What about Juan?' she asks.

'Juan, Ju-wanna-a pack up and ship out! He is dead to me.' he screams into the bedroom.

'Let's go!'

156

***

The Langham Hotel, London

As soon as Carlton and Alanna reach the hotel, they go up to the penthouse suite.

Walking into the room, everything is opulent. Among the couch, chairs, large bed, white crisp sheets, bay windows, champagne, flowers, gifts and MD and his assistant sit smiling.

'Ciao, darling. Ciao,' MD calls out.

They see MD sipping water. 'Christina and Harry told us to let ourselves in,' he says, while double-kissing her.

'MD, you are fierce. Carlton, you know this is Ireland's top hair stylist?'

'Pleased to meet you,' Carlton says.

'Wow, he is de-lish. Does he play for your team or mine?' MD asks.

'I think he is ball boy – a bit of both,' she jokes.

They all laugh in unison.

'OK, darlings, let's get started. Kim, go wash their hair and we will make beauties of them both,' he says to the quiet assistant.

Lulu, with black hair, red lipstick and make-up that reflects her style and career, enters. She's dressed all in black, carrying a wheelie make-up-filled case behind her. She's clearly prepared for the job. 'Sorry I was delayed. I had a later flight... because of a show in NYC.'

'NYC! My home! How is it?' Carlton asks.

'Fantastic!' she says in a Puerto Rican accent.

'Let's open the champagne!' MD says.

'Fo sho!' Carlton calls out.

With their hair wet, they dress in some robes and sit back in the armchairs, in position to get their hair, nails and make-up done.

157

'Who needs to go to a salon when you can bring the salon to you?'

'Toast to Harry Mac!' Calrton calls out They all clink their glasses, smiling.

***

Leaving the hotel, Alanna's red hair is bouncing. She is wearing a navy Lycra dress and wedged boots. Carlton is wearing a shirt and trousers with purple suede shoes.

'You look like a rock star!' Carlton exclaims.

'So do you!'

'I know!' Carlton confirms.

'*I love him!*'

'*I love Harry! A*nd we haven't even hit the shops!' he remarks.

'I love him too,' she replies.

'You do?'

'Well, I dunno.'

'Let's go. We have to meet our stylist!'

***

Design Studio, Dean Street, London

Alanna, your style is very cool, but we need to take this up a notch. Create a sense of sophistication in your look.

'She *is* soph-ist-icated. Alanna, you is *so* sophisticated,' Carlton reacts defensively.

'Oh, we know. We just meant *more* sophisticated. that's all,' Chantelle says in her posh London accent. 'So, let's measure you.' She wraps her tape around Alanna's waist.

'She has a fab figure, doesn't she? Check out that rack' Carlton screams out, watching the lady measuring her.

158

'Yes, fantastic,' Chantelle replies.

With that, the door is flung open and in steps in a man in an *Armani* suit, the best-kept man that Alanna has ever seen. *Ever.*

'Bonjour, Alanna. Pleasure,' he says as he double-kisses her. 'Je suis Rico.'

'Hey, hey, I am Carlton.' Carlton jumps up as if he has no choice.

'Carlton, fab.' He double-kisses Carlton too.

'You met your French match,' Alanna whispers.

Carlton nods. 'OMG. J'adore!' he mimics behind her.

'OK, Mr Mac gave us the green light to splash out today. Lucky you! Plan is… we measure you, and then we get to the King's Road, a few boutiques and some larger stores. Myself and Chantelle have called ahead,' he assures them. 'By the time you leave today you will be ready to meet even the Queen herself.'

Carlton looks at Alanna. *'Sista, this is the best birthday ever!'*

'I know!' She smiles back.

***

They move around from store to store with a driver, jazz music playing and champagne pouring, Carlton working on his phone calls and 'Just uploading to our blogs; Twitter, Facebook and Instagram, not including the gay sites, which you don't need to know of'.

'So you know Harry adores you!' Rico says to Alanna. 'I've been styling him for years, and his mum, but we have never worked on his ladies.'

Carlton's eyes look away from his phone as he says, 'Ladies? How many did he have?'

'Enough,' Rico says cleverly.

They both laugh.

'Yet all that matters, sista, is that *he is yo man now*!'
Alanna smiles and holds Carlton's hand. 'Yes, that's all
that matters.'

***

Selfridges, Duke Street
'OK, Rico, these places are nice, but, like, when are we
going big? I know you can do better than this,' Carlton
whispers to Rico with deeper implications.

'Relax. I'm saving the best to last,' he assures him.

'Well, I don't know about ye, but I'm starvin'.
Could we get something to eat?' Alanna asks.

'Hell, no! We are shopping... Woman, you can't be
no bloat when you're running designer fabrics against
your skin,' says Carlton in horror.

'A bloat. *Hahaha,* you're a funny lad, Carlton! OK,
well then I need a tea at least.'

'Sure, very soon darling, very soon,' Rico says.

They pull in outside the door of Selfridges on Duke
Street.

'OK, this is more like it!' Carlton says as his eyes
light up.

Without any hesitation Carlton runs ahead though
the golden doors with bags, people passing in and out
with bright lights shimmering. 'I'm home! Momma is
home....' he calls.

Everyone looks around to see who is screaming.

'Hallo, mwah, mwah, mwah, autographs later!'
Carlton screams. 'I have hidden it for too long. Fashion
is my drug! My counsellor would call you enablers, but
I would call you my friends.' He looks back at Rico,
Chantelle and Alanna, then runs through Selfridges
blowing kisses to all the staff.

'Is he for real?' Rico asks.

'Ye better believe it!' she assures him.

'So, why are you not running around like a princess? You have the chance to empty Harry's cards and have the best outfits, like a princess, Kate-Middleton style.'

'Oh, I know. I'm just taking my time. Plus, when I go for it, I go big,' she says seriously.

***

'Shall we do this?' Carlton calls out. 'Today you is Beyoncé and I am your main man Jay on a trip in London.'

'Bring it!

'Look at the Muslim women's shoes and bags. Under their *jilbāb* they have enough jewels to open a shop. Those ladies are the smart ones. You need to get yourself some of those jewels.'

Moving through each section, they have staff collecting clothes, shoes, and bags. Alanna passes through the designer section, knocks over a jacket by accident and struggles to bend down while holding a pile of dresses.

'Sista, you don't pick up the stuff. Everyone stops for you. You're in fashion world now... It's a monarchy system and right now you and Harry are the king and queen. You got so much to learn!' he says, hugging her.

'Let's hit the dressing room,' Carlton calls out.

As they walk in, they see two hundred or more outfits lined up.

'I am heaven!' Carlton exclaims, smiling.

'I am thirsty,' she says.

''Scuse me, we are so thirsty... any chance we could get some coffees and waters over here?' Carlton requests.

'Sure. Jessie get them water,' the in-house stylist calls to her junior, who looks happy to take this break.

'Thanks, Jess,' Alanna winks at her.

They spend an hour and a half trying on different tops, shoes, skirts, trousers, heels, bags, and jewellery.

Alanna truly feels special; Carlton is at ease. They do catwalk after catwalk.

Some outfits are 'horrendous' according to Rico, while some are 'marvellous'.

With at least twenty new outfits, ten new pairs of shoes, five coats and items of jewellery, they walk out with fifty-four bags being carried by the staff.

'Well, where to next?' Carlton asks.

'Are ye kidding me? Sure we bought so much.'

'Don't worry, sista. Harry has shares here. It goes back into the business,' he reminds her.

'Last stop is *Harrods*,' Rico calls out.

'Hell, yeah!' Carlton hollers.

'Harry has requested that you pick a dress. We are meeting the lady in *Vera Wang*,' Rico says.

'Hold up! Wha' did you just say? What kind of dress? OMG, this is your wedding moment!'

'Shut up, Carlton. We only just started dating.' She looks at Carlton, who has tears in his eyes.

'My Lani is going to get married.'

'Can we get some food?' Alanna says.

'No. Harry is waiting for us, darling.

'You gotta blow him away. You're soon to be the wife of a King,' Carlton reminds her.

She looks down to see various birthday tweets, Facebook and text messages, along with her Twitter followers increasing by one thousand thanks to Carlton's photo blogs from the previous few hours.

She goes to send her most important message:

Alanna: Harry, today you are my king,
I didn't think I could feel this happy on such a sad day.
Thank you, always.
See you soon X

Chapter 24

Tweet: @AStar My Girl, My Girl...
Talking about My Girl @TheTemptations

The Langham Hotel, London
Alanna, looking like royalty in her red dress, shoes and a final touch-up to her hair and make-up, is luminous. Jaws drop as she moves out of the lift and into reception, linking arms with Carlton. Harry, waiting mid-conversation, looks over to see his date, her hair curled backcombed and bouncing with an edgy fringe and *Prada* black dress with secret panels of leather under her high *Louboutin* heels. She smiles over at him and walks towards him in the sexiest way. He is impressed by this, but more with her sensibility to always dress for the occasion. 'Darling, you are stunning. I am the luckiest man alive to be joining you this evening.' He kisses her forehead and then her lips. 'Carlton, so great to see you,' he adds.

'Thank you for today. You're a very kind man,' she says.

Carlton agrees. 'Harry, it was the kindest thing anyone has ever done for me.'

Alanna nudges him. 'Oh, aside from Alanna on a daily basis.'

Laughing, Harry replies, 'My pleasure. Now, let's go. I am sure you two are starving.'

Harry holds her hand, smiling yet protectively close, while they are directed to their table.

***

When they reach their seats, Harry introduces her and Carlton to each of four men, including Hugh whom she met at the speed-dating event. Hugh looks much sharper than the previous time they met. Redeeming himself, he is now a man of pure politeness.

As they move through their courses, they talk of their day, their music, dancing, banking business and London life.

Midway through the meal heads to the bathroom, looking at her phone and seeing missed calls and texts from her family and Liz who were 'dying to hear about her big day!'.

A *Tweet* pops up from DJ Pronto:

Happy birthday! Loved working with you @AStar You're a real Star! Back in LA, living the dream. Dennis told me you'd be over soon, so let's get recording then. Kiss, @DJPronto

Then another text:

Jack: Was worried about you. Tried to call you a few times, darling. I want you to have the best birthday you've ever had. I know it's not an easy day. I want to spoil you. Wherever you are, Lani, I want ye to be happy. Love ya, x

***

As they move on to desserts and coffees, she watches Harry and Carlton interacting, knowing that with Harry there was something different. Watching Harry and his much older friends interact, she realises he is a lost soul in a tough world and all he needs is a partner who will support him. Rejoining the conversation, she hears Harry remark, 'Hugh, we are the hallmark of our parents' generation.'

'Hear, hear, son,' one of the partners with speckled white hair states.

'Such wise words for a young soul,' the other notes.

'You always were. Just like your father in his day.'

All three men nod in agreement.

Harry blushes.

They are all burly men used to late nights, and one drink leads to another. Before they know it, they move into the dining room. At one point Alanna, now drunk, smiles to see she is sat among such sophisticated men. Harry has treated her like a princess all night, along with Carlton, and she feels at ease with him. As if he is her other half. She'd only felt this once before, with Simon, and never since, so she knew they had something special.

Or else it is the expensive champagne.

As everyone says their goodbyes, the evening wraps after 2am. Stumbling into a cab, although they have a suite, she and Carlton agree to go back to Harry's place for a coffee.

***

Harry's apartment, The Shard, London

As they walk through the entrance of the Shard, Carlton screams, 'This is ma-hus-ive! Like a freakin' Toblerone bar!'

'I know I am very, very drunk, but I am impressed to say the least' Calrton calls out.

'Oh, I forgot you had not had the chance to visit it yet. You are always welcome!' Harry says.

They are all drunk, joking in the lift as they move up and up in the lift.

'Sista, my ears just popped.' Reaching the hundredth floor or somewhere near, Alanna is too drunk to notice as they move into Harry's place.

'Holy shit, you is rich! Like P-Diddy rich!'

'Carlton, calm down…' she urges Carlton.

'Let's get some music on.'

Carlton and Alanna run to the piano, and Carlton starts to sing

My girl, my girl…

Talking about my girl.

Harry sits on the couch watching, in awe, as if he is seeing a private jazz show.

'You two are so talented,' he says.

'Thank you,' Carlton agrees. 'You clearly is the best at your job, looking at yer place!'

'Stop it, Carlton.'

'Sorry to be rude, but I have a flight early tomorrow so I'll have to go to bed,' explains Harry. 'Carlton can go into one of the spare rooms. Will you show him there?'

'Of course. I will be in shortly,' she says. 'Follow me, Carlton. We need to get to bed.'

She directs him into the spare room.

***

Walking back out into the living room, she sees the sun rising and feels like nothing more than writing about the most magical day of her life.

Dear Sally,

Today was our birthday. I missed you terribly.

It's never easy.

Harry made it easier.

Things were magical.

Things were calm.

They were classy. There were no screams or tears or dramas, no highs and lows; it's always going to work out with him around.

I know that he is the only person who can give me everything that I dreamed of, including security for our family.

I've been dating this guy now for a few weeks. I don't know what it is about him but I think I am falling for him.

He passed my checklist:

Not a porn star or addicted.

Not a serial dater.

Not a sociopath.

Not mean with money (did I tell you about the guy Carlton dated, 'Spreadsheet Sam'?)

Not a loner, but not too cool.

Not too slim or too large.

No crazy exes or family.

Bonus: an extra-smart gene to not look or flirt with other women, at least whilst around me.

We have both lost someone (his dad is gone and I have lost you).

Always there for me.

Funny.

Kind.

Charming.

I know if ye were here you would say, 'What about Simon?'. Sure, he's amazing and ticks everyone's boxes, but he let me go. He knew I had to come here and he never asked to come. Simon will always be on my mind, but I have to let him go. He isn't what I want right now and he would never fit into this lifestyle.

Oh, then there's Jack. He's fab too and he plays for Dad's favourite team, Man United. Oh, Jack is amazing, but he is so far away in Manchester and never free.

Anyway, I must be kind to Harry. It's Harry who is the right man.

167

Today he treated me like a princess. I've never felt this happy or safe, only once before with Simon and never since. I know we have something special.

Miss you.

Love you, sis,

X

***

As she falls into Harry's bed, he wraps his arms around her as if the weather is cold and they have no other choice.

They both have many options, but they have chosen one another for a reason.

'I don't want to lose you,' she says with tears all over her face.

'Darling, you won't lose me.'

Hearing the sound of crying, he wakes up.

'Oh, don't be upset. Don't you ever worry. I am here,' Harry says while kissing her hand.

'Thank you, thank you, Harry,' she says as she moves closer to him.

Alanna looks at the clock. It is 5.18. She closes her eyes and drifts into a deep sleep.

Chapter 25

LUCE Studios, Covent Garden, London
'This is the final month of class. Each day and night should be focusing on dance and vocal rehearsals. As you all know, we have in-house photo shoots for each dancer's portfolio. There will also be new students visiting to audition, so please be professional,' Francesca instructs, while Nic nods behind her. 'Today is important for the new students too, so try to interact positively with them. Everyone, please move into the make-up room to get ready.' 'I have my artist and hair with me, so I will be OK,' says Alanna.

Francesca, displeased, says, 'Fine.'

'If there's enough time, my stylists can help with others,' Alanna adds.

MD whispers to her, 'Sista, I ain't no *pro bono* case. Hold back on sharing me out.' He winks at her jokingly. 'OK, the plan here is that you look the best! Lu, we are going to make this Irish lady *fierce.*'

'Don't forget me too,' Carlton says, running over. 'Glitter and glove me up,' He holds his metal Beyoncé-style glove.

The photographer takes photos, both planned and unplanned, trying to capture old and new students interacting together.

Tweet: *Photo of Alanna Star and Carlton Shoot Day!*

'Sista, our followers have gone up so well. You're getting like a thousand retweets, holler holler.'

***

As soon as they get their make-up done, Alanna and Carlton recall how they felt a year ago. 'So, tell us about open day,' MD says.

'Well, they lure the victims into thinking this is going to be glam, and instead it's sweat and blood,' Carlton jokes.

'I was so bleedin' nervous! I have never been as nervous as I was. But Carlton was amazing! He was the only person who was kind to me,' Alanna says, hugging him.

'Now it's time to see the new students, so everyone please be quiet,' Francesca says.

They watch with interest to see the students start their auditions.

'Hey, hey, hey, I'm Britney. I'm from the United States of America. I was head cheerleader, prom queen, head of chess, head of debating, and valedictorian. I love to help the sick and anyone in need. I always like to see the good in people. My parents always told me to give back to the less fortunate.'

'OMG, I am sure you give back in more ways than one,' Carlton says, referring to her tight outfit.

'I think she is also auditioning for Miss Teen America,' Alanna says.

'She is too happy and perfect. I am allergic!' MD says.

'Dancing is a hobby, and one day I hope to be a singer, dancer and of course an actress,' Britney continues.

'Darlin', you already are an actress. No one can be this happy!' Suzi the Polish lady says.

'*Hahaha,* don't be mean,' Alanna says.

'OK, thank you, Britney. Please go and dance,' Francesca says.

Britney starts singing, '*These boots are made for*

walking, and that's what they'll do, one of these days these boots are gonna walk all over you.' She moves around the floor with her body flipping like a gymnast, her hair swaying in sync to her perfect poise.

By the reactions on everyone's face, no one can deny how talented she is.

'Thanks, Britney. Next student, please,' Francesca says.

'I want to punch that girl in the face. I have never met such a fucking idiot,' says Suzi.

'She has talent. The only reason you don't like her is that you're so like her,' Carlton says to Suzi, who disregards him and looks back to the stage.

'The next person up is Chris from Boston.'

'Wazzup? I'm Mr C. C for cool as a…'

'So, myself, Lulu and MD are gonna hit the clubs. You gonna come?' Carlton asks under his breath.

'No, I need to get home to my man,' she says.

'Oh my lord, with MD and all these newbies I think I've died and gone to heaven.'

'*Hahaha…* You are too funny.' Alanna says. 'Have fun, hotties! I have a casting then something lined up with Harry, but I'll try meet you later. Thanks MD and Lulu, mwah mwah… I will see you all soon,' she suggests as she sneaks out of studio.

***

Carlton and Alanna's apartment, Chelsea, London
'Alanna, did you love the gig?' Harry calls out to Alannas bedroom.

'Ronnie Scotts was class – Thank you so much for bringing me!' she enthuses.

'You were amazing. I can't believe you played in front of the entire place' Harry calls out.

'Look, darling, please come out of the room. Are

you hiding something? Are you sick? You've been there so long!

'Plus, Emee told me you that I should be wary of your moods, you being an artist,' Harry says.

'Oh really, Emee says that...Emee, she can feck off. 'I'm Emee, I am so fecking perfect.' She wants to take me away from my man,' she mumbles in front of the mirror.

'What did you say, darling?'

'Oh, nothing, just saying I am so happy you're my man!'

'She has a point. I mean, sometimes your behaviour... well, it's a little contradictory. It scares me. You say you love your family, but you barely see them. You love people, or you want to be alone. You don't want to be famous, but sometimes I look in your eyes and there is a wild streak and something takes over you. It's the look of a kinky star, not a wife.'

'Ooh, Harry, and how would you know of what a kinky star looks like?' she says.

'Well, that's not the point Alanna,' Harry says sternly.

'Who's contradicting themselves now? Emee tells you about star signs, badmouthing me, then shares stories about you in strip clubs, women and badmouthing you. You're not perfect, but are we are supposed to listen to Emee about how we are supposed to act? She's an interfering...'

He explains, 'I'm sorry, you're right. I've just always had quiet girlfriends, and that stuff was for work.'

'Sure, I'm a nice woman. I just like a bit of adventure...'Stop analysing everything Harry. None of us are one way.

'So, let's enjoy now,

'All I know is that I hate having limits.'

'You give me what I need. In return I will always

172

give you what you need.

'Only if you can handle it,' she says as she walks out of the bathroom.

She claps to turn the music on.

'OK, Alanna. Ooh, I… hello,' he says.

'Last time you didn't get to enjoy this,' she says.

He was gasping for air. 'What?'

'Me doing what I love. How about I give you a new idea? How about you let me be me… And then you I can be your private dancer,' she says.

'Oh my gosh, Alanna,' he says, appraising her lace outfit, suspenders and heels. 'Wow. Oh, oh my lord,' he says as he pulls his shirt out from his chest.

'I will always be your private dancer.'

'Well, I think…' Harry cuts in.

'Don't talk. Just watch. Enjoy...' she says.

Chapter 26

Tweet: *@AStar@CStar*
Oh, everybody's starry-eyed
And everybody glows
Oh, everybody's starry-eyed
And my body goes @EllieGoulding

LUCE Final Show, Soho Theatre, London
'Welcome to the LUCE final show.' Francesca with her blonde hair and svelte figure is wearing a black dress, heels and red lipstick.

Nic, standing in a suit beside her, takes over, 'It is with great pleasure that we are here tonight celebrating our graduation students. What better way to enjoy these talents than a show?' he says. 'Each of our wonderful students will perform one of their own songs or scenes, then we will take a break, then students have prepared their diva dance... the closing act. We hope you have a wonderful evening.'

'Sit back, relax, and enjoy!' Francesca, always having to have the last word, closes the introduction as they move off-stage.

The large audience sits in the red velvet chairs, anticipating the show ahead. The spotlights flash up on stage.

Each of the students from Spain, Italy, Greece, London and America perform their own songs or acting scenes. They move from acoustic to jazz music and from scenes from 1920s scripts to modern-day monologues.

Carlton, using his best asset, his voice, sings:

It's 3am and you ain't home,
Well, I guess that means I'm all alone.

His voice is so emotional and breathtaking that tears well up on his face. The audience can feel it too.

Yet, life moves on and tomorrow I'll be out of sight,
I am a star, shining so bright,
Wait until you see me, in my spotlight…
Spotlight…
As the beat kicks in, so do Carlton's moves.
Spotlight, Spotlight… I'm in the spotlight.

He continues clapping, with the crowd joining in. Everyone is enjoying this moment, right down to his last beat.

Alanna, wearing all black with make-up and hair prepared by MD and Lulu watching back stage, follows suit. The piano is placed on stage as she walks out and takes her seat. She begins;

Finding you, finding me,
A new space, perhaps an affinity.
For people meet at that special time,
I never thought I would find someone that is only mine.

Finding you, finding me,
Waves of deep insecurities.
And passions of a life craving inside,
Now I am letting this out, with no fear of losing my pride.

Finding you, finding me,
The fears are potent ones, even if I can only see.
Yet, now it's the moment I must face,
Looking for love inside, our special space.
Part of me I cannot still express.

What you mean to me, is I can't speak without a
mess,
Yet finding you, I found me.
Thank you always, for you've set me free.
You've set me free,
You're the only one who could ever set me free…

Everyone watches in silence as her fingers touch each key. Her voice touches every note, the range so powerful that the entire room is present. As the photographs flash, she holds them all with her beautiful music. The passion and power in her voice causes everyone to sit up in their seats and clap endlessly as she looks back into the crowd.

***

As the second half closes, the audience takes their seats. Within minutes, the spotlight comes on and Carlton moves out on stage in a metal-style outfit, complete with eyeliner and glitter-filled hair in a Mohawk-style quiff. He starts:

All the single ladies,
All the single ladies…

He continues singing and dancing as he moves his hips up and down, with his right hand wearing a metal glove.

Now you gonna know what it feels like to really miss me

Carlton sings while he moves his hips across the stage like he owns it. Everyone in the audience is smiling, clapping and mesmerised by his talent.

If you like it you gotta put a ring on it!

He moves through the song with ease.

The Press flash their cameras. Within a flash he is finished. He moves out, allowing time for the next student to come on.

Twenty acts have moved through Tina Turner, Aretha Franklin, Michael Jackson and Fred Astaire, each individually impressive, unique and eye-capturing. For the final act of the night the music follows suit and Alanna comes out on stage head to toe in a red dress, her skin covered with diamonds and chunky-style stilettos with diamond-encrusted heels. Wearing black lipstick, her face is filled with glitter and diamonds matching her pointed black nails. There is a fearlessness shining out of her eyes. 'She's the most striking of the night,' is whispered through the crowd.

Everyone is speechless.

Harry too.

Assuming she will move into fast beats, as most of the other dancers did, silence fills the room as she lays her body on the floor.

The only sound is her voice against the diamond-encrusted microphone.

Paparazzi are flashing while her diamonds reflect back to the audience. She sings:

This girl is on fire...
This girl is on fire.

She moves across the stage like a snake marking its territory.

She's walking on fire...
This girl is on fire.

She continues with a rap while moving off the floor and shows her best dance moves in a subtle way. It is like being in a private show, one where you are not meant to look but just can't help yourself. It is the best show she has ever performed and everyone knows it. Lost in her moment, she continues until the end.

Looking up and out to the audience, it is clear she is finished. Each person stands up one by one to give her a standing ovation, including her parents, Liz, Harry, Emee and Jack.

Despite the impeccable talent of each performer, agents, Press, parents, and peers had no idea of Alanna's until this night.

Everything is coming together for her.

'A Star is born', with photos of her, is already being tweeted, headlining the digital media across the world.

***

Later that night the crowd moves to an after-party. The room is filled with flowers, champagne, outfits, Press flashes and glamour fitting for the Industry.

Press, newfound fans, friends and family surround Alanna. She stands with Carlton in a corner, smiling at each of the photographers, who take their photos and shine their light in her eyes.

Dennis grabs her. 'Well done, Alanna. Great performance. I forgot to say I have your contract here tonight, so let's get that signed before you get swept away by the wrong agent.'

'Dennis, this is not the time. I've been waiting months. Now it's your turn. I gotta go. Enjoy the evening,' she says as she double-kisses him as if they had just met.

Walking back to her mam and Liz in the bar,

dressed in a red dress and her diamond heels, she is glowing.

'You were amazing, love. I've never been so proud,' Mairead says.

'You're unreal, Lani. I've never seen you look so great!' Liz agrees.

'Thank you, ladies. I am so happy you made it,' she says, hugging them both.

'She was indeed,' Harry announces.

'Mam, this is Harry. Liz, this is Harry. Harry, my mam and my best friend Elizabeth.'

'Oh gosh, it is so lovely to meet you both. I have heard such wonderful things about you,' Harry says.

'Likewise, you've been taking great care of our daughter. Myself and her father are very happy,' Mairead responds, then turns to Alanna. 'Your dad just called and said well done. He will call you tomorrow when it's died down. You know he couldn't make it, as someone had to mind Brendan.'

'Plus, we'd be worried he'd fall apart if he saw ye half naked, *hahaha*,' Liz jokes.

'Sure. How is Brendan?' Alanna asks.

'Much better. He adores his school. I've never seen him so happy... well, since we lost Sally. Anyway, it's really all thanks to you,' her mam smiles.

***

Nic moves over and cuts into the conversation. 'Darling, you were fantastic! These were delivered for you! Enjoy yourself!' she says, handing Alanna two bouquets and walking on.

Alanna looks down to read the card:

Christina: Darling, sorry I couldn't make it. I had prior arrangements.

I am so proud of you.
You were born a star.
Christina
X

As she reads the second card, she starts to blush.

Jack: My Star.
Love you always,
Jack
X

Carlton comes running over. 'Sista, you were fierce. Sasha Fierce!'

'This is Carlton.'

'Hi, Harry,' Carlton high-fives him, then leans in to hug Mairead. 'OMG, Mrs O, I am so happy to finally meet you. You're like my second momma,' he says, hugging her tightly. 'Which man sent you the flowers?' he whispers in Alanna's ear.

'Christina and Jack,' she whispers back.

'Pass me over the cards. You're only gonna hurt them,' he says, taking them into his hand and looking up meaningfully at her mum and Harry.

She takes his advice, slips them into his pocket, then says to Carlton, 'I saw Christina there. She was in the back row watching me.'

'Sista, it's your imagination. You was on fire. You could have seen Queen Bee and would not have noticed.'

She looks to her phone:

Christina: Saw you on stage.
You're a star.
Very proud.
Lunch next week.

X Christina

While the Press continue to move around the room, they remain close to Alanna, knowing she is the one to watch. MD comes over to announce, 'Darling, you were fab, fab, FAB!'

Lulu nods in agreement as they clink their glasses of champagne.

'Alanna, can we get a photo with your entourage including MD, Lulu, Dennis, Carlton, your mum and Harry grouped together?' the photographer asks.

Alanna was being moved around from camera to camera, while Harry looks uncomfortable and stands back from the scene.

Meanwhile Jack comes closer with his entourage of men. 'Jaysus, ye're harder to get close to than Obama,' he jokes. Then he hugs her and whispers, 'Hope ye like my flowers. You are a star. I love you the most. I have something else for you, but I'm saving it for a big day.'

Too elated to take in what he has said, particularly in front of Harry, she nods saying 'thanks' and hugs the rest of the group that arrives.

The Press, seeing her and Jack, call out, 'Alanna and Jack, can we get a photo, please?'

'Sure.'

'Love to,' Jack agrees.

***

As the night moves along, the drinks flow, lights flashing, cards and contracts exchanged.

As if in a dream, Alanna moves around the room meeting casting directors, agents, parents of her classmates and her family. While talking to a casting director, she looks over to see Harry sitting at the bar alone.

'Please excuse me. It was a pleasure to meet you and I will send you my showreel and my contact details,' Alanna says.

'We look forward to it,' the blonde- and dark-haired ladies say in unison, smiling at her.

While she moves over to Harry, Carlton cuts in. 'Sista, all the top casting directors are here. I have so many auditions lined up. I think we have made it...'

'We are definitely heading in the right direction,' she jokes.

'Now or never, sista,' he says as they clink champagne glasses and move over hand in hand to Harry at the bar.

Dear Sally,

I can't sleep and have to tell you all about tonight.

My show... It was magical.

Every second. Before and after too.

For the first time in my life I feel ALIVE.

On stage is where I belong. Nothing else matters any more.

I finally know how you felt when you decided to be a doctor. You told me that helping people gave you a purpose. Now I have found mine. I wish you had been here.

Everything is perfect, except, well...

Harry and I aren't great. He is being weird. I think he wants a passive lady and we both know that's not me.

He is amazing, but sure I can't change for him. Nor him for me.

I think I got caught up in his kindness, yet he seems controlling.

Imagine me ever being controlled. HA!

Anyway, you gave me the courage to do this course and stand up there tonight.

Love you, sis.
My better half.
X

Chapter 27

Tweet: *@Emee But now you're*
You're looking like you really like him like him
And now you're feeling like you miss him miss him
Put it in your pocket don't tell anyone I gave ya
@EmileSande

Sushi Des Paradise, London
Alanna, Elizabeth and Carlton walk out of the restaurant, past paparazzi and directly to their car.

'*Z-Bar* please,' Alanna tells the driver.

'No problem, Alanna,' he replies.

'That sushi place, all the Press, your apartment… well, I must say it is very glam! Lani, ye've really hit it big. I hope ye don't forget about us back home,' Liz remarks.

Before Alanna has a chance to speak, Carlton cuts in, 'Sista, you ain't seen nothing until you head out with the ballers and, well, Harry. Harry's place, that's glam! Speaking of ballers, that lot turning up has become a regular, Lani. Jack has a soft spot for you,' Carlton adds.

'They are going out with you too, Carlton. I am sure at least one of the guys is after ye too,' she says as she winks at him.

Carlton blushes and keeps quiet while staring out of the window.

'Jaysus, I can't wait to meet the lads. A bit of rough and ready, the footballers always have that way about them,' Liz comments.

'Sure, but what about yer fella back home?' Alanna says jokingly.

'When on tour, sista! *When on tour*!' Carlton screams, then whispers, 'Alanna, don't deny you haven't thought of you and Jack?'

'No comment,' she says while looking at a message on her phone with a smile on her face.

Jack: Been thinking about your show all day.
You're amazing, Lani!
See you soon.
X
Jack

***

Z Lounge, Chelsea, London

As they move through the crowd and towards their table, they pass by a table with Emee and her friends, each sitting sipping a Mojito. They're tanned, blonde, and wearing black dresses.

'They are clones of one another,' Carlton whispers.

'What a coincidence!' Emee calls out.

'Indeed. This is Carlton and my best friend, Liz.'

'Loved your show the other night. I told the ladies it was very…' Emee calls out.

'Cheap!' one calls out.

'What did ye say?' Alanna reacts.

'Wild, Alanna. I said wild. Don't be bold, ladies. I never said cheap,' Emee comments.

'What did you say about Alanna?' Liz chips in.

'Sure, Emee. Well, when you or your ladies have the confidence to get up on a stage and sing with one ounce of the confidence we do, then you can comment. *Laters*!' Carlton calls out.

'Come on, ladies. Let's find some interesting people to hang with,' Liz adds.

They turn around to see Christina with two friends.

'Those girls are bitches, Alanna. I swear, if they say one more word…' Liz comments.

'Forget them. Mwah and mwah, so happy to see

185

you!' Christina says to Alanna.

'Oh my god! Christina, I haven't seen ya in years!' Liz calls out.

'Elizabeth Burke, I can't believe it. You've grown up into such a beautiful woman!'

They double-kiss one another. 'Thanks, same goes for you,' Liz says, smiling at her.

'Carlton, darling. Mwah, mwah, mwah!' Christina double-kisses him.

'Come on. Please come meet the casting directors I had mentioned. Seriously, forget them. They aren't your tribe!' Christina says, leading the way to those who are.

***

'Shall we get some more drinks?' Alanna asks.

'I need the loo,' Liz announces.

'Sure I'll go with ye,' Alanna says.

'OK, I will check out who I will have for dessert,' Carlton moves out onto the roof, smiling.

'Lani, I am so happy for you with everything that is going on, yet you must know, men rule the world. As soon as you get with a man with money… well, he owns you. Never give up on yourself, OK, Alanna?' Liz reminds her.

As they move into the bathroom, they see Emee and her two friends go into the same cubicle.

'Sssh, Alanna. It's Emee.'

They hear the girls making sniffling noises.

'Emee, this stuff is fabulous.'

'Harriet, you need to stop hogging the lines.'

'Anna, take some. What's with you?'

'I don't want any. I don't need this stuff,' they hear someone call out.

A few minutes pass they see Emee and her friends

186

make their way out of the toilets.

'Oh, our favourite friend,' Harriet says.

'Why are you always treading on my toes? Why don't you stick with your own tribe? Harry is too good for you,' Emee says.

'What are ye saying about Lani? The cheek of ye! With yer drugs, you're not half the woman she is. Say one more word and…' Liz says.

The cubicle opens and they all look around nervously to see who it is.

'You will live to regret it,' Christina continues.

'Ladies, I've heard everything. If you utter one more bad word about my niece I will have your reputation so ruined that you'll never get a job, or worst of all, a rich husband.'

'Oh, you're that actress,' Emee says.

'First and foremost, I am Alanna's aunt. So back off, or you and your classless friends will see the consequences,' Christina asserts. 'Do you understand? Apologise to my A, and if I hear of any future instances like this, you will only have yourselves to blame for your future shopping on the high street.'

'Sorry,' they say one after another.

'She is going to be the biggest star around the world… And one day you'll have to pay to see her, on stage,' Liz adds.

'Let's go,' Emee says.

Anna takes her time and turns around. 'If it's any consolation, I think you're amazing. You are so talented, and they are just jealous.'

'Thanks,' Alanna says.

***

East Village, Shoreditch, London
Alanna: Jack, we are on our way.

187

Emee is a bitch.
Seriously, I need to hang out with you asap!
See you soon.
X

As soon as they arrive, they see Jack and his friends and make their way to the bar. The music is pumping so loudly that everyone has to scream to hear one another. They move straight onto the dance floor.

Alanna and Jack are dancing closely. Carlton is dancing with Liz while smiling at the scene unfolding before his eyes.

Jack mouths to Alanna, 'Let's get some air.'

'Sure,' she says.

Holding hands to get through the crowd, they make their way upstairs outside the club, where lots of retro-looking groups are smoking and chatting on the streets.

'Are you OK after tonight? What happened?' he asks.

She explains…

'You don't deserve that crap. So what's happening with you two?'

'Who? Harry and myself?' she asks.

'Yes.'

'Well, I'm going to LA and he's going to follow me over. I'll be back by the summer unless things take off, but with my job I can't make long-term plans. I will focus on the next few months and take it from there with work and with Harry too,' she responds.

'What if I say I hate this guy Harry and I want to make plans and you to be in them?' Jack asks.

'I don't understand what you mean… I am going to LA and you're here.'

At that moment, a black car pulls up outside the club. Harry gets out.

'Alanna,' he calls out.

'Harry,' she says with a look of confusion. 'I thought you were still in Paris?' she asks.

'I flew in earlier and Carlton told me you were here so I thought I would surprise you... I've been trying to call you.'

She checks her bag and sees eight missed calls and some messages. 'Oh, sorry. I was taking care of Liz as it's her last night. Anyway, so great to see you!' she says nervously. 'Jack, Harry. Harry, Jack,' she introduces them awkwardly.

'Yes, we know each other,' Jack says.

'Yes, we do,' Harry says.

'So, do ye like football?' asks Jack.

'Yes, he does. Harry supports your team, Man Utd.' she says.

'Well, I have a box and some shares, so yes, I support and own, you may say,' Harry continues.

Realising the tension, Alanna continues, 'OK, lads. Liz, Carlton the guys are downstairs, so let's go down and enjoy Liz's last night.'

'Sure,' Jack says as he moves towards the entrance and back down the stairs.

'OK, Alanna, please stay for a second,' Harry grabs her hand as if to mark his territory. 'I really missed you. I was thinking we could just go home as I haven't seen you since your show. Plus, Tom has the car ready to go. When the others are ready he will come and collect them,' he offers.

'Sure, sounds good,' she says, holding his hand and walking towards the car.

***

'So, Emee says she saw you and you were looking great!'

'Oh, how kind of her... Did she also tell you that

189

she and her friends were snorting cocaine and verbally attacked me tonight? She told me I am not good enough for you,' Alanna says.

'Emee? Emee is a darling. She would never say that to you,' Harry says defensively.

'Ask Carlton or my friends.'

'Look, Alanna, someone in your position may be overreacting. I think you're stressed out. Carlton tells me you're struggling with money, the agent and contracts, so it's probably a little bit of anxiety. Don't worry. We can sort all that out,' he places his hand on hers reassuringly.

'Harry, my aunt Christina was there and your friends humiliated me in front of my family and friends. Why should I put up with that?'

'Is this a pity party for Alanna?' she screams.

'You should be ashamed of yourself. Class doesn't come from money. I have nothing to prove to you and your loser connections. *Nothing to prove*!' Alanna screams with her face going redder and redder to match her hair.

'Oui, oui, Alanna. Don't stress. I'm sorry. Let's go home and get some sleep?' Harry suggests.

'Don't stress! *Don't stress*? How dare you insult me, call me a liar and then tell me to sit here and take this calmly! Let me out of the car! *Let me out of this car now! Tom, pull over, please!*' she screams.

'No, Alanna, I'm sorry…' Tom pulls the car over to the kerb.

'Alanna, it's not safe to let you out here. Can't I just drop you home?' Harry suggests.

'The street is safer than being attacked in here,' she remarks. 'You and your friends may have money, but you lack class. The truth is you don't deserve me. I'm priceless,' she says, slamming the door and storming down the street towards a cab.

Chapter 28

Tweet: *@CStar*
What you won't do, do for love
You've tried everything but you don't give up
@JessieWare

The Tea Room, Harrods, London
Carlton and Alanna sit in the tea room in Harrods. Looking around, they see a glamorous dark-haired, green-eyed woman walk in. In fact, everyone notices this woman holding an array of bags moving through the café. The woman moves closer to Alanna, then comes straight over to double-kisses her.

'Hi, darling,' Christina says to Alana.

'Hi, Carlton' Christina says.

'Mwah,' he double-kisses her back. While she kisses Alanna, they both turn to hear a scream from Carlton. 'OMG, you have *the* wrap dress, DVF latest collection.'

'Yes, Carlton, new collection, no need to scream it,' Christina states.

'Grabbed you this for Christmas,

'And one for you,' Christina hands Alanna and Carlton a Harrods bag each.

'Honestly, Christina, you didn't need to do this.' Carlton rips open his bag. 'OMG, D & G glasses! I am going to look super-fierce! Darling, you are amazing!' he double-kisses Christina again, whose face indicates her intolerance to close contact.

Alanna opens her gift up while Carlton pulls it out through the wrapping, 'Stella McCartney chainmail limited edition bag!' he screams.

'I don't know what to say. Thank you.' Alanna hugs her aunt, but pulls back when she sees her face.

'Anyway, congrats. You were stunning...'

'So you were there?' Carlton reacts.

Ignoring him, Christina continues, 'Alanna, the ladies the other evening were two of the top casting directors in Broadway and Soho Theatres in London. Plus, I have the agents lined up for here and LA. I have some contacts. What's your plan?'

'Well, I am with Dennis,' Alanna reminds her.

'I mean, who is this Dennis? What has he lined up for you?' Christina cuts in.

'Well, they are doing a show,' Carlton cuts in.

'What show? What are his fees?' she asks curiously.

'Well, Mam has talked to him,' Alanna assures her.

'Mam? Oh god, Alanna. No disrespect, but you know your mam has no idea about this business. She's my sister, but she has no idea.'

'Look, he is meant to get 15–20 per cent, but no more.

'So, how much are you making?' asks Christina.

'Well, £10k for the record. Then a few hundred from modelling stuff, but that went on rent. Oh, and he's covering my rent now.'

'Do you have contracts?'

'I'm fine. We signed one early on,' Alanna says.

'OK, well, I need to see that. You don't sound fine… Look, Alanna, you need to get your own album out and get rid of this has-been!'

'You said it, sista! FYI, I don't have an agent, so that would be great if you could…' Carlton adds.

'Well, send me the contracts and I will take a look,' Christina ignores Carlton.

'OK, sure I'll get it off Mam,' Alanna agrees.

'So, with the men, who's this Harry guy?' Christina asks.

'I am with Harry. We are trying things out, and the other guys are just friends,' Alanna assures her.

'Oh, don't forget the footballer!' Carlton reminds them.

'Well, footballer or banker, you can have any man you want. Do not settle. Focus on your careers, make your own money, your own mark, so neither of you will ever need a man!' she advises.

'Sure, I am doing that.'

'Men are not worth it!' Carlton says as he stuffs a croissant in his mouth.

'Anyway, I know you were at the show, so why didn't you stay? Mam would have love to see you....' Alanna asks.

'We need to ask a question,' Carlton remarks.

'Depends, darling. I am busy now…' Christina responds.

'Look, Christina, we both wanna know why you and Mrs O don't talk? I mean, it's *ridic*. You're both super-cute, super-cool…' Carlton leans forward with curiosity.

'Quite simply, I was in a band with your parents. We toured Ireland. Your mother and I both sang, yet she was the lead. I played violin and did back-up singing. Your dad was on the piano. It was fun… yet I always wanted more. So I looked around and I got a casting for a theatre show here. I got it and took it. It was the opportunity of a lifetime to break into the Industry. I wanted her and your father to come over; I was paving the way for us all.

'Anyway, she got pregnant that year. Then with Brendan being autistic, she felt she didn't have the same chances, so she studied teaching and took care of him. Look, I was always too big for Kerry. She was so suited to there. Simple,' Christina states.

'Wow, intense!' Carlton exclaims.

Alanna stares out to space…

'Look, better you learn younger: life ain't easy. You

make choices and you live and die by them...Yet you gotta do what you love. Never let anyone stop you!' Christina advises. 'Anyway, I gotta run. Step-kids need me.' She stands and leaves £100 on the table.

'Christina, don't do that...I will pay...' Alanna says.

'Darling, I am paying. We all know you are not there yet, so avoid the dramatics. Spot me when you're A Star,' Christina says standing up

Alanna and Carlton both stand up to say goodbye.

'Mwah, mwah, mwah... laters!' Christina blows air kisses and moves out as fast as she arrived.

***

Winter Festival, Hyde Park, London
Alanna and Harry walk through Hyde Park to the Winter Festival gig hand in hand. Aside from the Press following her and Harry, it has been a romantic day out. The weather is fantastic, the music is blaring, and Harry has VIP tickets preventing any unnecessary crowds or queues.

Moving through the VIP ensemble, she looks around to see free drinks and food laid out. Comfortable seating, private DJ... it is all natural to her. Destined to mix in the upper circles, she is naturally placed in between the models, footballers, DJs and bankers.

'Hi, this is Alanna,' Harry introduces her to 'old work colleagues'.

'Nice to meet you,' she says, shaking the hands of the head-to-toe groomed wives, girlfriends and friends of Harry's. 'So who's in the line-up?'

'Lily Allen, One Direction, Jessie J, David Guetta, and Example,' Harry's friend replies.

While listening, she sees Jack and some waif blonde in the crowd. She stares long enough for him to see, yet not long enough for the crowd to notice.

As the conversation continues about business, the Royal baby and Alanna's songs online, everyone turns to hear.

'Lani, Lani! I didn't think you'd come!' Jack says, while he runs at her. 'Alanna, me love! How are ye? Jaysus, so great to see ya!' He kisses her near the lips, so close to then that everyone is taken aback, yet he's careful not to get close enough for Harry to react.

Within minutes Jack and Alanna move away from the crowd and continue chatting away. Harry watches in amazement at the speed of the conversation that flows out of their mouths.

Shortly after, Alanna moves back towards Harry.

'Gosh, you two surely do talk,' Harry remarks.

'Harry, we are Irish. We chat. It's a given. Anyway, let's go get some food. I am starving.' She leads him to the buffet.

'Sure, darling. Great idea,' he agrees.

***

As the gig ends, the evening gets dark while Alanna gets drunker and drunker. 'Let's get another drink! Yay! I love London!' she screams.

'Alanna, we are going back to a party. Will you come?' Jack asks.

'Sure. Let's do it! Party!' she screams. 'Harry, let's go. Jack can come with us!'

'OK,' Harry says. 'Are you sure you don't want to go home?'

'Home, home... whatcha talkin' about? Home? *Hahaha*. Where there is a party is my home!' she replies, slurring her words.

'Alanna, are you OK,? You're drinking quite a lot. I am so sorry for hurting you, but we can work this out. You have proved your point. I am so, so sorry. I love you with all of my heart,' he whispers to her.

'Chill out, Harry. I'm fine. Just let me be me!' she screams.

***

Knightsbridge, London
They pull up to a large house in Knightsbridge.

'We are here,' the driver calls out.

They walk through the house, which has large white slates, white and black furnishings, chandeliers and art throughout. Most prominent is the grand piano in the central lobby.

'This house is fantastic, Jack! I was looking to buy a house on this exact street,' Harry states.

'It's the house of the captain. Top class. Clearly we both like the same quality things,' Jack replies.

'Perhaps we do, yet there's a huge difference between liking and owning,' Harry says while holding Alanna's hand and walking on.

As they move in the house is filled with crowds from the gig.

'Everyone here is so glamorous,' Alanna says.

'Depends what you call glamour,' Harry remarks.

'Alanna, there is a piano here. You have to play for us, darling.

'You're a singer, you have to play us a live show' Jack calls out.

'Go on Lani, sing for us,' everyone was looking over and there was a scene.

'OK, sure, why not?' she says as she stumbles through the crowds towards the piano and takes a seat while the crowd gathers.

She sets her fingers on the keys and sings out in her slow jazz-esque husky voice:

Hey baby, baby, oh my baby,
Need you,
Hey baby,
You're my world,
My life…

Everyone moves closer to her, falling silent as her voice sounds throughout the house. Harry and Jack are both mesmerised by her.

I wanna love you,
Need to love you for life,
One day, I will be, will be, will be,
I will be your lady, your lover, your wife.
Yes, yes, baby, tell me, tell me…
Tell me that you'll want me for life.
Tell me you're feeling this too,
That you need me through and through,
Oh baby, tell me it's you,
It's only and forever me, it's just me and you.
Say, yeah, yeah, baby, tell me it's true…
I wanna love you,
I wanna love you,
Love, love, love you…

As she shuts the lid of the piano, she stands up to see over three hundred people looking at her in amazement. They all cheer, scream and whistle, surrounding her and saying well done and honouring her.

'Wow, you're so talented, Alanna! Jaysus, I can't believe you're not on the telly!'

'Ye're a lucky man, Harry,' Jack says.

'I know,' he says while kissing her on the forehead and pulling her tightly to him. 'The luckiest.'

Jack is almost speechless, 'Well, I… I… I'm going to see some of the lads so I'll catch up with you in a bit.'

'Sure, see ya in a bit,' Alanna says.

'I'm so proud of you,' says Harry, turning to Alanna. 'Tonight I realised something.'

'What's that?' she asks.

'That I want to be with your forever,' he affirms.

'Really?' she asks.

'Yes, for life,' he says.

Chapter 29

Tweet: *@AStar I can't believe I'm your man,
I get to kiss you baby just because I
can@MichaelBuble*

Mandarin Oriental Hotel, London

As Alanna moves out of the car and into the hotel reception, her hair flows. She is wearing a *Chanel* blazer, black dress, high patent heels and a demure lipstick. Harry looks to her, smiling.

'Like a fine wine, Alanna, you get more beautiful day by day,' he remarks admiringly.

She smiles back, but clearly forces it while she adjusts her camera, which now feels like a normal part of her attire. 'Darling, you still appear slightly upset this evening. Are you OK?' he asks, concerned.

'Look, I am sorry about our arguments and for not believing you. Emee told me some of her friends were taking drugs and I know we both upset you. You must know I am not into that scene, but unfortunately we live in cosmopolitan London, and like in every big city there will be drugs. Particularly in the industry you're in,' he explains. 'All I can assure you is that this stuff will never ever pass near myself or our inner circles, and that's all I can guarantee, Alanna.'

'Thank you, Harry. I really appreciate you clearing that up, as I don't want to be around that scene. My parents brought me up with strong Catholic values. False arrogance from drugs is never something I will be impressed by. Class is not something ye can just buy your way into; you earn that by keeping your beliefs,' she states.

'As always, Alanna, your argument stands alone. I do but agree. Irrespective of classes and backgrounds, it is large mind versus small mind. It's up to you to decide where you want to fit.'

'Harry, I want to fit wherever ye are, but I need you to defend me. We are a team,' she says.

He kisses her passionately. 'Alanna, I love you so much, my partner. I would love you to be my partner, for life,' he says. 'I would be so proud to be with you, never forget that.'

'I love you too. Thank you for making me feel safe,' she says.

There must be a catch.

As he leads her to his mother who sits at a table with a sour face on, Alanna felt this might be it.

***

'Pleased to meet you, Alanna, again. Particularly with clothes on this time. May I add, beautiful clothes,' Anne remarks.

'Nice to see you again too.'

'Splendid to see you, Mother. You're looking charming as always,' Harry says solicitously.

'So, Harry tells me that you're a dancer and do a bit of singing. What a delightful hobby to entertain you until you start your real job of producing children and raising a family,' Anne comments.

'Sorry to disagree, but I don't see it as a hobby. I am a dancer and also write, sing and play some instruments too, which has taken years of practice and still requires ongoing practice. I don't feel just because I have kids it should stop my passion and career,' as she scans the menu. 'Mother, as much as I cherish your worldly views, please let's move away from Alanna's choices of career and children, particularly at such a premature time. Alanna and I have not discussed kids yet, so please let's talk of something different.'

'In fact, my mam worked right up until late into her pregnancies. Not a bother for her,' Alanna cuts in.

***

'How was your trip to the Bahamas? Did Margaret and the ladies join you?' Harry enquires of his mother.

Alanna cuts him off, 'Sorry to interrupt again, but I think the Bahamas and Mags are quite irrelevant in comparison to my future as a mother, so let's talk it through,' she continues. 'I assure you that I am talented at what I do. Plus, ye should be happy that I want to work; it shows I have no interest in marrying your son for his money, as he tells me most women in his past would have liked to. Unlike them, I am independent and will always wish to be if I can. If I or we decide to have children and I change my options, that will be only a choice for myself and my partner.

'And while I am on the topic of my partner, do you know that Harry is extremely talented at his job running his father's company and gets little or no credit for the wonderful work he is doing? Meanwhile all these shareholders are in the newspapers being acknowledged for your son and late husband's work. Maybe we can chat about that?' she says sweetly.

'Alanna, I think you should calm down a bit, mother doesn't deserve this,' Harry says.

'Yes, but she does have a fair point, Harry,' Anne confirms.

'Did you know that he's developing technology apps that can change the way trading is done? Or that his apps are being used in the music industry? Also, that he is now helping to get involved in a charity for autistic children that I work with?'

'No, I knew of no such things,' Anne concedes.

'Together, I believe we are a fantastic couple. So, if and when we have children, they will be equally fantastic.' Taking a deep breath she faces her boyfriend and his mother, both calmly smiling back at her. 'Tonight we should celebrate Harry and I being fantastic,' she says before shouting out, 'WAITER!'

All eyes look over to the roar from the young woman as the waiter runs over, reacting to Alanna's feisty manner.

'Your most glamorous champagne, please.'

'Our favourite, please,' Anne confirms by smiling to the waiter.

The waiter hurries back and within a few minutes the sound of glasses is heard.

A union has been created.

The evening progresses with ease, and Alanna excuses herself to go to the 'ladies' room to freshen up'.

***

'Oh, she is so charming, Harry. Where did you find this one? A step up from Emee! I'm so pleased your cousin married her. She wasn't a nice lady. Not good enough for you,' Anne frowns. 'As for this one… well, she is a handful, but a beautiful and intelligent one. I also see softness in her eyes, which you need in a woman. She reminds me much of myself when I met your father. I like her.'

'Really, Mother? You think so? Oh, I am so pleased! It means more than you know that you approve. Alanna is often rough around the edges, but she is so loyal and is a princess. She has the makings to be a queen, just like my mother,' Harry kisses his mother's hand.

Meanwhile, Alanna is adjusting her camera in the bathroom. She calls Dennis, 'Look, I don't want to do this anymore. We said one or two tapes. We never agreed his mother. It's not fair.'

'Fair? Fair? *Hahaha*, darling, the Industry isn't fair, but you gotta toughen up. Keep playing wifey and we'll get this show out. You'll be rich and famous in no time.'

He cuts out.

***

Sitting back down at the table, Harry kisses Alanna's hand and looks at her with a glowing smile. It is clear that she has made a great impression. Blocking her nerves, she accepts the rounds of drinks all evening, and is impressed by Anne's ability to hold her drink. Sending Anne off with double-kisses, she finds herself in a cab back to Harry's.

'Your mam has such a dynamic personality. Honestly, the evening was much more enjoyable than I had expected.'

'I'm glad you think so. I always knew you would get along. You're so alike – both loyal, beautiful and bright women.'

If only he knew, she thinks to herself.

As she rests her head on his shoulder, they move through the streets towards home.

It is clear that they have magical charm, and anyone in their company would notice how they can't stop touching each other. There were little gestures all evening, which may not have been there at their first moment of meeting, but now they come more frequently. As they move in and out of the streets, Alanna sees swooshing lights, blurs and spinning, but

203

with Harry she is safe. He holds her hand and she knows she adores him.

***

Harry's apartment, The Shard, London
As soon as they get in the door to Harry's apartment, they kiss passionately.

'I want to prove how much I love you,' murmurs Harry. 'Wait here.' He comes back in with a box from *DeBeers.*

She opens it to find a diamond chain with matching earrings. 'Wow, these are stunning! Thank you so much... I adore them,' she says while he fits them on her.

'I adore *you*,' he says as he places her on the kitchen island, kissing her all over. 'I love you. I want all of you and would do anything to help you see that I can make you happy.'

***

'Let's go,' he says to her while he leads her into the bedroom. As he undresses her, he kisses every part of her and puts his hands all over her lace underwear as her toned body is revealed. Together they are laying naked one on one, kissing slowly, intimately, intensely, better than anything she has ever experienced before. She feels like she can be herself with him. He is the same. She isn't scared anymore. He will take care of her. She knows he will always take care of her.

Chapter 30

Tweet: *@BStar Sometimes I feel like throwing my hands*
up in the air
I know I can count on you
Sometimes I feel like saying "Lord I just don't care!"
But you've got the love I need to see me through
@Florence

Harry's Apartment, The Shard, London
Three days later, she has spent the whole time at his place. Waking up naked between his sheets, she smiles as calls up 'This can't be real!' her Kerry accent pervades so loudly it may have woken him. She is sure he is opening his eyes and closing them again.

Ignoring this, she slips on one of his oversized shirts and walks outside with her iPad looking at the view of London.

Enjoying the moment, she smiles as she begins to write.

Dear Sally,

This wasn't meant to happen. I am a career girl; I am all about the music. I wasn't meant to go this route of waking up naked with the most handsome, wonderfully sexy, funny charming, perfect man.

I have always had feelings for him and now I know they are love. Yet I was never the loved-up kind of girl. I'm the tough one that scared the crap out of all the boys back home.

I was the top of the class with men. You were top in terms of academia (well, both of us were). Simon knew that too. Anything we wanted we set our minds to, worked hard and in the end always got it. Mam and Dad instilled in us that 'anything is possible, with hard

205

work and two feet on the ground'. Hahaha, do you remember those days, sis?

With Mammy and Dad as schoolteachers, I now see we had such a nice childhood. Brendan being autistic was never discussed. It was just Brendan; he was different but that was it.

Do ye remember we would play him songs on the piano and sing to him?

You were so patient with him when he had his fits. You were the one person who could help him. You were destined to be a doctor.

You would have been the best.

Love you, sis.

X

***

She falls back to sleep on the couch, dreaming and reminiscing about the past...

As she wakes, she looks at her phone.

Dennis: Every night, Alanna, you create a better show. The producers are impressed with you. In fact, they call you a natural. The deal is signed. We have Harry's mother on camera. You have sealed the deal, the show is due to be released as soon as we meet the directors in LA.

They have your launch party ready once we arrive.

Alanna Star is coming to life!

Dennis.

Alanna, shaking, drops the phone onto the ground and moves in circles, feeling a huge wave of guilt.

Dear Sally,
I don't know what to do.

206

I have everything I want.

Amazing family and friends.

Carlton's fees will be paid.

Graduated from LUCE.

Yet when my show comes out I'm going to lose Harry.

It's only a few dates…

Maybe he won't mind?

Maybe he will understand?

I can't ask him for money.

Or can I?

I want everyone to think I can do it on my own.

You know me.

Maybe I can cancel the show?

Maybe I can explain everything about Brendan and you and he will understand.

Miss you, sister. You would have known what to say.

Harry comes into the room as Alanna is sobbing hysterically, holding her iPad.

'What's wrong, Alanna? Oh, darling Alanna, tell me what's wrong with you? Please tell me. Did my mother upset you? Is it me going to Paris? I can cancel. I won't go.'

'No, no, she was lovely,' Alanna sniffs. 'And no, it's not Paris. You have to work. That's not it.'

'Is it money, darling? Please tell me. I will give you anything you need. Anything!' he screams.

'Well, it's not just that. It's just… well, remember I told you I am going to LA for a show?'

'Yes, you said it's entertainment. I am assuming a dance show,' he says. 'I'm very happy for you. I am sure they will love your voice and you'll get a great agent. Yet if you don't, don't cry. We shall get you one when we come back.' He holds her hand protectively.

'Well, it's not that kind of entertainment.'

207

'What do you mean?'

'Well…' She looks at his face. So tough, yet deep down so innocent.

'Are you OK, Alanna? Is Dennis upsetting you? Is he forcing you into something illegal?' he says. 'To be honest, I don't trust him. Or Jack. Carlton is the only friend you have around you,' he says.

'I'm fine, Harry. I think I'm just tired. The show will be OK. Christina is helping me with contracts.'

'OK, well, I was going to tell you this when I got back, yet maybe this will make you feel better. I have done some research and so I bought a place in the Palazzo, West Hollywood. It's a great investment, and if you plan on working there, I want us to have a home from home. I have arranged visas so we can stay there up to three years, but with a plan to move back into our new place afterwards. I want to help you do what you love, as you will help me in what I love.'

'Oh, Harry. I love you so much.'

'There will be room for Carlton, plus I want you to be safe if I'm not here,' Harry adds.

Harry's phone goes off.

'Take it, Harry. It's work.'

'What do you mean the stocks have gone down? Darling, can you give me one second?'

'Sure…'

'Well, tell them I'm on my way to the plane,' he says. 'Darling, I have to go, unless you want me to stay?'

'No, you need to go,' she says, smiling.

'You stay here and get some rest. The key is there. Stay until I get back. Are you sure you're OK if I leave?'

'I'm fine.'

'I'm so glad. You know my father used to say to me: don't fret, everything will work out in the end. Everything always works out as it's meant to.'

He kisses her forehead as he moves out of the door.

'I'll be home soon.'

'I miss you already' she says with tears streaming down her face.

Chapter 31

Tweet: *@AStar And when that love comes down*
Without devotion
Well it takes a strong man baby
But I'm showing you the door
'Cause I gotta have faith @Jack @GeorgeMichael

Alanna and Carlton's apartment, Chelsea, London
Alanna answers her phone as Jack calls.

'Darlin', I am so excited you're coming! The press officer will meet you at the front gate. I have a car picking ye's up so they will drop ye straight there. I won't be on the phone, but you will come meet me in the players' lounge after the game, OK?' Jack asks.

'Sure, sounds great,' she confirms.

'Lani, I'm so delighted that ye're coming to watch me play. Ye keep cancelling on me, and as much as Carlton is a fun replacement... I want ye there,' Jack says.

'I promise I won't cancel. It's just been a busy time.'

'Anyway, I'm really excited to see you! I'm gonna score ye a goal. Wait and see...gotta go. See ya later,' he says, hanging up.

***

Alanna and Carlton prepare their make-up and hair as per usual in the bathroom, mirrors side by side.

'OK, sista, I am in the loop. I know all the WAGs' names and personalities,' Carlton informs her.

'Some will be your friends, but most will ignore you.'

'Imagine dancers on speed who haven't eaten in days and with lots of power,' Carlton suggests.

'Well, they didn't get that seat in those stands from being no nice girl...'

'You better believe it that they ain't letting you come in and get their men,' he says.

'I don't want their men,' she says, laughing.

'They ain't knowin' that! Imagine, these ladies are like the directors on Broadway. They are the brains of the operation. They act all pretty and aloof, but they manage the stars and together they run the show! So you gotta put on the fierce side to ye today. Imagine castings. Imagine claws out... Imagine *America's Next Top Model*, Tyra-style!' he says to himself in the mirror.

'Not sure if it's you I'm more worried about, or them,' she says, laughing sarcastically.

***

Manchester United v. Chelsea, Fulham Broadway
With the VIP pass, they travel by car, moving past the crowds rushing out of Fulham Broadway Tube station. Alanna watches the touts selling flags and merchandise. Seeing people wave and whistle at the car, Alanna wonders, 'Do you think they recognise us from my record? Or maybe things with Jack, or...' She looks around to see Carlton waving and blowing kisses at the fans. 'Carlton, what are ye doing waving at them like that?'

'Lani, we are WAGs. So to these fans we are just like the Royal family. Keep waving... you're in the loop.'

'Ye're bleedin' gas,' Alanna jokes. She looks around to see the excitement in everyone's eyes. 'Do ye know what? I think you have a point!'

'That I'm a queen...? Gosh, sista, you haven't seen the half of it!' Carlton states.

'Well, that too, but that the players are really performers like us.'

'The WAGs are the directors. The wives and the coaches and managers are the agents.'

'They are adored by all. People pay to come and see them... Yet each minute counts and they are only as good as their last game or show. It all makes sense...' she says thoughtfully. 'I now know why he wants me here! My man Jack, when I miss his games, it's like him missing my show... I would be so upset!'

'Hold up, hold up, I thought he ain't yo man?' Carlton asks. 'Don't go meddling, sista. We talked about this!' she says in a New York accent.

He laughs, seeing the glint in her eyes.

***

Manchester United V.I.P Area, Chelsea F.C., Fulham Broadway

'OK, this is Tara, Tamara, Steph, Lucia and Denise,' Carlton introduces the ladies seated in the players' lounge. 'This is my lady A Star. FYI, she ain't here to take yo men!' he screams out.

Blushing, Alanna says, 'Pleased to meet you.'

'Nice to meet you.' Two or three posh London and some Essex accents are heard.

Alanna is drawn to the kids and waves down to them. 'And what are your names?'

'I am Sophie. He is Stuie, and that is...'

'My name is Daniel. My dad is a player. Is your dad a player?'

'No, well, my friend is a footballer,' she responds.

'Is he your husband? Mummy, I don't understand.'

'Anyway, who wants to come with me to get some drinks?' she suggests to the three young kids. 'Is that OK?' she asks the mothers.

'Sure, by all means... Please do!' they all smile in agreement.

They bring Daniel and the kids into the bar.

'Sista, I see wifey and mummy written all over you,

'What's with you today?' Carlton asks.

'I love kids. Especially Daniel. Look at him; he is so helpless. Reminds me of Brendan.'

'Brendan who?'

'My brother. He is autistic,

The one I've told you about for months,' she says impatiently.

'Oh yes, so many of you Irish, like rabbit families so hard to keep up,' he jokes.

She moves back over to join in with the kids.

***

'OK, kids, let's go watch the games?'

The crowds scream and jump up and down. The waitresses are serving food and drinks while everyone sits watching the game intently.

'So Jack has it bad for you. Do you know that?' Denise says. 'He is really smitten.'

'All the women love him, but he has no interest. It's all about you.' Tara says.

'That's really sweet,' Alanna replies.

'OMG, sista, I told you this months back. Sometimes I worry about your memory, gurlfriend' Carlton rolls his eyes.

***

'So, Carlton was showing us your music and dance

blogs. Pretty impressive. We hear you're going to LA and you've got a record out. That's pretty cool,' Tamara, the slim blonde lady, states.

'Who is your agent? I am doing some fashion shows. You could play.

'I also do some charity things,' Denise says.

'Her agent is a douche,' Carlton responds for her.

'Yes, he's not great. I'm in the middle of trying to get rid of him, to be honest,' Alanna agrees.

'Well, let us know.'

'We gotta support each other. Take our cards.'

'Sure,' they say as they each pass their card over to her.

'Thanks, I'll definitely be in touch.'

***

Just then Jack scores. Everyone screams and jumps up and down.

Carlton screams, 'My man and Jack. They did it! Go hotties!'

The women are looking around. 'So, who is your man...? You must be dating one of the guys!' they ask.

'A queen never reveals her secrets,' Carlton responds.

'He's with Jean,' Alanna says.

'What? But he has a lady and two babies at home!'

'Yes, but that's all a cover-up,' Alanna says.

'Carlton, is you serious? Is this why you're at these games?' Tara asks.

'I thought you loved football... Or us?' Denise says, laughing.

'Sista, I ain't got no clue what yo's are talkin' 'bout. The only balls I came here to see are...'

'Carlton, there are kids around!' Alanna warns.

'*Hahaha!*' they all laugh at once.

'He is our favourite gay *ever*! Queen Carlton!' Tamara calls out.

'Let's get a round of champagne. The guys will be off soon, so let's get some more in. Don't want them to get jealous,' Tara winks.

***

Jack runs into the players' lounge towards Alanna.

'Lani, Lani… so happy to see ye!' He kisses her on the lips without any hesitation while she quickly pulls away. 'I scored for you! I promised I would score for my Lani.'

'Well done! You did amazing out there,' Alanna says.

'What de ye's want to drink?'

'Whatever you're having.'

'Well, done Jack! You did amazing today! Please can I excuse her for two?'

'Sure, Carlton. I'll get you the same.'

'Thanks, Jack.'

'Come with me.' Carlton takes her out into the hallway. 'Sista, this life suits you. You could do your dancing on the side and have no ties.'

'But I'm with Harry. Not everyone can cheat like you,' she says.

'Wha' you say?' he snaps back.

'Ye heard what I says. Why with all the men in the world are ye meddling with someone else's man?'

'I ain't meddlin',' he says, looking at the ground. 'He ain't her man; he's mine. He told me he was leaving her for me.' Tears well in his eyes.

'Do ye think he'd agree if we asked him now? Look, he's not even comin' over to you!' They both look at the French dark-haired man at the bar. 'Until he

215

confesses this, you better step back. It's not fair. On you, on his wife, the kids. It's his mess and you're all losing. Carlton, you have everything to offer a nice man. Why do you think so little of yourself?' Alanna asks.

'It's called LSE. My therapist calls it low self-esteem. I eat because I'm unhappy. I'm unhappy 'cause I eat,' he says with tears streaming down his face.

'Poor Carlton. Well, next time you feel lonely, you come to me – I am your drug,' she suggests. 'Let him go,' she adds.

They look over to see Jean leaning towards his girlfriend, kissing her and staring into her eyes. Carlton has tears streaming down his face.

'Come on. You are way better than him!' She gives him a tissue.

**

Jack walks over...

'Let's celebrate!'

They all move towards the bar. Jack holds hands with Alanna.

'This feels right. My team, my goal and my lady' Jack says.

Carlton, smiling, looks out of the window pretending not to notice, Alanna's hand in Jack's.

'Do ye think we will ever fill a stadium like this?' she asks Carlton.

'I hope so, one day,' Carlton muses. 'Imagine the crowds calling out our names. 'A Star and C Star are on next!' he calls out, voiceover-style.

'Let's keep the faith,' she says.

'Let's never lose our faith,' Carlton says, smiling back.

'Gotta have faith.... Gotta have faith' Jack starts singing as they both join in.

216

Chapter 32

L.L's Members Club, London
Dennis sits behind his black Ray Bans, as usual hiding from any eye contact with anyone. 'OK, Alanna, I have booked our trip to LA. Everything is covered. We are all good to go. Here is the final edit, as you requested. The editors are going to put some more in but this is mainly it.'

He hands disks over to her, and she takes them, hands shaking.

'We will launch this soon. Plus, I have some castings lined up, then you can start working on an album,' he states. 'I know that Harry insists on sorting your accommodation, but that's all he has a decision on. Remember, I am your agent, your main man. He can't get involved in this,' Dennis insists.

'OK, I thought you would want this back.' She passes over the camera to him.

'Be a bit more discreet! There are people around,' he says.

'What are you talking about? Sure we work in media and it's in a bag, ye mad thing. Ye're so bleedin' paranoid!' she laughs. 'Before we move on, we have agreed this show is about dating in London, not Harry's family.'

Dennis nods.

'I still don't know why it's taken so long. I mean it's only one episode.'

'Yes, it's just the director has been held up with another show,' Dennis explains.

'So when am I getting paid? You've given my family a few grand, but you have never paid me for my song. It was top on *YouTube*, number three in *iTunes*... I should be raking it in!' she says, the volume of her voice rising.

'You had a wonderful home, Alanna, designer clothes for free, and lots of Press. The best is ahead. All in LA,' he says, smiling.

'Look Dennis, what if I said I don't want to do this? What if I said I don't want to go to LA and I am happy here? Would ye pay me then? Where are the feckin' contracts? It can't always be about *feckin' LA!*' she screams. 'My mam says you've never sent them back to her, so I am talking to my lawyer. Plus I've been writing lots and I think I need to move on. We want different things.'

'Don't even joke. You're *my* artist. *I made you!*' He slams his hand on the table and screams so loudly that the entire room stops and stares.

'Calm down,' she says.

'Alanna, you have a contract. Your parents have money for your brother. I'll send them the contract and more cash.' His nose starts bleeding again, all over the table in pools of blood.

'What the feck? Dennis, we need to get ye to a doctor? Or the hospital!' she says.

'Give me a minute,' he says as he holds his nose with tissues and moves towards the bathroom.

She moves immediately out of the restaurant, handing the waiter £50. 'Can you tell him I left? Please don't let anyone see that mess,' she says to the waiter, who is in shock about what they have left behind.

'Sure,' he agrees.

'Thanks,' she smiles and runs out.

***

L.L's to King's Cross Eurostar Station, London

Friday peak time was never going to be easy to get a cab, thankfully, with her Irish charm and luck and the red dress she was wearing, one pulled in.

'Thank you so much. You saved me, sir! Saint Pancreas, please.'

'You're too beautiful to miss, darling,' he jokes.

Blushing, she says, 'If you take the shortcuts, I'll give you a big tip!' Alanna, now a pro in London, knows what to do to charm him.

She decided to text him.

Alanna: Hi Dennis, had to leave. Harry is taking me away.

See you soon or in LA.

Alanna

The taxi man's glint is seen through the mirror as he speeds off on his mission.

As she prepares her make up, a few minutes later she looks down to see a text pop up.

Dennis: Sure, see you in LA.

Don't do anything to mess this up.

D

***

The cab journey, like many before, entails a quick change of shoes, from flats to stilettoes, and the use of baby wipes as Alanna changes from her daytime face to stunning glam goddess. She knows how much this trip means to Harry, particularly after all they've been through, and she wants to look her best. Now she has her man, she never wants to let him go.

'Alright, lovely, we are here. £10, please,' he requests.

As promised, she hands him £10, plus a £10 tip and with a flick of her hair pushes out her wheelie bag and steps out of the cab.

Looking out into King's Cross station, she sees Harry standing awaiting her arrival. Looking her way, he walks towards her in his suit, his black hair moving up and down, his green eyes glowing, wheeling his bag behind. Alanna, waves back, realising more than ever how handsome he was.

Every man and woman stares in amazement as they run towards each other.

'My man!' she screams.

'My love!' he responds.

Her butterflies come up again.

'Paris awaits us, princess,' he kisses her. They see cameras flashing and realise it is just tourists. 'No paparazzi... just us,' he says, joking but also giving a sigh of relief.

'No press, I swear,' she assures him.

They kiss deeply until they are interrupted by a French accent ringing out across the station. 'Final call to board the Eurostar. Final call, thank you. Final call.'

'Let's go, Alanna!' he says as he holds her hand and leads her towards the check-in.

***

'Tickets, please,' the mousey-brown-haired petite woman calls out. Harry takes the tickets out and hands them to the woman.

'Passports, please?' He hands his passport to the lady and turns back.

'Alanna, passport, please?'

'Are you joking?' she replies.

His face is hopeful and unassuming. Her accent gets stronger and the speed at which she speaks is as fast the

220

train about to leave. 'No, like, I never knew of this. When we get a train from Kerry to Dublin with Mam or my friends, like, we never need one. And so I thought... well, I didn't really think at all, to be honest. I just never thought of this,' she says innocently.

Realising she is serious, his face shows a sense of disappointment.

'Now I have ruined the whole trip. I'm such an idiot!' The tears stream down her face in floods, and Harry hugs her, seeing how upset she is.

'Oh dear, oh my dear Alanna. What will we do with you?'

'You should check train times for tomorrow instead. Please go back through security or else stand to the side,' the lady suggests.

'Let's go,' Harry says as he looks at Alanna, who still has tears streaming down her face.

***

Harry, following some intense arguments in French with the security guards, gets them released back into King's Cross, which is quieter now that all the crowds have left for the day. His arm remains around her as they walk outside.

'I'm really sorry,' she says again.

'I know you are,' he smiles.

'For everything,' she says.

'I forgive you, Alanna. I will always forgive you,' he smiles.

Picking up his phone, he dials his driver. 'Tom, we are taking a rain check on the Eurostar tonight. Can you or one of the guys pick us up? King's Cross? Yes, ASAP. Please tell Sue to sort the plane; we'll be going to Paris as soon as it's ready. Tell her to call me with details. Many thanks.' He hangs up 'Now, let's get home and get some rest. We have an early start.'

As he puts his hand into the small jewellery box his inside jacket pocket.

'We have a big day ahead. A big day indeed,' he says.

Chapter 33

Tweet: *Paris @AStar Oh you look so beautiful tonight*
In the city of blinding lights @U2

Harry's apartment, The Shard, and Heathrow
At 5am after a light sleep in Harry's home, various alarms later Alanna and Harry clap on the lights, shower and dash out to meet their driver waiting outside the house. Thirty minutes later they are boarded on a private plane.

'Harry, I have never seen ye this nervous. Are ye OK? You poor thing... you didn't sleep a wink. Close your eyes and get some rest or if you don't feel well, we can go home?' she offers.

'No, no, no. I do not want to go home!' he reacts uncharacteristically.

Alanna, in shock, pats his back. She knows there is something bothering him. 'OK, no problem.'

As soon as they are sitting, the hostess offers drinks, and within minutes Alanna looks out of the window, holding his hand. 'This is our first trip together. Also, my first time on a midget plane,' she says, smiling.

'Midget plane! *Hahaha*! Oh darling, you make me so happy,' he says.

'So why didn't you take me on the plane rather than a train in the first place?' she asks.

'Well, I hope that we have our entire life to travel on my planes. I need to know you're happy with just me,' he smiles and looks deeply into her eyes. 'Don't you worry if things will be different after you go to LA?' he asks.

'Well, no, but sure ye're coming over so we will be together.'

'I'm scared of losing you, Alanna. I don't want to stop you, but I see the paparazzi and the footballers and agents all pulling away at you, and then you're doing this show. Well, I feel like there are parts of you I don't know yet. Or parts of you that I will never know.'

'After this show, I don't want to be famous or to be around that scene. I will continue my singing and dancing, but I will focus on what I love: writing and singing. I love music as much as my family and you. Oh, and my family… well, they can't wait to meet you.' She kisses him for the longest kiss she could remember.

***

As soon as they land in Paris, Alanna shows Harry her iPad. 'I wrote this for you,' she says.

As I take flight,
This is a new part of my life.
With you, beside me, happiness is surely in sight,
The past was hard and lonely with so much fight,
At times I felt I had to no one there,
Yet it all changed with one stare.
Now you've opened my secret door,
Love is there, a love I would have never known before.
The future may be great, or tough, no one really knows,
We'll never know until the day comes along.
For now, you are my moment, my love when at home or on show,
With you is where I feel I belong,
Each day you will be my passion, my beat,
The reason I will keep writing my songs.

Harry has tears in his eyes. 'I love you so, so, so much.' He kisses her. 'You are my everything.' He holds her hand and helps her off the plane.

***

On the car journey to the hotel Alanna answer answers a call.

'*Sista!*... Guess what? I got a job!'

'Aaahhh!' she screams. 'Where?'

'In LA!' Carlton calls out.

'LA?' she repeats. 'Are you serious?'

'Yes, I am serious,' he says.

'We will both be in LA!' she says.

'We will *both be in LA*!' he screams. 'Yay!'

'Yay!' she reacts.

Harry has his hands over his ears while politely looking out of the window.

'So, I will be running a dance studio...' Carlton elaborates. 'I have some meetings with agents lined up and I have heard through friends in NYC about a dance movie casting in LA that we *must try out*!'

'Carlton... Us in LA... I can't believe it!*Ahhhh!*'

'*Ahhhh!*' he screams back.

'OK, gotta go. Call ye soon. Love you,' she says.

'Love you too.'

They drive through the streets of Paris.

'Je suis desolée, mon petit chou,' she kisses him and leans into his chest.

'Je t'aime,' he responds.

***

Le Jules Verne, Paris
'Cheers, to us,' he says as they clink their champagne glasses. 'This was my dad's favourite restaurant.'

Looking out over the view of Paris, Alanna replies, 'He had impeccable taste.'

'So, what happened to your dad?' she asks.

'He had a heart attack. Very suddenly. It was very sad for Mum. I was working in Hong Kong and travelling a lot, working crazy hours. Dad always wanted me to work for him, but I wanted to prove myself. Anyway, they say it was stress.'

'It's very sad,' she says.

'I do wish I had worked with him, as maybe I could have taken some of the load off him.'

'So you feel guilt?'

'Sometimes, yes,' he concedes.

'I understand how you feel,' Alanna admits.

'What do you mean?'

'Well, I've lost someone close to me and I can't help blaming myself.'

'Is this Sally?'

'Yes, but I'd rather not talk about it tonight.'

'All I do know, Alanna, is that you owe it to a person you've lost to make the most of every day. Guilt gets us nowhere.' He puts his hand on hers.

'I wish you could come to Kerry, but I know you have work and yer mam this Christmas.'

'We will work it out, don't you worry,' he assures her. 'Alanna, tell me about your sister? Carlton told me, and I can't imagine how hard it's been for you.'

'She was my better half, and since she died... well, I'm on a search.'

'For what?'

'My better half.' She smiles as tears fall down her face.

He hugs her. 'Darling, you're so brave. So very, very brave.' He wipes away her tears.

***

As they move through the streets of Paris, Alanna asks, 'Have you ever heard of *The Symposium?* '

'Plato, yes. I studied it in college. Fascinating man,' Harry responds.

'You know he believes that people were originally totally round creatures, like balls, then we annoyed the gods so much and were split apart into two. Since then each half has been trying to find its other half. So, true love is that feeling. I like that idea,' Alanna says.

'So, you think we all have a soulmate?' Harry asks. 'Like serendipity?'

'Yes, but I don't believe it always works out. I believe a series of decisions can affect how this works out. Sometimes people make bad decisions – really bad ones,' she responds.

'What do you mean?' he asks.

'I don't want to remember anything but magic about this night, so let's forget it. Let's enjoy here and now,' she says.

Hand in hand they walk through the streets of Paris, taking in the beautiful architecture.

'Voilà!' Harry says.

'Wow,' she breathes.

'Aren't these magnificent?' he questions.

'On first reaction they look like Mam's pipes in the boiler. Yet I am always open to art,' she says.

'*Hahaha*, darling, this is one of the most decadent galleries in the world: *La Pompidou.* '

'You speak such fantastic French,' she observes.

'How do you know? You don't speak French,' he reacts.

'Je parle un petit peu,' she responds.

'Wow! Tu es bien a parle a francais. Je t'aime,' he says, kissing her.

227

***

As they drive around Paris in the convertible, they pass the *Champs Élyseés.*

'Gosh, the people here drive like crazy,' she says.

'Darling, don't worry. You're safe with me,' he reminds her.

Their car manoeuvres in and out of streets.

'Louis, pull in. Here we are. Merci!' he thanks the driver.

Holding hands, kissing and stopping for gelato, they smile, happier than ever walking towards the the Eiffel Tower.

'Jaysus, that's pretty high. I thought it was going to be teeny.

'Sure ye woman Mona was tiny, and this is massive.

'The French are great magicians at fooling us, aren't they really,' Alanna says.

He laughs at her. 'Only you would say that about these iconic statues... Darling, you're one in a million. Really, I have never met anyone like you. I love you.'

'I love you too,' she says.

'Let's head back to the hotel.'

They hold hands as they go back to the car to meet the driver. Harry checks his phone, 'Just want to check in with Mother to see if she has arrived safely. Bonjour, Maman...' he says.

Alanna looks down at her own phone and sees a message from Jack on What'sApp. It includes a photo of him smiling with his sisters. They start to chat;

Jack: Darling, I miss ye a lot! Where are ye? My sisters are in London and want to meet you.

Alanna: I'm in Paris with Harry.

Jack: Oh.

Alanna: Let's catch up when I'm back.

Jack: Darling, ye're in Paris. Ye know you're not going to come back the same person?

Alanna: What do you mean?

Jack: He'd be a fool to not make you his. I just thought it would be me.

Alanna: What do you mean?

'Darling... darling, Come here.' Harry reaches for her.

Dropping the phone into her bag, she moves towards Harry.

'This was my summer house growing up.' He kisses her on the forehead. 'Maybe we will have our own summer house here one day.'

Looking down at her phone, she sees the end of the message from Jack.

Jack: As a wife, he wants you as his wife. So do I. I love you Lani. We need to be together.

'Maybe we will,' she says, with tears in her eyes looking to her phone. She lays close to him as they glide through the streets of Paris and back towards the hotel.

Chapter 34

Tweet: *@AStar @Harry*
My first love
There's only you in my life
@DianaRoss @LionelRichie

Hamman Spa, Ritz Hotel, Paris
'Bonjour. Welcome to the Hamman,' says the beautician with curly black hair and cute freckles on her cheeks. 'So, I have laid out all the products. You start from left to right. I will leave you together to enjoy your treatment.'

They move into the steam room.

'Harry, if I didn't know you, I would think you're trying to get me naked!' Alanna jokes.

'I don't need an excuse,' he says cheekily.

'Oh really?' She rubs mud in his face.

'Yes, really!' He takes the mud and throws it at her.

They continue to throw mud on each other, laughing hysterically.

'I love when it is just us,' he says.

'Me too,' she says.

'Tous les jours,' he says as he moves close and kisses her.

***

Alanna, walking out of the bathroom in a robe, sees Harry rushing to get dressed with his hair still wet.

'Darling, I have booked a salon and spa for you to prepare for this evening. I have to go collect Mum,' Harry says. 'She always recommends this as her favourite salon, particularly for galas and things. She may even join you later. They can do your make-up, hair, etc. I'll leave it to them. See you later. Bisous!' he says as he kisses her and leaves the hotel room.

'I'm in heaven!' she screams.

Looking at her phone, she reads the messages and photos from Jack over and over while staring at photos of her and Harry.

***

As she walks into the salon, an opulent room with marble floors and mirrors, where everything is sparkling clean. It is obvious who the clientele will be in there.

'Hi. I am Alanna O. Here for an appointment.'

'Je suis desolée...' the woman looks at her appointment book and shakes her head.

'Well, I have an appointment. Perhaps it could be under Alanna Mac?'

'Oui, bien sur. On y va!' the brown-haired lady takes Alanna through the room and into a finer one, where she sees a team of stylists waiting for her.

A man with light brown hair, framed glasses comes forward.

'Bonjoooooour!' he calls out at her while grabbing who face and grabbing it as if she is a child. *Tu es belle, belle, belle!'* He kisses her on both cheeks. 'Je suis Jean-Luc,' he says, enunciating the words clearly to ensure that she understands.

'Je suis Alanna. J'adore!' she points to the salon.

'Merci. It is such a pleasure to meet you. Harry has told me only wonderful things about you,' he says.

'Oh, you are so kind,' she responds.

'So, we shall get your hair and make-up done... oh, and your feet look dreadful! We shall do these too. Get to work, team!' he says pointing to the chairs for each stage of the process.

Sitting back into the chair, Alanna picks up her phone and dials. 'Carlton, you will never guess where I am. *Dans la salon,*' she says in a French accent. I have people pulling at me... my hair, make-up, even my feet. I feel like I am on one of those home make-over shows.'

'OMG, that is too funny. Sounds like the Mardi Gras, except they'd be wanting to touch more than your feet,' he jokes.

'*Hahaha*, you're mad!' she reacts.

'Seriously, though, you know he is grooming you to be his wife?' he says.

'Why is everyone talking wives?'

'No reason,' he says.

'Miss you here,' she says.

'Miss you too... But... gotta go have a date. We met online. It's *amore*! Oh, and when you get your gift, send me a photo!'

Carlton hangs up. She looks back to the magazine she was reading and smiles.

***

She returns upstairs in her polka-dot summer dress, smiling with her hair up, pearls in the sockets of the buns, navy nail varnish, beautiful make-up and eyelashes. Walking into the hotel room, she sees a note sitting on a Harrods suit holder on the bed: *Je t'aime.*

'The Vera Wang dress from Harrods!' she screams. 'Wow, wow, wow... I can't believe it!'

She removes the polka dress, while carefully placing the floor-length dress over her head, ensuring not to ruin her hair.

The navy satin dress with a lace cover moves over her chest, and as she looks to the mirror she sees a drop-down back. Placing her diamond heels on, she looks at herself in the mirror and smiles.

'I look like a princess,' she says out loud.

She takes a selfie and sends it to Carlton and Liz, then sends a message on What'sApp

Alanna: MD, I am cheating on you with another stylist, but you can't be angry… getting my hair done in Paris. BUT if it's any consolation, they are fab so I hope, I just hope you approve. A x

***

'Sure, I'll send it to you, Jack,' she says out loud.

Jack: I have never seen anyone more beautiful. You're so beautiful, Alanna.

'Darling, you are you're the most beautiful woman I have ever seen!' She turns around to see Harry standing there while the door closes. 'I really, really I love it. I really love you. You know I always want to be with you. Do you know that?' he says.

She hears a beep and looks down to gets a text;

Liz: You look like an angel.
I'm with your mam and dad.
You've done a great thing; your parents got another lodgment from Dennis.
They are very happy. Brendan is so happy in his new school.
You're an amazing person, Alanna.
A true star X Liz

***

Soon after she starts to arrange her dress, shehears another text pop up:

MD: OMG - You are like a queen. Damn!
Irish goddess…
When on tour, darling… I'll let you off ONLY as he
has done a fab job!
See you at Christmas in Dublin ;)
X MD

'Are you OK, Harry? You look very pale,' she asks, watching him getting ready.

'Yes, it's just tonight is a really big night for me.'

'I know it's your dad's ball, so of course you will be nervous,' she says while she adjusts his dickie bow. 'I wish I had the chance to meet him,' she says.

'He would have loved you… You're so classy and strong, just like Mum. That's why he married her,' he says, smiling and looking into her eyes.

***

Hotel Le Meurice, Ballroom, Paris
As they move into the ballroom, they see sash drapes and over a hundred tables full of white tulips. The attention to detail throughout is impossible to miss. The windows all face an opulent, gold-encrusted stage veranda, moving out onto an equally stunning garden.

Alanna is transfixed by the room, and savouring the jazz being played by the band in the background. 'Look at the gold paint, the old furnishings, the décor! It's like a scene from heaven,' she gushes.

'I know. It is beautiful, just like my date,' he says, taking her hand and leading her towards the table as she moves her eyes around the room.

'Ah, Harry, great to see you!' a table of middle-aged men call out.

'Great to see you too!' he shakes hands with each of them. 'This is my partner, Alanna. Alanna, this is Tom,

234

Ben, David and Theodore and their lovely wives,' he sweeps his hand to include the women sitting at the table.

'Pleased to meet you all,' Alanna replies.
'We shall talk later, fellows,' he says, once again taking her hand.

***

As Anne move towards them, she has a sour look on her face. 'Mother, so lovely to see you!' He stands while he double-kisses her.

'Nice to see ye again,' Alanna says.

'Oh, darling, lovely to see you. Money really suits you,' Anne jokes.

'Excuse me?' Alanna frowns.

'Mother, don't be silly,' Harry says.

'Sorry, I can't hear you. The band are playing loudly,' Alanna says while they all take a seat.

***

Harry stands up and walks towards the stage to give his speech. 'On behalf of my father Mr Mac, I would like to invite you all here in aid of the Mac Cancer Research Foundation. Being in Paris, I would speak in French, but father always insisted that if giving a speech it was best spoken in your native language. So I shall continue,' he smiles. 'It gives me great pleasure to be here this evening to celebrate the work that we have completed over the previous twelve months. As you can imagine this charity is close to our hearts. Each year I work with the board to invest in the most suitable projects we see fit. Once again creating research and hospitals to care for those affected by this tragic illness. Words cannot convey this, so the books on your desks provide images of this work – photographs of the patients who have benefited from the cause over the previous twelve months.

'I am here merely to share and support their stories, yet the victims and doctors... well, they are the true heroes and heroines. So let's raise a glass today to the board, the doctors, nurses and most of all the patients,' he finishes, holding up a glass.

'Hear, hear,' people from the crowd call out while chiming their glasses.

'As always I must thank my mother, who is the reason I am here today, and for her support of my father. A toast to Mother,' he says, raising his glass again. 'One last thing, could I ask you all to raise your glasses to my beautiful girlfriend. Alanna, please come to the stage.'

Alanna comes forward and climbs the steps up onto the stage.

'Alanna, my dear, since we met, each day I have fallen more and more in love with you. I have done nothing more than imagine you as my wife.' He puts his hand in his pocket. 'In the hotel where my parents got married, in a room filled with all the people that truly matter to me, I would like to ask you to share this dream and be my wife,' he proposes.

'Oh, yes, yes, of course, Harry!' she says as she kisses him.

'I am the luckiest man alive. Thankfully that didn't go terribly wrong!'

'A toast to the bride-to-be!' someone shouts out as everyone else sighs and cheers.

'Come here, darling,' he says as he places the large circular diamond ring on her finger. 'I have never been so happy,' he says.

'Me neither,' she agrees.

***

'We must dance!' Alanna requests to Harry. She initiates a ballroom dance and the crowd cheer as they watch the happy couple, so in love. Moments later, Harry sees his mother storming off from the table.

Harry cuts their dance short. 'Let me check on Mother. I will be back very soon, my darling.'

She takes a photo of her ring and sends it to Carlton.

Within a minute Alanna makes a call.

'OMG, OMG, OMG! Saw photo. OMG!' Carlton screams.

'*Carlton! I am ENGAGED!*'

'I know, I picked the ring – or *rock,* should I say. *Hahaha,* it is *so* big, sista. Just as you like them!' he jokes.

'I love it, Carlton. Thank you for everything!' she says. I gotta go. I will see you tomorrow.' She hangs up.

Without hesitation she calls her mam. 'I am engaged!'

'We know. We wanted to call you too. Dennis gave us lots of money, Alanna. Your father wants to talk to you.'

'Hi, Dad.'

'Hi, Lani. Look, you must know, Alanna, that we are very proud of you,' her father intones in his Cork accent. 'With your engagement, your college and also Brendan can now go to his school and Mam can work part-time. We love you very much and will celebrate when you're home.'

'Love you too,' she responds and hangs up.

She soon hears a book from Twitter with photo of her ring

@AStar, soon to be Mrs Mac, A Queen can you believe it? @CStar

***

237

Alanna, noticing Harry's return, moves towards the reception to hear him.

'I know, Mother. I know you may not love the idea of me being married, but she is an angel. Only time will tell what is ahead, but I love her. I am not marrying her to make her stay. I know she will stay. She will make a great mother like you,' he states.

Pretending not to hear, she walks over to Harry.

'My future husband,' she smiles. 'We have lots to celebrate. Come on, darling, let's have some privacy. Please excuse us for the evening, Mrs Mac.' Alanna takes Harry's hand and directs him to the lift.

She walks to reception and addresses the receptionist. 'Please send your most expensive champagne, strawberries and all of your desserts up to room 310.'

'All the men must stop contacting you. Many broken hearts will be had now that you're mine,' he smiles smugly, kissing her in the lift.

'Yes...'

She gets a message on Whats' App.

Jack: Is it true?

Alanna: I'm engaged!

'I love you, I love you so much – so much it's going to hurt,' she tells Harry as she looks up to the ceiling, tears welling up in her eyes.

'I love you too, darling. Don't cry, we have only happy times ahead,' he says, kissing her eyelids. 'I will always make the pain go away,' he says.

'I love you always,' she says.

***

Lying in lace on the bed while Harry lays asleep, she looks at her iPhone. Smiling at hundreds of Twitter retweets, she hears a beep come in.

Jack: My heart is broken. You're my one. I want you to be happy. Yet it was meant to be us. Jack x

Dear Sally,
I'm engaged!
I really do LOVE Harry. I want him for life.
I am safer with him than anyone before.
How can I tell him what I've done? Is it too late to back out?
Brendan and family have the money. So many thoughts went through my mind. It's only one show, one episode.
Perhaps he will never find out?
I knew I could tell him the truth and maybe he could help with Brendan and I could stop working in the Industry?
I love him. I don't want to lose him and couldn't bear the thought of any more loss. If the show was released, I may never lay next to Harry like this again. I don't want to lose him. That's not what I want.
Yet sometimes I am not sure what I want at all.
Love you, sister.
X

Pulling Harry close with tears in her eyes, she closes her eyes and falls asleep.

Chapter 35

Tweet: @*AStar Hey, those flashing lights come from everywhere The way they hit her I just stop and stare* @*CStar* @*JT*

Aer Lingus Flight, London to Killarney
Looking out of the window of the plane, Carlton is rambling hysterically about his latest man. 'So, like he says he wants to be with me, but, like, I dunno as he says he can only talk to me on Sunday or every second Wednesday. Like, I know we are leaving London, but he's busy and I don't want to appear needy so I think I'll go with it and see how it goes.'

At this point Alanna's attention has drifted, as she is reading her iPad, a piece she wrote a few weeks back:

People running by every day, different faces to me,
Smiles or acknowledgements yet nothing to say.
As time is previous all must move fast,
Forgetting the now, it has us passed.

People move on and never say goodbye,
Without a card or a note or an address to say hi.
Moving forward or so it seems,
They are missing this moment in search of these dreams.

People want love but won't give it a chance,
To others around who may share their romance?
Or intellect or hope for a present moment shared,
Yet, if they don't fit into their future, not one more moment is shared.

People are sprinting by me, forging through,

It all gets so much.
My head is heavy, my eyes too,
One day the people will stop for just a special
moment in time...
Yet, I will be gone, now is my time to shine.

'Anyway, *Ms Evernote*, I swear you have, like, either a serial dating thing going on or you've written a few albums. You're never over that dang thing. I am jealous you're not giving me attention and you won't share that with me.

'One day I will. It's my album,' she says, smiling.

'So, do yo miss Harry?'

'Sure, it will be weird being apart.'

'You two are, like, joined at the hip,' he admits. 'On the other is Jack, *hahaha!*' he jokes.

Although she is excited to visit her family, she knows already that it is going to be hard not to see Harry over the coming weeks. She has never felt this way before.

'What about Jack? Bet you're excited to see him?' he asks.

'Sure, I am.'

***

Alanna nods, trying her best to not appear judgmental. 'Darling, you have three dates in a day – too many is as bad as too little. It is a losing battle and a pattern only you can break. You are online dating to the extreme. You must have a premium-plus account,' she jokes. 'Honestly, do what's good for you, Carlton. You know I will never think any of these guys are good enough for you. When you are up dancing on Queen B's tour, you will find the right one.' She takes his hand.

'My wifey, what would I do without you and your wise words?' They both smile.

As they move over the Irish coastline, Carlton screams, 'Oh my lord, it's so *green*... just like the movies!'

'The entire flight is looking at ye, Carlton. Sure, it's no wonder, you're tall, handsome, green eyes and as gay and loud as Christmas, *hahaha*,' she jokes.

So much for keeping a low profile! Yet, her cover is blown as children behind her take photos on their iPhones, while a familiar paparazzi face on board watches their every move.

'There are paparazzi on board so let's try keep our secrets to ourselves,' she whispers.

'Sure, sista. Where are those paps? We are on a private holiday, so I will kick their asses if they even try to take a photo of you.' He sits up smiling in the hope that they will.

She laughs. 'I know ye too well.'

***

Landing in Kerry airport, they move out of the door to see flashing lights as both paparazzi and fans take photos.

'Alanna, look here! Look here! No, this way,' she hears.

Trying to hide, she moves as fast as possible towards her mam. Carlton, enjoying the attention too much, decides to bow at the crowd and perform a pirouette. Alanna, as always and with pleasure, allows him his time to shine.

'Mam. Maaam, Maam! Maaaaam, over here!' she screams as she runs towards her mam. *Mairead. You are one of my best friends – My rock.*

'My Lani! Ye look so grown up, I didn't recognise ye,' exclaims Mairead.

They hug closely for a few minutes while the photographers focus on their special moment.

'Come on, Carlton!' Alanna beckons.

They move swiftly out of the airport and over to the car.

'Where's Brendan?' she asks.

'At home with Dad. All the excitement would be too much for him.'

'You're right. Carlton is enough to handle!' she jokes as they reach the car.

'Mam, skooch over. I want to drive. You go too slowly and I want to get out of here.'

'Oh, I understand, Mairead. It must be since the accident. Well, at least you're brave enough to drive,' Carlton says.

Seeing paparazzi moving towards the car, Alanna speeds out.

Carlton, in the back, says in amazement, 'Oh my lord, you're fast, Alanna! Mrs O, your accent is so fab. The people are so smiley and Ireland is just *so green!* I love it here already!' he screams.

***

Fixing his gaze out of the window a few moments later, he proposes, 'So, what's the party tomorrow for? You and who else, Lani?'

'Celebrating my sister,' Alanna says proudly.

'What. Which sister?' he asks. 'Oh, I see. Sally? Oh, you poor ladies. Sorry, me and my big mouth.' He wraps his arms around both of their seats.

'I am here for you both,' Carlton assures them.

Mairead says. 'I am very happy to see my daughter Lani.'

243

Alanna feels relief to be back, but is nervous about leaving again as she holds her mother's hand tightly.

'Oh, another green field... oh, and another... Oh, and there's a tractor. Oh and another...' Carlton continues.

'Carlton, let's just rest assured that they are all green,' Alanna says, half-joking but half-serious, smiling into the mirror.

***

O'Riordans family home, Killarney, Ireland
Driving into the entrance of her childhood home, Alanna breathes heavily, overwhelmed by feelings. Slowly shaking, anxious and feeling slightly faint, she smiles, trying to cover it up.

Carlton notices immediately. 'Sista, don't worry at all. You are with me! You haven't been back since that time, so it was going to be an emotional trip. Feel those feelings,' he advises.

She sees Brendan and her dad in the entrance of the house. 'It will be worth every minute to spend time with my family, especially Brendan!'

Seeing him wave to the car made it all worthwhile. 'Brendan, *Brendan*!' she screams.

'Alanna, Alanna!' he says while jumping up and down with excitement hands over his ears.

Reaching the door, like a mother to a long lost child, tears pour down her face and she embraces him. 'I missed you so much. My darling Brendan. I love you so much!'

He hugs her back.

'Gosh, she's going to make a fabulous mother one day, Mrs O,' Carlton comments.

'Yes, indeed she will,' Mrs O agrees.

'As will you, Carlton,' she jokes

'*Hahaha*. You better believe it, sista! I'm destined to be a Queen, like you.' He puts his arm around her, leading her into the house.

Chapter 36

Tweet: @AStar @CStar
All I want for Christmasis you
@MariahCarey

O'Riordans family home, Killarney, Ireland
'Lani, come downstairs…'

'Sure, Mam. Carlton and I are getting ready.' She hears a text pop up on her phone.

Jack: Can't wait to see you.
X

As she is reading this, she runs downstairs…

'Someone is here to see you!' her mam calls out.

'Harry! Harry, I knew you'd come! Harry…' She stops dead at the foot of the stairs. 'Jack! Jack? I can't believe you're here. I mean, I thought you were with your family?'

'What a nice welcome!' Jack responds.

'Oh, sorry,' she grabs him and hugs him tightly. 'So great to see you, Jack. Come in, please come in! I am so happy to see you. This is Mam, who you met in London. This is my brother Brendan. Carlton is changing and Dad… Dad, come here! You have to meet someone!' she calls out.

As her dad walks out from the kitchen, his eyes grew wide with excitement, while Alanna and her mother look at one another, smiling.

'Dad, Jack. Jack, Dad… Think we will leave you two to talk about what ye know best: football!' they say in unison.

***

Killarney Church, Kerry

As Carlton and Jack enter the local parish with Michael, Brendan, Liz and Mairead, Alanna senses the tension with the 'famous and foreign visitors'.

'Sista, ye may as well have ran naked through the parish, as everyone is staring,' Liz whispers.

'Carlton, Irish people are the bleedin' kindest but in some corners of the Emerald Isle some folk are not ready for ye,' Alanna says.

The congregation at Mass that day has to deal with something very different to what they are used to:

Carlton: age 28, 6 foot 2, African American from New York, dancer with bad-ass attitude.

Jack: age 24, 6 foot Irish footballer for Manchester United.

Alanna: 5 foot 11, age 20, singer, songwriter, presenter, dancer, Irish superstar.

The grannies stare over, whispering. It's clear that everyone in the church is staring at the O'Riordans.

'Child, you better stop staring at me or I is gonna come over there and give you a piece of my mind,' Carlton says to the little red-haired child staring and pointing at him. The child fearfully sits down quietly, snuggling into his mother.

'What is with you white people?' he whispers to Alanna. Yet Carlton whispering is never a whisper, and heads turn once again.

'At least he'll give them something to chat about,' Jack whispers to Lani.

Alanna and Jack laugh, knowing too well that Carlton will be the talk of the town for months – if not years – to follow.

***

'There's Simon,' Alanna says.

'Who? That guy walking past?' Carlton points to Simon, who walks past with his sisters. Outside the church, every person arrives to shake Jack and Carlton's hands and also curious to see which one is 'Alanna's husband from the 'Big Smoke'.'

Realising it is not one of these two, they are interested in the newbies at Mass, and Carlton is enjoying every moment.

'Lani, I'm going to head off. Have to make dinner in me ma's. So glad I got to meet your family,' Jack says.

'Thank you so much for coming,' Alanna says, hugging him.

Her father and mother shake hands with Jack. 'Pleasure to meet you.'

'See you in Dublin soon,' she assures him.

'Anytime you need me, Lani, I will always be here for ye,' he reminds her as he walks towards her car.

Just then Carlton runs over. 'Gosh, I feel like a president visiting! You Irish people are so friendly. I don't know what a lot of them are actually saying, but I am sure it's something sweet, as they were all smiling.'

***

Alannas House, Killarney, Ireland
'Where are the lads?' Alanna looks out into the road and sees the guys moving up and down.

'They robbed O'Sullivan's tractor and are doing some sightseeing tours of the neighbourhood,' her mam calls out. 'Oh, and Harry called while you were sleeping, so I said you'd call him back.'

'OK thanks, Mam. I am going to take a trip to see Sally…'

'Are you OK to go alone, darling?' she asks.

248

'Yes, I'd like to see her by myself,' Alanna assures her.

***

Killarney Church Graveyard, Kerry

Kneeling at the grave, Alanna talks to her twin. 'So, that's it Sally, all my news. As ye know I miss ye, like every day. You're missing out on some craic here. OK, I gotta go, sis. I love ya and speak to ya soon.' Alanna has tears in her eyes as she walks away from the grave. Just as she turns around, she sees Simon and is unsure how to act.

'Jaysus, Mary and Joseph, it's you! I can't believe it's you!' He is in shock. 'You look so beautiful,' he says, referring to the cream *Chanel* suit, leather skirt and mid-heeled boots, along with her organised hair and subtle make-up. 'You always did.' He looks down at the ground like the first time he asked her on a date.

'Thank you,' she says, blushing. 'Being a dad suits you. She is an angel,' Alanna remarks about the child, looking at the uncanny resemblance between them.

'Suzie is really sick, so Ali is staying with me. She's a handful, but sure worth it,' he says proudly.

The little girl moves in and out of his legs and pulls at him, looking intently at Alanna as if she was going through a government inspection.

'You're such a decent man. Never change,' Alanna states.

'So, how are you? I hear you're engaged?' he asks.

'Yes, recently in Paris.' She shows him her ring.

'Congratulations,' he responds.

'Thank you, Simon. And for you? Have you met anyone special?'

'Yes, well… no, this is my woman now. More than enough to handle.' He smiles, holding the children's hands. Slightly nervous he continues, 'Anyway, must be off. We're heading down to the village to see my sisters. Good to see you. Take care, Alanna.'

'Please send all of your family my love,' she responds as he moves back towards the car.

Chapter 37

Tweet: @AStar *I'm always gonna be the best thing you never had* @Beyonce

Muckross Lakes, Ireland
Alanna sits by the lake watching Carlton and Brendan play in the water as she writes in her notepad.

> *Sitting here in Killarney to a beautiful sight,*
> *Friends in the lake, happiness is moving through me.*
> *Smiles, laughers and jokes throughout,*
> *Love in the friendship are heard in their shouts so loud,*
> *Passion, pain, love is seen here through their days,*
> *Bringing them together to this golden moment.*
> *All is good, all is fine,*
> *The weather is rough but life is kind,*
> *I drop my pain with the pen,*
> *My heart and mind are on the mend.*

'Back in a few. Myself and Alanna are going for a walk,' her dad announces to the guys. 'Come with me,' he says in his pronounced Cork accent.

Saying nothing the entire trip, Alanna follows her dad as they walk along the Killarney Road. After ten minutes they stop.

'Do you see this land, Alanna? I bought it for you and Sally, and one day I was to build a house each for you both. Both of ye and your little sprogs one day,' he smiles.

Alanna looks at her father with tears in her eyes.

'I thought you would marry Simon, and Sally would be with Michael, and you'd raise lovely families here.

Yet things change. We have lost our Sally and nothing is going to bring her back.'

At this stage Alanna is sobbing. 'I can't believe we will never see her again,' she says.

'I know, dear. I know. Yet you are here and that's my point. We all have plans and dreams and sometimes life throws a spanner in the works and ruins them. We have to be strong. We have to move with the way life takes us. Like Brendan,' he says. 'If you love this lad Harry, then do whatever it takes to make it work. The day I saw your mam on stage, I knew she was the woman for me, and I never gave up. If you're not sure and you love music, then follow your dream. You have all the chances that your mam and I didn't. As soon as Brendan was born we lost that freedom. Yet we wouldn't give him up for the world. So you have to take this chance... follow your heart, love. This land will be here for you and one day you will build on it. If not, that's OK. Now I want you to do whatever makes you happy. We will always support you,' he says, hugging her.

Alanna looks at her dad with tears streaming down her face. She wipes them away. 'Thanks, Dad. I will make you proud.'

'Now let's go. You have to get on the road to Dublin before it gets dark,' he says while putting his arm around her shoulder and leading her back to the lake.

***

Killareny to Dublin, Ireland
Waving goodbye to her parents and Brendan, who are all standing in the driveway, Alanna sobs hysterically with her head in between her knees.

252

'Sista, goodbyes are never easy, but we must learn to live on the road. They are in your heart. That's all that matters,' Carlton says.

She remains silent for an hour or so.

Texts from Simon arrive in between her tears as she drives through storms on the motorway to Dublin.

Simon: It was so strange to see you. You broke my heart, but I could never be with you.

I don't want a showgirl. I want Alanna – the young Kerry lady who didn't need all that stuff. I will never change my feelings, but the situation isn't right.

Oh, you should be back here with your family. It's not right what you're doing, running away from yourself.

Simon

***

As they move on the Motorway 'OK, I said you can drive if you drop the phone. Sista, have you not seen those ads on television?' Carlton scolds. 'You need to keep your eyes on the prize. Think of Sally. Give me that phone.' He grabs it out of her hands and checks what is on the screen. He looks up after reading the message and responds with, 'Oh no, he *didn't*!' in the most flamboyant tone ever.

Alanna, with tears smudged all down her face, nods as if to say 'yes, he did'.

'Sista, you is telling me that he is not liking your fine ass because of some technicality and your wonderful job? Dump, dump, dumpster. He is not a real man. Alanna, you is the best. You have everything a man needs and you is a fine kisser. The best I had. Queen A, you have the ability to turn even the gayest men straight, so forget him. *Fo-get* his *stup-pid* ass!'

Carlton throws her phone into the back and puts on some Motown music to change the mood.

***

Continuing on down the motorway, Alanna remains quiet thinking about Simon, Harry and Carlton.

'Ye know that was the first time you have mentioned what happened that night,' Alanna puts her hand on Carlton's.

'Darlin', we have Jack star, Jack in Dublin, then you have a trip to LA, Dynamite Dennis and Handsome Harry, along with any man on the Tube if all else fails. I can't fight against all of that.'

They both laugh.

'Sure ye can,' she says.

'What ya thinking about?' he asks her.

'Harry and how happy he makes me feel and how I will be seeing him soon. Ye know I'll always love Simon, probably like every woman would always have a place in their heart for their first love.'

'Tell me about it, sista. Yet time to accept that and move on. Harry needs you to move on,' Carlton says. 'Let's get some Christmas tunes on and get in the spirit!'

'Christmas is over, Carlton,' Alanna reminds him.

'Oh yeah. Well, for next year then.'

'I used to want you so bad..

I'm always gonna be the best thing I never had' comes on high volume in the car as they both join in.

Alanna turns to Carlton smiling knowing he has created a playlist of Beyonce songs to entertain them on their drive.

Chapter 38

Tweet: *@Jack And if you have a minute, why don't we go,*
Talk about it somewhere only we know?
This could be the end of everything,
So why don't we go somewhere only we know?
Somewhere only we know @LillyAllen

The Shelbourne Hotel, Dublin, Ireland
Lifting up the covers in the hotel, Alanna looks up to see Carlton in a luminous pink sweatband, matching shorts with dark leggings with a bright smile bouncing around the room.

'Wow, someone is bright!' She calls out.

'I have already done a jog around that stunning park. Mr Stephens or whatever it's called again,' he says. 'I hear the Irish guys are charming, so I want to get some attention. Ya know, get to know your fellow men,' he says, laughing.

'Yes, they are charming, but please let me sleep,' she says, going back under the covers.

'Sista, we are performers. We need to train. Plus, we are hitting LA in less than a week... You gotta look fierce!' he says, mimicking a lion. 'Get your sweats on and get your fine ass down to the gym.'

'Dread... I don't want to go,' Alanna says.

'OK, we can do another lap of the park,' he compromises. 'OK, let's do that. I need air.'

'Give me five... Is there any chance that this may be a paparazzi moment and nothing to do with my health?' she calls out.

'Never!' he says smiling.

***

Fade Street Social Restaurant, Dublin

'OK, we have covered the Guinness factory, the History Museum, the park, Grafton Street, the Book of Kells, live music... what else?'

'Best to last: let's get stupidly drunk, proper Irish-style,' Carlton says. 'Even more crazy: let's play truth or dare and do a shot or knock back at every truth or dare?'

'Wow, truth or dare, drunk-style. That sounds promising. You start,' she adds. 'Truth?'

'When you met me, what did you think of me?' he asks.

'I thought you were the most handsome man I had ever met. I had no idea what Americans were like other than a few passing in and out of town. The nicest in our studio by far!' she announces.

'Drink up!' he screams.

'OK, truth or dare?' she asks.

'Truth,' he requests.

'What do you think of me, Harry and the camera? Sorry, that's a really selfish one,' she admits.

'Sista, I don't know how he's going to react. I mean, we haven't even watched the tape. Why haven't we watched the tape?' he questions.

'I know, Carlton. I'm scared,' she says.

'Don't worry, Lani. Look how happy your family are. You've done the right thing. You needed the money,' he says.

***

'We can watch the tape together, so are you relaxed now?'

'Well, I have a feeling there is something missing. Why would Dennis want you to film only few dates with Harry?'

'It is not Harry. It is about dating in London, isn't it?

'Do you have the contract?' Carlton requests.

'Yes… well, no. Well, we have a kind of contract back in the hotel room,' she says. 'My plan is to go over there and get this tape back.'

'Sista, I don't think it's that simple.'

'How do you know?' she worries.

'Well, I've grown up in the Industry – lived it, breathed it, even lost my dad to it… You may think I am an idiot, that I sleep around and fall in love, and that I don't care. But I give people what I expect back.

'Yet, I am more than that. I love the Industry. It's my life. My mum is an acting coach and my sister will be a singer, so my family is part of it. The Industry is the real me. I don't know who I am without it. To make it in this you have to be a certain type… Trust me, these guys are not nice guys like you know. They will eat you alive. Look, you've chosen your career over love and that's your choice… You're going to be a star!' he says, smiling.

'Don't you think you can have it all?' she asks.

'No, darling. Something's got to give. So just enjoy the ride,' he reminds her. 'Let's get rich and successful and we can buy our men!' he jokes.

She smiles, but with effort.

***

'Truth.'

'What's the story with nosebleeds? Dennis was rampant with them! No one seems to care in the Industry!' she says.

'That's drugs, honey! Sometimes I think you're so naive! Do you remember the day we arrived in the apartment and I convinced you to take the wall bed as it would be like a Bond Girl?'

'Yes.'

'Same applies here. Sometimes you're in a bubble... but in the greatest of all ways,' he says.

A What's App message arrives.

Jack: Hey, Alanna, I am back for a Sports Against Racism Event.

I'd love to see you both. We are just hanging out.

Heading to House Club. Please meet me and my sisters there!

'Jack wants to meet,' she says.

'OK, let's go. Do you think it's a good idea, though?' Carlton asks.

'Why?'

'Erm, *hello*! Jack loves you, you know that? Isn't it gonna be hard enough to say goodbye to family, that loser Simon, then Harry too, without adding Jack into the mix?' Carlton asks.

'Ah, sure he's just a friend,' she jokes. 'Do you ever think of being with him?' he asks.

'No. I'm engaged to be married' she says, pointing to her engagement ring. They see flashes and hear calls of 'that's yer one! Yer won the singer!' someone calls from the table nearby.

'Oh *dram*, what dram!...' Carlton says while subtly smiling for the cameras. 'He loves your fine ass,' he says.

'OK. Dare.'

'I dare you to kiss Jack and admit to yourself who you really love... Then you could live in London being a WAG, you could be a millionaire's wife or you could choose the best option: to be with me!' he jokes.

'I love your romantic notions, Carlton!' she says, laughing.

'No matter which man you choose, I will have a rich and amazing best friend to hang out with,' he says.

'Who says I won't make it on my own?' she argues.

'Oh you will... Yet it's always nice to get there with some nice perks.' He smiles.

'Sure, anyway, let's get back and change and go meet Jack,' she says as she signals for the bill.

***

House Club, Dublin, Ireland

'Jack, we are here!' Carlton calls over whilst the paparazzi flash their cameras on the Irish stars.

Jack and his two blonde sisters walk out, in the highest heels, to the flashing. Alanna wears skintight leather jeans, *Louboutins*, a fitted black top and a blazer. She waves over to Jack and his sisters. They move closer.

'Jaysus, she is a ride!' says Jess, the buxom sister in Lycra.

'Sure you're bleeding tiny... That camera must be the biggest liar! Sure you're like *min-ute*' she reminds her.

'Jaysus, she is much more beautiful in reality. I swear you're a bleedin' ride ye are,' Lu exclaims.

'Yes, she is,' Jack says proudly as he kisses her forehead.

'My Lani,' he smiles.

'Jaysus, ye're bleedin' massive!' Kim says.

'Massive?' Carlton asks

'It means gorgeous in Irish slang' Kim assures him.

'OK, leave her alone, ladies...' Jack cuts in.

Carlton's face drops. 'Seriously, you ladies look B-star amazing! Nice to meet you, ladies...'

'This is Carlton, my best friend,' Alanna says.

'Jaysus, step aside! You're fitness,' Jess says.

'Are you gay?' Kim calls out.

They both nod.

'For fuck's sake, why are all the best ones taken?' Lu says.

'You ladies have the coolest street slang. Can you teach me some?' Carlton asks.

'Sure, no bother,' they say as they make their way inside.

'Let's go inside,' Alanna continues.

'Lani, stay here with me for a sec,' Jack asks.

'OK, Carlton, go on in and I'll be inside in a few,' Alanna says.

'OK, boss,' he says, winking back and mouthing '*dare*' with his mouth.

They move up the stairs up to a couch while the paparazzi remain flashing.

***

'Well, how are ye's? Are ye having a great time in Dublin?' Jack asks.

'It's super, we are having a ball. Thanks for all your recommendations,' Alanna says.

'No problem. How are you, darlin'?' He hugs her and kisses her forehead.

'I'm great!' she says, pulling back.

'Lani, you look so beautiful. I miss you so much... Jack says as he moves closer.

'I miss you too,' Alanna cuts in.

'I worry about you, you seem so quiet. What's on your mind?' he says.

'I've been so busy with football, but you know you're like my bleeding family... I really miss you and feel like I haven't been helping ye like I said,' Jack says with his face looking upset.

'I know you're with Harry now, but I… well, I can't really believe it. You were meant to be my…' Jack says.

'Your WAG?'

'Well, yes,' he says, laughing but also looking at Alanna to see her reaction.

'Can you see me sitting around behind your shadow?' she asks.

'No, but it wouldn't have to be that way. I would give you everything. Anyway, look at Posh and Colleen and the other girls. They call the shots. I love you, Alanna, more than I knew I could.'

He takes out a ring box.

'Oh no, Jack, don't do this. We both know I'm engaged. I'm going to LA for a few months to work, then going to London to get married, move in with Harry, have babies… That's the plan.'

His face goes pale. He puts the ring box in her hand. 'You talk about soulmates. I am street. I don't bleedin' care about yer man Plato. All I do know is you're marrying the wrong guy. You're my soulmate. We both know it. Even Carlton agrees,' he finishes.

She has tears in her eyes.

'At least I'm honest enough to say it as it is, Lani. Why are you scared to love me?' He kisses her and they remain tightly together until Alanna suddenly pulls away.

'You're scared of losing me. You can't marry someone because they are safe!' he argues.

'Just take it… I can't hold onto it. 'It was a gift. Keep it as a memory of your truth,' Jack says as he walks inside trying to hold back his tears.

***

261

'So what did she say?' Lu says while she leans over the bar trying to use her assets to get the barman's attention.

'Ah, ye bleedin' pet. She's not right for ye... Ye know the right lady would never say no.'

'Sure, Jacinta told ye she would even do WeightWatchers to look like a WAG. Don't rule her out,' Lu says joking while she hugs him.

***

'Ah, jaysus how are ye?' Carlton screams. Sitting around a table of cocktails, Carlton continues, 'How are ye, love?' while the table erupts with laughter.

'This Carlton is a bleedin character.'

'Hey, sorry to ruin the buzz, but I need to go!' Jack says.

'Ye dry arse,' Jess calls out.

'There ain't no way you're leaving now,' Carlton says.

As they look around, Jack walks away from the bar.

***

The Shelbourne Hotel, Dublin, Ireland
Meanwhile Alanna is back in the hotel room, crying. As she opens the box, the tears flow as she sees a ruby with twelve diamonds encrusted around the central gem. She looks closer to read the engraving:

My soulmate. I love you, Alanna. Always. Jack.

She begins to write:

Now I know why I'm here,

262

Feeling the sadness of you is clear,
Family are it all, love, laughter,
Agreements big and small.
Now I know why I'm here,
Your strength, creativity and soulfulness, etched into
my skin,
I must be brave, this battle I must win,
Now I know why I'm here.
Your courage, kindness and support,
I was blinded with pain,
Yet now the door has opened and I can see this
happiness from afar.

Chapter 39

The Shelbourne Hotel, Dublin, Ireland
Hours later, Carlton stumbles back to the hotel, falling into bed beside Alanna.

'I don't know much about your future. Yet all I do know is…' he pulls a hairbrush from the behind his back and blares the music from his iPod singing:

I know, I know you must follow the sun,
Wherever it leads…
Remember life holds for you one guarantee,
You'll always have me…

He starts dancing around the room, slightly stumbling with hiccupping.

Ain't no mountain high enough,
Ain't no valley low enough,
Ain't no river wild enough,
To keep me from you.

They sing together, laughing and smiling at one another.

***

As he places the disk in the player he turns to Alanna 'So let's fight this fear and check this tape,' he says. 'I think I should look at it first. 'Let's hit play.'

He watches the scene of Alanna in *V Bar* and smiles. 'You look fantastic on camera'.

Text flashes up: *'How Low Will You Go to Get Rich and Famous in the Industry?'* Then they see Alanna and Carlton and cutaways in the apartment.

'What the fuck!' Carlton screams.

Alanna who has her eyes covered 'Oh no, Carlton! What's wrong?'

'What the fuck is this? We are kissing. He has you half naked here and in bed with Harrry. How did he get this footage?' He calls out.

'You've been set up. *We've been set up.* He has hidden cameras all around our house!'

Alanna starts screaming hysterically. She calls Dennis, screaming down the phone as it goes straight to voicemail, 'I saw the clip!

'What the fuck is this? You have set us up! Call me back. *Call me back*!'

'Calm down,' Carlton says. 'Tell me all you know.'

'The show has signed off and is being edited within a few weeks. Dennis told me I had possibilities to record an album or work on an American dance show. My dreams were coming true. My only fear was telling Harry. I had only filmed a few scenes, and Dennis told me we could use the event and one or two dinners with Harry just to prove that dating worked. I am meant to be so happy, but how can this be happening?' she speaks so fast and hysterically that she nearly faints.

'I don't know what to say, sista,' he says. 'This is the Industry…you always gotta be one step ahead. One step ahead.'

***

Dennis name flashes up on her phone 'It's him calling,' she says.

'OK, say nothing, you hear me?' Carlton says.

265

'Hi. Got your message. Darling, don't even try this crap,' Dennis says. 'It's too late. The deal has been signed. I would advise you to get over here. We have castings and deals to sign... If you act stupid, I will call your parents and tell them how you got your dirty money. See you in LA.' He cuts the call.

'I am going to fucking kill him!' she screams, her face turning red.

'Give me the phone! Give me the fucking phone,' Carlton says.

'I have so many emotions going around in my head,' she says laying back on the bed breathing heavily.

'Sista, calm down. Just calm down. You know he is calling your bluff. He's an agent. The bad kind. He plays a game; you just need to beat him at his own game, OK?'

'What do you mean?' she says, wiping away her tears.

'You will play dumb. You will call Christina. She will sort this. Then you will get your ass over there and get the rest of the tapes and you will do whatever it takes to get this back and *sign nothing*. You knew he was a fucking snake. Darling, no agent records tunes and gives you no cash or proper contracts... You gotta be tougher,' he says. 'Don't get mad, and don't get even. Get what you want.'

***

Dear Sally,

Tonight feels like a blur. I had a panic and thought about Mam, Dad, Brendan, and you. Oh, how I miss you dearly. Sometimes I think you're here guiding me. Sometimes I pray to have my old life back.

My life with you.

Us all in the local church, happy with our local friends. You would be a doctor, and I would be a dance and singing teacher.

Sally, you would have two babies; I would have three. They would all be friends, of course. We would bring them to the local school and Mass on the weekends. We could be happy like everyone else.

I never wanted this life, selling my soul for money? Fame? Who have I become? The Industry isn't fair.

Love you.

X

Chapter 40

Tweet: *Happy New Year@AStar I Belong To You, You Belong To Me @LennyKravitz @Jack*

Shelbourne Hotel, Dublin

'Look, Alanna can't let this eat you up. Christina is on it. You need to enjoy tonight. You need to put it in a box, wrap it up, get to LA and sort it out before it goes live. Tomorrow is a new year and a new day and you'll be in a new continent and a new chapter for you,' Carlton says.

'I know you're right,' she says.

'Now, we have MD coming to do your hair and his stylist so you need to focus on looking fab!' he says as he hugs her.

'I have something to show you,' she says as she leans into her bag. 'Take a look.'

He opens the ring box that she hands him...

'OMG, I do! Yes!' he says.

'Carlton, stop being funny! Jack gave me this,' she explains.

'Now they both gave you rings. That's *big!*'

'Yes, but this so hard. I love Jack. I know he is the right one for me. Yet, I am already engaged, What will I do?' she says.

'Here's an idea. In the morning we gotta go get them valued, then whoever spent the most loves you more. Simple.' He smiles.

'If only,' she says, hugging him.

Seconds later they hear a buzz at the door.

'Hello, my darlings.' MD and LuLu come in. 'Show me the outfits and masks!' demands MD. 'Let's make superstars out of you both!'

***

Masquerade Ball, Residence Members' Club

As they walk into the ballroom hand in hand, masked ladies and men are everywhere. Alanna wears a red satin ball gown with a red and black mask and black gloves, with her hair half up, half down. Carlton wears a suit, his hair spiked, black eyeliner on and a red mask.

'Look, it's Jack and my ladies!' Carlton says as he leads Alanna over linking arms.

'I can't believe you all came,' she says to Jack and his sisters.

'Ah, Jaysus, how are ya?' Carlton says.

All the girls erupt in laughter.

'Come on, we have lots of people we need you to meet,' they pull Carlton away.

'Look, Jack, I am really sorry I am just scared,' she says.

'I didn't mean to scare ye. I'm sorry, I know it was a big deal,' he says.

'No, it wasn't you,' she responds.

'What's up, Alanna? Can I help you?'

She has tears streaming down her face.

'Tell me babe, what's wrong?'

'Come outside with me.'

'Tell me, babe, what's wrong? Tell me!'

'I did a show and it's not good. They set me up. They've set me up!' she screams. 'He lied to me. My career is over. My family will disown me.' Her make-up is streaming down her face.

'Darling, you look at me. Look at me right now,' he instructs.

She removes her mask to see his eyes.

'Whatever you've done, I will always be here for you. I love you, Alanna. Love means fighting for that. I will break anyone's back who hurts you. I will fix this.

It's breaking my heart that you're engaged. I want to see you happy, but…'

They turn around to see Carlton cut in 'Excuse me for interrupting, Lani, but your main man is here,' .

She wipes her face. 'I have to go', she kisses Jack on the cheek. 'Thank you for everything.'

Harry walks over, looking upset. 'Darling, sorry for arriving late, but my flight was delayed. Where have you been?'

'Oh, I was catching up with friends.'

'Sure,' Harry gives a dirty look to Jack, then adds, 'You're safe now' as he puts his arms around her.

'Yes, I am.'

***

'Countdown…3, 2, 1'

'Happy New Year!'

Harry kisses Alanna as confetti falls over the entire ballroom.

Amid kisses, songs and glasses chiming, everyone is smiling and enjoying the special moment.

'Harry, I have something to tell you.'

'Darling, tell me anything.'

'I have that show coming out.'

'Yeah, your dance show about studio,' he says. 'Are you excited?'

'No, I'm scared,' she says.

'That's normal, Alanna. I wanted you to know I've had a talk with Mum and she apologises. After Dad passed, she always fears me leaving her, but she's come around. In fact, we were both saying how we love you. I will always love you for the honest person you are,' he says and kisses her. Paparazzi flash. Confetti falls. Kisses are exchanged. Truths are told. Lies are told. A new year begins.

Chapter 41

Tweet: *@AStar So, honey let me love you down*
There's so many ways to love ya
Baby I can break it down
There's so many ways to love ya
@Jack@Usher@WillIam

Dublin Airport, Ireland

'Sista, you sure you don't want to come to NYC to see Momma and Mel?' Carlton asks Alanna.

'No, I have to get this sorted.'

'I will be there in three days, so you be strong, sista… We are in this together.'

As they walk through the airport, dressed in black with dark glasses, the paparazzi are everywhere.

Carlton grabs Alanna and shrieks, 'LA, baby!'

The screams catch the attention of the photographers, who flash insistently at Carlton's smiles.

'I will see you soon, hot stuff … Can't wait!' he says.

Harry takes her hands. 'I will be out by the end of the month once I have the deal closed. We can prepare the wedding. You focus on your show,' he says, smiling and kissing her. 'I am so happy I have found the woman I will spend the rest of my life with. This is the beginning of something very special,' Harry says, kissing her.

'OK, lovebirds, we gotta go. NYC and LA awaits us and we ain't go no private jet… yet!' Carlton says blowing air kisses while moving towards customs.

'Remember… Don't get mad. Don't get even. Get what you want!'

The three move in the directions of flights to Paris, NYC and LA.

***

Alanna looks out of the window and sees that the plane is on the runway. Realising she has to turn off her phone, she looks down and sees tweets and What'sApp messages from the previous few days.

Mam: Great to see ya, darling. Call us when ye land. Love Mam, Dad and Brendan x

Dennis: See you soon, LA awaits you.

Hearing a text pop up, she looks down again.

Jack: Alanna, I love you. I can't lose you. I need you here. You can't go to LA. You can't marry Harry. He is so wrong for you. We both know it's meant to be us. Don't leave me. Jack X

Her phone shows up Jacks number as he calls over and over.

She feels her chest close up as tears well while she tries to answer the call. The air hostess shouts in an LA accent, 'Ma'am, please turn off your phone. Ma'am, I don't think you hear me correctly. We are on the runway and are about to take off. All phones must be off, otherwise I will have to remove this from you.'

Dropping the phone, Alanna turns pale as it slides under the air hostess's feet.

***

The plane takes off and flies faster and faster in line with Alanna's breathing.

'She is having a panic attack!' screams the lady beside her.

'Ma'am, ma'am! Are you OK, ma'am?'

'I can't get married. I can't do this. I'm marrying the wrong man!' Alanna jumps up, trying to get her phone. She is now hyperventilating.

The air hostess calls out, 'Alice, get this lady some water. She's having an attack.'

'The poor child, she says can't get married. She's having a panic attack. We have all been there!' says the woman to the hostess.

'Don't do it! *Get out quick!*' some man calls.

'You heard him,' says a woman two rows up.

'Everyone, please remain calm,' the hostess calls out.

A few moments later, they hand her a glass of water.

'Darling, take this,'It's my best friend V – V for valium.'

Alanna takes it without any hesitation, and soon after feels suddenly calm. Forgetting all of her troubles, she fades into a sleep – a deep, quiet and happy sleep.

***

Dublin to LA Flight, Aer Lingus
Five hours later she wakes mid-air, hazy and unsure what is going on. Holding her heavy head, she looks next to her, realising she is hugging the woman on the seat beside her.

'Oh, I am so sorry!' she announces, jumping back on to her seat.

'Dear child, you poor thing. We all heard about the marriage,' the woman says, grabbing her with a hug like a bear hugging her cub.

'Been there! Anyway, here's your cell. You dropped it. I hope you feel OK after your sleep? Can I get you anything? A drink? You need something strong!'

'Sure,' Alanna says.

'Will you have any family picking you up?'

'I am in a hotel,' she says.

'Oh no, we can't have that. I can get my husband to drop you to your destination.' Before Alanna can respond, the woman unbuttons her belt and is facing the back of the plane.

'Frank!' she shouts across the plane. '*Frannnnnk*!'

A middle-aged man jumps up from his deep sleep. 'Yes,' Frank answers.

'We gotta drop this little gem off once we hit LA.'

'OK honey. Anything you want, honey,' he says fearfully.

Turning back around smiling, the woman says, 'All sorted. You will come with us, you poor little lady. Now, let's get you a drink.' She pushes the button to call the hostess. 'Can we have some champagne, please? And some snacks: potato chips, chocolate and whatever you got. And lots of it! Thanks.' She smiles at the hostess.

***

Within minutes Alanna and her new friend Kate are sipping champagne and making small-talk.

'In case you're wondering why myself and my husband are in separate seats, it's because I can't bear his snoring. He doesn't know a thing.'

As Kate turns again, smiling and waving back to her husband, he returns her smiles and waves back.

'He thinks they mixed up the seats again. Marriage is the best thing in the world, but you gotta learn some

274

tricks when you get married. It's called survival. One of them includes our friend V,' she says, winking.

Looking at the messages on her phone, Alanna knows she has to be strong and get to LA to get this contract signed.

Survival is something Alanna is learning hard and fast.

Chapter 42

Tweet: @AStar Hollywood (Hollywood)
Ooh it's the lights (Satisfaction)
Satisfaction! (So addictive) @JayZ

S Hotel, Los Angeles, America
Waking up feeling jet-lagged, Alanna's mouth is so dry she feels she can barely speak. Realising there is nothing in her mini-bar, she leaves the room to find a drink. Wearing nothing but a silk nightdress, she is taken aback by the crowd in her room.

Two or three models are wrapped around two older men, and it is like a scene from a movie. R 'n' B music is playing and lights dimly lit set the mood.

'Darling! We are having a skiing party. Come join us!' Dennis says.

Skiing in LA? I must be very jet-lagged.

'We thought you'd never join us with your company,' Dennis says. 'These are some of the agents I told you about. Get your beautiful ass in here and meet everyone.'

'Beautiful ass… will kick *your* ass,' Alanna mutters under her breath.

On further inspection, she sees each person snort lines of cocaine off the table. Her palms start to sweat, her heart beats fast and she forces a smile.

A man lifts his head, brushes some white powder off his nose and gums says, 'Honey, you is a fine ass.'

'Isn't she, Tony? I told you,' Dennis says.

'Yeah, oh yeah. She is mighty fine,' he says, slurring in his Texan accent.

'Alanna, here you go. Take this drink. Especially prepared for you,' Dennis says, smirking.

Looking around to the two blondes and the brunette laughing like in unison. Each is intoxicated, half naked, and half asleep, leaning against the other men.

Sitting in the chair with Dennis, Tony grabs her and attempts to kisses Alanna 'She's my lady, hands off. Well, at least in front of me!' He high-fives the other men and laughs.

Alanna texts Carlton:

Alanna: They are having a skiing party and being so feckin sleazy. I feel like punching them all, the perverts.

A text pops up:

Carlton: Darling, that's another name for a Cocaine party. Please don't take any drinks or anything off them. Think of the contract and discs, do whatever you have to do get it sorted but be smart.

I will be there soon.

X CStar

In utter shock, she remains silent for the rest of the night, listening to stories about the business that are being shared.

'You know she's in rehab *again*.'

'Has-been!' Tony calls out.

***

They continue snorting more lines as room service is eaten, music plays, followed by a stint of dancing by the models. Alanna, feeling spaced out, starts to dance around the room. She feels free. Within an hour she is sitting on Dennis's knee, her brain flashing in and out of moments by the lake, lying in bed with Simon, kissing him.

Her mind is racing through lots of thoughts and images as she flashes through dreams.

Eventually they hear, 'Shit, it's 7am! We have to make this shoot by noon. Let's go!' On Tony's orders, everyone gets up, says their goodbyes and leaves.

'This is business, darling. Suits you!' Dennis says, moving towards her. 'These guys are the ones who will make or break you. Literally.' He laughs with an evil tone.

***

Dennis places his iPod on shuffle, and Alanna sidles along and moves around the room in circles as if on her own special stage that no one could see.

Watching her, transfixed by her every movement.

'You have the voice of an angel,' Dennis admits.

'You are a star, Alanna Star. My star. You're the only woman I have ever loved since Anna.'.Walking over, he kisses her… 'My A's, my beautiful A's.'

***

Moving back to the room, he prepares drinks for her again, and he moves his hands up and down her body. Her eyes are rolling back, and she was heavy, under his control.

'I love you,' he says.

As soon as she sits down, he places his hand on her leg, and without any hesitation moves it slowly up her lace dress, looking her intimidatingly in the eye.

'Darling, you are mine now and we will take over the world together. Are you ready to be a star? Stick with me and I'll make sure your name shines in lights,' he promises.

As Jack and Harry continuously tried to reach her. She drops her phone and falls asleep on the couch next to him, drifting into a deep sleep.

Chapter 43

Chateau Marmot, LA

As Dennis pulls the car in, they walk inside to meet the casting directors who she recently saw. Many stars are having lunch or perusing others walking past. Within minutes and without any in-depth discussions, a contract is drawn up.

'I have a cheque for $50,000. Your show will be sent for pilot and launched within the next four weeks.'

Alanna feels sick, but acknowledges the cheque while focusing on passers-by such as Ryan Reynolds, Richard Gere, and Kate Hudson. Her face is full of confusion.

'OK, so we need you to sign here, here and here.' Tony hands her a pen while the three men look at her, expecting a response.

***

Alanna's mind goes into overdrive as she tries to read the contract.

'Please excuse me. I need to freshen up,' she says.

Sobbing in the bathroom, she sees the Kardashian sisters walking out. 'Are you OK?' they ask. 'You are very pretty. LA likes that, so get your make-up fixed up and get back out there! Sista, he isn't worth it.'

Alanna picks up the phone and waits for a dial tone.

'Jack, something strange happened on this trip. I feel spaced out. Sick. My thoughts are pacing around my mind.'

'What do you mean?

'What has he done to you? Harry? Has he hit you?' Jack asks.

'No, it's Dennis,' she says quietly.

'What do ye mean, Dennis? That gimp. What the fuck has he done to you? I will break his face if he has touched you. Tell me what's happened!'

'I don't remember,' she responds.

'What do ye mean, you don't remember? Darling, you need to tell me everything. No matter what it is, I will fix it.'

'Well, I stayed in the hotel and I think he has drugged me. I am here with him now to get a contract off him.'

'What the fuck? Get out of there. Don't deal with him! I'll deal with him and his bleedin' contracts. Your safety comes first!' he assures her. 'Where is Harry? Why is he not with you?'

'Well, he had to take care of business,' she admits

'You should be his business,' he says angrily.

'Well, it's not his fault. He can't find out about the show,' she says.

'What a wimp! You are his lady. His lady for life, Alanna. You need a man who will save you from this shit. Anyway, you listen to me. Get out of that place and call me. I will sort you a hotel, flights… I'll even come out. Send me the name of where you are and all the people you're with. I'll sort them too.'

'OK, thanks,' she says, relieved.

'For nothing. This is my job. I'm so happy I can help you, Lani,' he says. 'Call me as soon as you're outside.'

As Alanna walks into the bar, she sits next to Dennis and keeps the act going. 'VIP, champagne and canapés, this is only the beginning for us!' Dennis announces as he clinks glasses with Alanna and the other men. 'We have so much to celebrate.'

Judging by the reaction on her face, his excitement was unrequited. 'I know you're confused, probably thinking about what to do with this guy Harry, but he's a big man. He'll handle it and move on. There are much better out there. You got what you wanted. We got what we wanted from him and now you can forget about him. Now you're a star.'

'I will never forget about him. You don't fucking own me!' she screams.

'Darling, no, I don't own you. But who will want own a slut who wears cameras and sleeps with random men, especially their agent?' he smiles.

'You fucking wish!' she shouts.

'It's all on camera, my dear. You foolish girl. It's no surprise, coming from an idiot family.'

Without any hesitation, she gets up and throws the champagne all over him, screaming, 'You can say anything about me, but you even try for one second and disrespect my family and I tell ye, now ye'll be a dead man walking!'

The entire bar glance over and back as if this is a typical scene from a set.

'I'll never disrespect them as much as you already have.'

She grabs the contracts and rips them up. 'Ye can all fuck off if ye think I will sign these and work with any of ye perverts. You should be so lucky!' she says.

'Hell, yeah, this is what I am talking about!' someone shouts from the crowd.

Shaking, she runs out.

***

Chatot Marmot to Palazzo Apartments, Los Angeles
She gets the nearest cab organised by the valets.

'Palazzo please. West Hollywood.'

Texting Jack;

Alanna: I am safe. I will call you soon. XXX

She looks down at her phone to see WhatsApp messages flooding in:

Carlton: Sister, I have just arrived. I am so out of it. Where you at?

Alanna: On the way. I don't feel well. I feel spaced out.

Carlton: It is jet-lag?

Alanna: No, it's not that. There is something weird happening.

Carlton: Has he drugged you, darling? Did you sleep with him?

Alanna: No!

Carlton: Thank the lord! See ya soon.
X

As she arrives, she passes the courtyard, recognising some actresses and actors, mainly from reality TV shows. The sun is shining, people are smiling, and music is playing, stars all around.

It is exactly like I had expected.

Dear Sally,

I am in LA. It's been a crazy start. I am not sure what will happen. I could stop now, move back to Killarney and still be a success. Brendan is sorted. I could teach. Live a simple life. Yet I haven't had enough. I need to make my mark. I love the music.

It was all about the love of music, after all.

Chapter 44

Tweet: *@CStar I'm friends with the monster that's under my bed,*
Get along with the voices inside of my head,
You're trying to save me,
Stop holding your breath @Eminem @Rhianna

Palazzo apartments to LA Studios
Alanna, after spending the morning in the gym and then in the salon getting careful grooming, knows she is ready to go.

'Where you off to, miss?' says Bill, Harry's driver. 'Somewhere very special by the looks of it, Mrs Mac!'

'Oh, LA Studios, please, sir,' Alanna responds.

'OK, ma'am, I'll have ya'll there in no time,' he says, smiling back.

As they pass through the streets, Alanna stares out of the window reflecting on the last three days while watching the bright cars and billboards flashing past.

She looks down at her phone.

Liz: Darling, best of luck in the casting!
You made it to 'Hollywood' so you're already making it in the Industry.
Take the pressure off and have fun!
Skype soon,
Liz
X

Alanna moves up the twenty-five floors via the lift. With each floor the light passes onto another number, and her hands start to shake as she goes up and up. She reaches the reception, where a very slim blonde-haired lady is seated typing ferociously at her keypad.

'Hi, I am Alanna. I am here for the casting,' she explains.

'Good for you. It's the room over there.' The woman points without even looking up from her screen.

'Thanks,' she says despondently while moving towards the glass room.

Walking in, she sees a diverse group of people, ranging from twenty-one to in their thirties, all shapes and sizes. Each is on their iPhone or iPad, all in their own world.

***

A tall lady enters, and without introducing herself she starts pointing around the room.

'OK, so you're pretty. May need to lose a few pounds but we can work on that. Can you act?'

'What, ma'am?' A red-haired lady with a Canadian accent responds.

'Can you act? Do I need to spell it out?' the tall woman replies.

'Well, I suppose you could say I can... can... can act. I... I... I was the lead in all my school plays...'

'OK, next!' the casting woman passes her and moves her pointed finger around the room. 'You, man, you gotta learn we don't take overweight dancers unless you're signed up for a certain role. Please come back when you sort out the mood eating. We are not here to feed your habits. Next! Big nose, great for stage, too big for camera... Next! We know you were born in the 1980s but here's a secret: the perm is not in, sista! Next!

'Seriously, how in your right mind did you think you would be picked? Go home and book in with a new guidance counsellor as yours obviously lied,' she says to the plump blonde-haired girl at the back of the room who looks up from devouring a bag of Cheetos. OK, think we are done here.' She looks around the room. 'You, you, with the red-brown hair,' she screams, pointing to Alanna. 'Come over here... Follow me.' She points a finger out of the room.

Alanna, used to the ruthlessness of castings, follows her with ease.

'The rest of you deadbeats, don't give up the day job! Lesley, next time I ask you to arrange a casting, do your job. I've never seen such a room of incompetent and unattractive idiots in my life,' she says to her assistant, who looks as nervous as those in the casting.

***

Alanna stands in a white studio with wooden floors, mirrors and speakers the size of TVs, waiting for the casting director to continue.

'I'm Chloe, by the way,' she introduces herself and hands Alanna a script. 'OK, take this. Imagine the love of your life has just left you for your best friend, you just found out you're pregnant and your world is falling apart.'

'The theme here is loss, failure, and abandonment,' Lesley shouts out.

'OK, Lesley, we are not on Oprah here. So, embracing those feelings, say those lines off until we tell you to stop.'

Having done an acting module in LUCE, Alanna embraces the role without hesitation.

'How could you do this to me? What about our future? Our plans? The house? You can't leave me... You can't do this to me, to him,' she says this with tears coming down her face, holding her tummy as if she's pregnant.

'OK, not bad. Not bad at all,' Chloe says. 'Lesley, put on some music…'

Within seconds R 'n' B music comes on. 'You're in a bar, you're trying to win your man back and claim your territory in a new dance squad. Show me how you would work it.'

'I have my own music. Can I use that instead?'

She plays a song that she sang and recorded in LUCE studios then added in remixes with Nic. She knows the perfect routine to go with it.

'I like her. She's ballsy,' Chloe says to Lesley. 'Sure. Pass it over.'

They hit play, and Alanna flips around the room, her body, hands and feet hitting every beat. For three minutes she creates a show, bringing the stage and music to life.

'She is a star!' Chloe whispers to her assistant who nods in agreement.

***

'I must say, I am impressed by you. I love this whole Irish get-up you got going on.' Chloe points her finger up and down. 'So who's your agent?'

'I am between agents,' Alanna explains.

'OK, well, take my card. Send me your reel…'

'Sure, I have a blog with lots of reels and demos of my songs. I'm a singer and writer too so I'll send you some stuff.'

'Sounds good,' Chloe nods.

Just then a strikingly beautiful dark-haired Brazilian woman runs in the door. 'Hey, hey, Chloe. Have I missed the casting?' she says.

'Becky, no, you're good, Becky. Come in,' Chloe says.

'OK, you can leave, Alanna,' Chloe says.

'You look amazing, Chloe. It must be your new man!' Becky says, double-kissing Chloe.

Alanna looking back is starting to believe;

It's not what you know, it's who you know; It's the Industry after all.

***

Santa Monica Beach, Los Angeles

'Hey darling, how are you keeping? How did the casting got go?' Harry asks.

'It's tough here, Harry.'

'What do you mean? Is Dennis doing anything?'

'No, I have left him… Christina is working on that, so don't worry,' she assures him.

'Yes, but I need to see copies of your contract. Don't be embarrassed about the fees, etc.'

'No, it's not that,' she says. 'Anyway, we met this girl who lives in the palazzo. She's a journalist, but she works in one of the clubs too,' she explains.

'OK, be careful with her, Lani. Agents and journalists have a reputation of selling their mothers to make a buck,' he states.

'Isn't that the same for bankers?' she challenges him.

'Sure, you're right. Sorry for generalising,' he says.

'No problem. Anyway, can't wait to see you!'

'Go enjoy yourself, my love. I'll be with you soon,' he says.

'I wish you were here now.'

'Me too, but Mother was ill so I will be here next week. We have so much to celebrate and to prepare for the wedding! Oh, and I have news.'

'News?' Alanna's hands are sweaty and her breathing is pacing.

'I have found us a house in London. Check your phone…'

She looks down to see messages. An image of a white three-story house in Knightsbridge pops up.

'Wow, what can I say?' As she looks up, she sees Carlton rollerblading past and she waves over. 'Thank you, thank you so much!'

'Our home, for life,' he says.

'Love you,' she says to Harry.

'Love you too,' Harry responds while holding her hand.

***

Alanna calls Christina.

'OMG, Christina you were right about the LA Industry!' she says.

'Told you, darling. It's like London except people are eating less and taking more. Grow some extra layers, just not pounds, *huhuhu,*' she jokes.

'Did ye get a chance to look at the contract?' Alanna asks.

'Of course. I've read the contracts and still can't believe you agreed to cameras. You're wilder than I thought! My lawyers are on it!'

'Well, do be in touch.'

'Be careful out there. It is a tough place and stay away from the cameras,' Christina warns. 'Oh, and try and get a show and we will have an excuse to visit!'

'Toodle-ooh. Thanks for everything. Bye,' Alanna says.

'Bye.'

The phone cuts.

Laying back on the chair, Alanna scrolls through Twitter comments, including one from Jack:

@AStar Saw your video reels on your blog. Miss you, Jack x

Chapter 45

Tweet: *@AStar*
Well, I don't like living under your spotlight
Just because you think I might find somebody worthy
Oh, I don't like living under your spotlight
Maybe if you treat me right you won't have to worry
@JenniferHudson

Palazzo Apartments, Los Angeles

Harry wears a tucked-in white polo, sailor shoes and khaki shorts, holding a wheelie bag and laptop case. 'I'm looking for Alanna. Does anyone know where Alanna is?' he asks.

'*Baby*! My Harry !' Drunk and in a bikini, she runs for him and wraps herself around him. 'I'm, like, so happy you're here,' she says, kissing him. 'Come meet all my friends: Belle, Joshua, Kelly, Kendell, Fibs and Carlton. And this is …oh, I can't remember his name!' she says, slurring.

'Darling, I missed you like crazy,' he says, facing her.

Some remain in the pool splashing each other while others are drinking on lilos.

'Watch me!' she says as bombs into the pool. Harry stands still at the edge in shock, while Carlton comes over and hugs him. 'Harry, I missed you! What's up, man? You seem pissed?'

'I came to see my darling, not to paddle pool…but she…' Harry says.

'Oh, OK, I get it,' Carlton says. 'How 'bout you two lovebirds go up and catch up?' Carlton screams.

'Yes, let's go upstairs,' Harry calls out to Alanna. 'We clearly need to catch up.'

***

Waking up from a nap, Alanna lies beside Harry. 'Oh, I have such a bad headache. Yet, I have my Harry here!' she says, hugging him tightly.

'Lani, I thought you were wild, but you've really pushed it here,' Harry says. 'Let's go out and see some sights!'

'I'm going to chill here. I'm so tired,' she says.

'Rise and shine!' Carlton storms in. 'We need to show our guest around! Come on, up you get, Lani. Don't be selfish!'

'OK, I'm coming. Give me a few minutes,' she says reluctantly.

'OK, but I have a class to teach and people to meet, so don't take too long!' Carlton says.

***

As they get into the convertible Harry has rented 'Harry we have started to do some freestyling do you wanna hear?' Carlton asks.

'Sure' he says.

'OK, one, two, three, go…' Alanna says.

'Her name is Lani and she's amazing at her beats,

She is from Kerry, yet, she can make a track like J-Lo from the streets' Carlton adds.

'Carlton is the main man, he loves the high life,

Yet, you know he has had it all, trouble and strife' Alanna continues

'Hollywood,,, Hollywood, Let's take it higher' Carlton and Alanna join in, laughing as Harry looks away.

***

Beverly Centre, Los Angeles

Harry, Carlton and Alanna move around the stores, and Carlton screams either 'Oh!' or 'Wow' as they pass each one.

'Carlton, are you screaming for the stores, or the men?' Alanna jokes.

He smiles back while Harry looks disappointed.

'Let's go try on some dresses to fit your hot bod!'

'Sounds like a plan, Harry. What d'ya think?' Alanna looks at Harry.

'Sure,' Harry says.

***

Alanna walks out of the changing room in a tightly fitted *Ellie Saab* turquoise dress.

Harry watches in amazement as each inch of the dress wraps around her curves. 'You look incredible.'

She smiles back, as if she knows she does too.

They walk out of the shop, Alanna clutching her bag with the dress in one hand, while Harry holds the other hand. For the first time it feels uncomfortable.

'I'm tired and want to call Mother, so can we head back?' Harry asks.

'Sure, I gotta hit class too,' Carlton says.

They drive back through West Hollywood.

'Carlton, do you need a lift to studio?'

'No, I'm all good. I'll make my own way.'

'No, we will drop you, won't we, darling?' Alanna says.

'Why not?' Harry says.

***

Palazzo Apartments, Los Angeles
Driving towards the apartment, they see paparazzi all

around the gate.

'Not for you, I hope?' Harry asks.

'No, not yet,' Alanna whispers.

As they move inside, walking by the pool courtyard which is full of people.

'So he's an actor... Him too... him too... and her, she's a dancer,' Alanna introduces Harry. 'Isn't this place like Italy?' she says, pointing out balconies overlooking the courtyard.

'You may say so,' he says.

Miki runs over in the tiniest white bikini filled with red stars and her hair poofing out from the pool water. 'Alanna, they say B is here today. She's at a party upstairs with her baby. There are paps everywhere.'

'OMG, I have to call Carlton!' Alanna says, dialling his number. It goes to voicemail. 'Carlton, please answer. Beyoncé is here. You gotta meet her!'

A text pops up:

Calrton: At a casting, didn't want to tell you but it's looking good.

Thanks for letting me know about B.

I will be back ASAP

X

PS I think it's a sign from God I am not there as I don't think I could be in the same room with her without being arrested... hahaha.

***

Palazzo Apartments, Los Angeles

Alanna and Harry lay in bed face to face.

'I missed you so much. I'm so happy you're here,' Alanna says. 'But you seem so quiet.'

'You seem so loud,' Harry responds.

'I *am* loud,' she says defensively, sitting up on the bed.

'You were never this loud in London. I feel like I don't know you anymore...You have all these new sides to you that I never knew,' he says.

'How exciting is that?' she responds, smiling. 'You'll never be bored!'

'Maybe I will. Maybe I find this all so focking boring, A.What's up with this, and your hair done, your pointed nails and your bad-ass drunken attitude?'

She laughs. 'I never thought you would say that word! *Hahaha!*' she laughs.

'Well, it's true,' he says in a serious tone. 'You're not the woman I knew.''

'Let me be,' she says.

*****

Carlton runs into the apartment screaming 'So, tell me everything!

'What was Beyonce like? Pretty? Nice? Diva?' Carlton asks.

'Who?' Alanna asks.

'Queen B, of course!'

'Oh, I don't know. We went out for food... It was hectic with fans and paparazzi here,' she explains.

'That will be us one day so you better get used to it!' Carlton says.

'OK, I've picked a table at the *Viper Room* for us all,' Carlton says. After a dead silence he reacts, 'Oh, gosh, you look tired, Harry. Why don't you two get some rest? Spend some time alone? Looks like you need to catch up.'

'Are you sure?' she says.

'I will hit the gig on my own. Or may ask someone from class to go or that hot guy by the pool, or Miki...

yes, she is up for anything! OK, lovebirds. I'm gonna go or I'll be late. Have a good one. Mwah! Mwah!' He blows air kisses and leaves.

***

'Look, I know things are different than in London,' Alanna says. 'But we are the same. You have nothing to worry about. I am still the same me. Your wife-to-be. The lady of your dreams! You're helping me live mine and I will always be thankful.'

'Yes but you're so wild here. You're hanging out with the wrong crowd, Alanna. I thought you were here writing an album, doing castings and working on your craft. Not sitting by the pool with stripper-type women who drink all day.'

'I am not drinking all day. I'm just having a bit of fun, OK? I've had a serious year or so and I'm entitled to have some time out every once in a while. I'll be back in training next week and the writing is ongoing, sure, I've nearly finished an album. I just need to get it recorded. I'll never give up on my dreams. Or us,' she says as she kisses him.

His face looks sad as he kisses her too.

'You're just tired. Get some rest and you'll feel better tomorrow. Everything is always better in the morning,' she says.

They lie side by side but far apart.

Dear Sally
I'm not sure what's happened but I have lost Jack.
My better half.
Where are you now?
I let you go and now I am half the woman you and I were meant to be.
I need you here, lying next to me.

297

I feel a pain without you by my side.
My love, my life.
You're all I want.
I'd rather love and lose than never have tried...
My better half...???

Chapter 46

Tweet: *@PerezHilton:*
Stand back @KimK you have met your match @AStar
NO. 1 YouTube video of all time!

Palazzo Apartments, Los Angeles
Carlton runs in the door with the newspapers, screaming. 'Alanna, Dennis has released the show online, big time!' He gasps for air. 'Christina may have stopped this show on television yet, has used tapes online. Plus, it includes some party in LA, in our house, everywhere. We are both naked too'

'What? What!' Alanna grabs the papers to have a look at what he is talking about. 'What do you mean?'

He pulls over her iPad and plays the YouTube links to their show.

'The Fame Game... How low did she go?' and similar icons pop up.

Looking at her iPhone, she sees sixteen missed calls from Harry, some from her parents, Liz and even Simon.

'This can't be real.'

***

Immediately Alanna calls Harry.

'I am so sorry, Harry. After Sally died I had to get a job to help my family. Dennis offered me money and it all happened so fast and I wanted to tell you so many times but I just didn't know how. Also, I think Dennis drugged me in LA. I haven't felt right since. I don't remember any of those scenes. I know you're going to break up with me and things are over and you'll hate me forever. I understand if you hate me, but I want you to know that I do love you. I really do.'

'I am angry too. He has taken over the news with cameras revealing my life too!' Carlton calls out.

'I am on my way,' Harry says and hangs up.

'Harry is coming back,' she announces.

'Sista, you need to get some wipes and heels on and do what we always do: smile and wave to the camera,' Carlton says. 'Oh, sorry, I don't mean literally wave to the camera. Sorry, that is not funny is it?'

***

Within minutes, Harry arrives at Alanna and Carlton's place and charges through the door.

'All I know is whichever DJ, so-called gay best friend – no offence, Carlton – you've kissed or flirted with or spent time in bed with, it has to stop,' Harry says.

'None taken.'

'I am a nice guy, but I am not an idiot. I can't be with someone who is playing around – a cheap woman who wants to be a star but sells her soul to get a quick fix. Are you that desperate for money? What did you think would come out of this show? It's so cheap. You're a lady, Alanna. Or at least I thought you were. If you want to be famous, then go this route. You didn't need an agent or cameras. Don't you believe that you are talented enough on your own? I could have helped you do anything you wanted. What kills me the most is you could have asked me for help!'

***

Within moments a Skype from Simon pops up and Carlton answers.

'Tell me, Alanna, what is it? What scares you so much? You can go on television to the world and spy on people, but I and we both know it's not you. You're not happy. You're a shadow of the person you once were. What is going on with you? Are ye on drugs?' Simon looks really concerned. 'You have to trust me, Alanna. I loved you from day one. The confused girl with the red hair and freckles. Through thick and thin. You've yourself and your family. You need to get back here. I will take care of you. Your family and me. We are all worried about ye.'

In shock, Alanna and Harry react together.

'Who is Simon?' Harry demands. 'Oh gosh, I have to leave.'

At that exact moment, Simon cuts off.

'OMG. Momma, it is like *Jerry Springer*!' Carlton calls out.

Harry runs out, and just as Alanna tries to chase him, he turns around. 'Please leave me alone. This is over. You are not who I thought you were. You lied to me. I loved you and let you in closer than anyone. I can't do this. You never loved me. Your only love is the Industry.'

Hysterically crying, she chases him down the hall.

He turns around and adds, 'For the record, I would never marry a slut.'

She can tell by his face that there is no point in chasing him, and tears stream down her face as she lets him get into the lift. Falling to the ground with Carlton trying to hold her and Miki running out, she knows it might be the last time she ever sees him.

'This can't be real.'

***

Dear Sally

I feel lost, alone and in pain.

Now it is the first time since you've left us that I have felt this. There is pain all over me. I can't explain or understand why I feel this bad yet I know there is nothing I can do about this.

I just have to accept it. BUT I CAN'T. I know if you were here you'd be so calm.

You never would have done this.

I've sold my soul for money. Everyone said I would, but I didn't think it would to me. I didn't do it for success but still I didn't stop myself.

I've shamed our family and friends. I've shamed myself.

Dad is calling it 'dirty money' and told me you would never do this and you were the better half of us two. He is right. You were and will always be better. You would never have done this.

You would never have run away.

All I know is I have to fix this. I have to. I am going to become known for something special. I am going to write the best album anyone has ever heard. I am going to make this all better.

I miss you so much.

I miss you.

X

Thinking of who to text, she goes with her instinct.

Alanna: Call me, Jack

Within seconds, Jack calls. 'Hi, baby. Are you ok? I'm sorry to hear about the show.'

'I know,' she says, sobbing.

'*Wow*! You're wilder than I thought!'

'It was a set-up,' she says.

'Sure everyone knows that. Alanna, we love you still back here. Everyone knows you're a brave lady. You needed the money for your brother. Family first. Don't you ever worry about what people think, once you and your family are safe. Don't you mind those fuckers in the Industry. If I didn't have football, I'd be over. We have our final few games but if you want me let me know. Please just ask me if you need me.

'The only thing that makes me sad is you didn't ask me for help. You know you should have asked me for the money; I'd give you the shirt off my back if you ask me. Yet, I'm always here for you. You're a star.'

'Thank you,' she says.

'Don't let anyone make you believe anything else. Let me know what you need… You're never alone.'

The phone cuts off.

'This isn't the life of a star' Alanna says as she lies back into the couch sobbing.

Chapter 47

Tweet: @*AStar Take me away*
I wear my heart on my sleeve
Always let love take the lead
I may be a little naive, yeah
You know I'm drunk on love
Drunk on love @Rhianna

Miki's apartment, Palazzo, Los Angeles

'Now you get yourself together,' Christina says. 'I have sent my top lawyer to nail this bastard. I mean he had cameras planted in your bedroom, your bathroom. It is illegal. The focker is going down! Also, I have press officers to cover this up, darling…'

'OK, thanks,' Alanna says.

'We are mentioning Sally and how you were in a bad place. You will be staying in that apartment. I have arranged for the money to be sent to Harry for the rent. It is covered for the next six months, then you have to do it on your own, Alanna.'

'I don't know what to say,' Alanna says dolefully.

'Well, all I ask is for you to get a job, keep working on your skills and become a star. You have the chance to be bigger than any of us. Grab this chance, Alanna. You hear me? Don't let me down!' she says.

'Thank you. I promise I won't. I just wish that the rest of the family were so forgiving,' she says.

'I've called your mam to get her off your back.'

'What? You two have barely spoken in fifteen years!'

'Well, I did it for you. I've explained the business to them and how this is all part of the Industry. Give them time. They are starting to understand that it wasn't your fault. Don't come back for a while. I need you to be strong, OK? You've made a mistake, but get back to your art.'

'I am. I promise you. Thank you so much. I won't let you down...'

'I won't let you give up because off some idiot.'

'Speak soon.'

'Yes, speak to ye soon.'

Phone cuts.

***

Alanna sits crying, dressed in a black Lycra tracksuit, on a leather couch between Carlton and Miki with both their arms around her.

'It's OK, lovely. This is so LA. I mean, everyone has their own show. What an idiot that he can't keep up. He should be super-happy that he has such a hot and fab lady!' Miki says.

'I still can't believe Dennis did that to me. Everyone must think I'm a slut,' Alanna says helplessly.

'Ok, most of it was just you and Dennis,' Carlton says.

'What about the secret cameras in the apartment? The shower? I mean the Irish people will think I am...' Alanna says.

'Forget about them. People that matter won't care and they know all those shows are made to look dramatic,' says Miki consolingly.

'You said it. Listen to her, Alanna. She is talking sense,' Carlton agrees.

'Now I've lost my agent, the love of my life and my family are ashamed of me. Who knows if I'll lose my course too and my best friend will probably leave me,' Alanna sobs.

'You wish,' Carlton respond. 'Your man will come around. So will your parents. All ya need some rest,

305

some ice cream, more chocolate and you'll be all good in the hood!'

**

'Hallo, A Star's phone,' Miki answers Alannas phone
   'Alanna, it's your lawyer,' Miki calls out blushing.
   'Thanks,' Alanna says, taking the phone.
   'Hi Alanna. We can confirm that on all accounts, in terms of a show on television and online, Dennis never had the contract. We confirm that the clip is off YouTube, and you shall get compensation for damages. This will take some time, but I will keep you informed. We are claiming circa $500,000 against your artist's reputation, for the abuse and time wasted with him. We shall keep you updated.'
   'Many thanks,' she says.
   'Take care.' The lawyer hangs up.

**

Alanna wakes at 5.30am, spooning Carlton on Miki's couch. Having cried so much, her eyes are so swollen she finds it hard to see. Stumbling back to her apartment, she looks at photos of her and Harry, then her with Sally. She takes her iPad to the courtyard, where she sits by the pool to write the three most important emails of her life.

Dear Harry,
I am so sorry for hurting you.
I should never have got engaged to you.
You deserve someone who loves you unconditionally.
Look, I don't expect you will ever understand what I have done.

We may never talk again and I have lost the love of my life because of one show.

Yet I can't say I regret it.

Not everyone comes from your background, your opportunity, and your wealth.

I will never have these opportunities... well, at least not until I met you.

Sally died and our world fell apart.

She was going to be a doctor. She was going to help my parents mind Brendan and I was going to be the fun sister who went to performance school, taught dance classes and maybe one day made an album. I make choices and think about them after.

Yet now it's all on me. I had to do this. I needed to get money. I was too scared to ask you and it was too far gone to tell you the truth. If I had told you, who's to say you would not have left me and then I would have no you and no money.

I never doubted my talent, but I know enough after a year of castings to see that even the most talented may never make it in the Industry. I see incredible people every day, struggling to get by. I couldn't be one of them. My family couldn't struggle because of me.

They deserve to be happy.

Brendan especially.

All I do know is I made this choice before I met you. Before we fell in love and before you changed my life.

I know it is too late but I never wanted to hurt you. I am so sorry I have.

My family are safe and we are suing Dennis.

I have lost you but I would rather that than Brendan to suffer.

It's all part of my plan.

Now I will focus on my art and create work that I am proud of.

I always thought I was good enough for you and still do.

I hope that you meet someone, and I hope she can love you even half as much as I did.

I wish you so much love.

Alanna X

***

Dear Simon,

I know things are not great between us, but please take care of my parents in this mess. I never wanted to hurt anyone, including you. Please forgive me for leaving you. I will always have a place in my heart for you. You deserve to be the happiest man and loved back as much as you give.

Be happy.

X

***

Dear Jack,

It was and always has been you.

I realised I never would have done the show if I was with you.

I feel so terrible for hurting Harry, I shouldn't have hurt him.

You're right: I love you.

I always loved you.

I didn't want to tell you as everything I love leaves or has pain so I thought it was easier this way.

I would love to be yours.

You're the one.

Love you.

X

***

Palazzo Apartments Poolside, Los Angeles
Alanna watches the slight lady practising yoga, who is rolling up her mat.

She smiles at her.

Alanna smiles back.

'At this hour you must be working on something serious in your mind, young lady?' the woman asks.

'Just some emails and songs for my album.'

'Ya know, I pictured you as a party girl, not a writer. I've seen you running in and out here at all hours. If writing is your thing... well, you need to slow it down.'

'Everyone here is trying to be a star. Make sure when you get your big break that you have enough energy to keep shining! I'm Mindy, by the way,.' She sticks her hand out to shake it.

'Alanna, pleased to meet you,' she responds.

'Yes, I know. Did you ever walk into a room and feel so alone? Like everyone had an idea of you before you even speak?' Alanna says.

'Yes, darling, I surely have had that.

Everyday we have eyes on us in the Industry,

'But focus on what matters to you.

What is your burning desire?' Mindy asks.

'Music and writing and performing. I was born to do that. Anyway, I can't believe you have noticed me. Oh crap! I'm sorry if I was in your face. It's just that I have only just moved to LA and...' Alanna says smiling.

'Darling, we all have excuses to run. If I can give you one piece of advice: protect your energy. These people don't care about you. Don't give that to anyone who doesn't deserve it. You need to stop throwing it around,' Mindy advises.

***

Now sitting side by side Mindy asks
'So, what separates you from the rest?'
'I'm authentic,' Alanna says.
'Through your words and music I need to feel what rocks your soul. If you feel it, then everyone else will feel it,' Mindy says.
'You're right,' Alanna says.
'So, show me this piece you're working on?' she asks.
'You're not a journalist are you?'
'*Hahaha*, no, I'm an agent. You're more clued in than I thought,' Mindy says while looking down at Alanna's iPad to read the song in front of her.

Bubbles fizz and lines are made,
It's a life of fun and the showbiz trade,
Or perhaps a life that everyone wants to live,
Except I hear the sound but not the taste,
It's my life and moments I don't want to waste.

Bubbles and lines are often found,
Laughter and smiles are all around,
Music and words are the surround sound,
Yet I hear them all as if far away,
I can't go back there, happy here alone I stay.

Bubbles are passing and lines soon disappear,
The night gets busier and people crowd in,
The love and lust, in preparation for the sin,
Although the wild life appeals to me somehow,
I stay away; my time is busy here for now.

Bubbles in the end of the glasses no more,
Memories of moments in the night before,

I am awake as others they lay to rest,

I sit here alone, with the pen and my music close to my chest,

With my songs, with me and them, is where I am at my best.

'This is great work, Alanna. Very passionate. You keep that up and cut down those parties. When you're ready with that album, let me know,' Mindy says as she walks back towards her apartment holding her yoga bag.

'I am ready, I have never been more ready' Alanna says to herself looking back down to her songs. So engrossed, forgetting to hit send on the three mails.

Chapter 48

Tweet: @AStar Damn Girl She's a Sexy Chick
@DavidGuetta @Akon

Playhouse Hollywood, Los Angeles

Alanna walks through the club straight into VIP and is met with kisses from Miki 'Darling, mwah, mwah. You look fantastic!

'Thanks so much for doing me this favour. I know you're not into this... but you'll do so well.'

'So, tell us, what's your secret to staying slim?' Miki says.

'Stress, have your life shared online and you'll see the weight drop off. hahaha' Alanna responds sarcastically.

'OK, sista, please go and get changed into something a little nicer on the eyes.' Miki drags her... She is in a PVC leotard with fishnet stockings and over-the-knee boots.

'I'm managing the dancers but I'll join in here and there.

'You're going to make $1,000 dollars. Easy money!' Miki assures her.

'Sure,' Alanna reacts sarcastically
'Easy' and 'money' never come hand in hand.

'Let me help you.' Miki assists Alanna into the leather swimsuit-style outfit, then Alanna adds glitter paint and heavier make-up.

'Look, sista, you ain't gonna make a penny if you keep on this face.

'I thought you were doing me a favour?' Miki asks. 'You're a dancer, so this is no different to a show or music video.'

312

Alanna straps on her boots, looks up and smiles. 'Happy, happy,' she says sarcastically.

'Photo time,' says Miki as she snaps full lengths photos of Alanna and herself in their outfits.

'OK, I am heading out now.

'I'll be back in a few minutes to show you your stage, mwah!' Miki says as she struts out the door.

A What's App message arrives from Carlton:

Carlton: OMG, sista, what's with the get-up on you?

Miki has tweeted you in some hooker shit!

You look loko! Get out quick!!

Alanna: I'm helping out dancing – Dread!

Carlton: Hahaha, oh good lord! OK, sista, good luck in your classes… Take care of my students. I'll be back in a week. You better behave!

P.S. Jack called again. I'm on Team Jack. Call him soon.

X

Alanna: Enjoy NYC.

Good luck in the casting!

Say hi to your mum and Mel.

X

***

Playhouse, VIP, LA

Alanna dances on a podium while the crowd cheers her on. Miki walks past, taking photos while she flirts with tables of men.

'Damn, she is fine!' she hears a group of guys call over.

'She certainly is fine!'

'That's Alanna, Alanna… *Alanna!*' DJ Pronto screams.

Alanna looks down, trying to work out who it is through the smoke and crowds. Seeing Pronto in black jeans and a shirt with gold jewellery, she smiles.

'What are you doing here. Alanna? This doesn't suit you,' he says. 'Get down! Get your fine ass down from there!' He helps her down. *'Get your stuff and get out of here, Alanna!'* he says, screaming through the music and crowds.

Looking over at Miki, Alanna calls, 'I am leaving.'

'That girl is out of her mind on drugs. Let's bounce,' Pronto says.

***

Mel's Diner, Los Angeles
'Rough about that show being released. Seriously with that and this dancing, what's going on with you?' Pronto says, watching her sip a milkshake. 'Are you taking drugs? Do you need some help?'

'No, not at all. I had to help out my family. They needed cash,' she admits.

'We made a bomb on those sales…' Pronto says.

'Maybe you did, but I certainly didn't,' she explains.

'He never paid you your cut? Are you kiddin' me? I need to get my men to sort this one out. You need to be smarter, Alanna. You should have called me. This is business, and in business you get paid. Capisco!' he smiles.

'Capisco!' she responds.

***

'So tell me, how did you make it in the Industry?' Alanna asks.

314

'You know there are two types that make it: the talkers and the doers. You get off your ass and you make shit happen,' he says. 'Like every industry, some people skip the queue. They do drugs, they sleep their way in, use contacts, but most people are there because they have talent. Plus, they work their asses off. I am one of those. I got myself off the streets of Chicago and made it happen. My dad walked out, and I was the older brother of five so I had no options. They needed me to step up. So I did what I was best at... music,' he admits. 'You, on the other hand, seem like you've had it nice.'

'It wasn't as hardcore as yours, but my brother is sick and my twin died. I had to "step up" as you say, to take care of my family. So we are really not so different after all,' she says, smiling.

'You is so street. Let's get your fine ass home,' he says, holding her hand leading her to his car.

***

As she lay in bed with tears streaming down her face, she reads over and over Jack and her conversation.

Jack: Hey, Lani

I've been trying to call you for days.

Alanna: Sorry it's been so busy here, I'm teaching classes and writing my album.

I'm arranging a trip back to Europe soon. Carlton and I were hoping to go to one of your final games of the season.

Jack: Lani, I've met someone.

Alanna: Oh, really? OK

Jack: She's lovely.

I have training but let's talk later.

Best of luck with your work,

Always here

X

Dear Sally,
Will I miss him; will he miss me?
What does it matter now?
I was never happen. I feel so wasted.
And used and lost.
Nothing is worth that, I know deep down.
Now it's me alone and free.
Not sure if I am happy or want to cry.
I confided my love in him and now it's over.
Choices have come and gone. I must be strong.
I hate this sorrow.
I hate this pain.
I'm not sure why this feeling is here or if it will ever end.
Why me?
They say I have it all.
Just when I'm everything seems to crumble and fall.
It's always high or low it seems.
I am searching for somewhere in the in-between.
I want it all, happiness in life.
I don't know how to find it anymore.
I'm feeling low, sitting here sobbing on the floor.
I work so hard, every single day.
I'll keep on writing on my way.
Tears will come and go.
But I can't, no, never let my dreams go.

Chapter 49

Tweet: *@Miki @Carlton You wanna hot body,*
You wanna Bugatti,
You wanna Maserati,
You better work bitch @Britney

Waffle House, Los Angeles

'The smell of LA is different to anything I have experienced before,' Alanna calls out.

'Sista, you is in love and that smell ain't LA. It's called waffle house syrup!' Carlton laughs.

'Welcome to the waffle house. I am Jim. In the waffle house, our aim is to make sure you'll always be happy, I am always happy,' says Jim, the ever-smiling waiter.

'Wow, that's a big claim,' Alanna says.

'Can you tell us your specials?' Miki asks.

'Sure. Butter, blueberry, raspberry, strawberry, berry-berry, choco, vanilla, cinnamon, choco-vanilla, syrup, Oreo, gluten-free, sugar-free, dairy-free, … there are a few specials. But let me know what you guys like and I will make sure you get it,' says Jim.

Alanna's jaw drops. 'I didn't even know this amount of waffles existed!'

'In America, we have it all!' Carlton says confidently.

'Wow, I will have choco-vanilla waffles, please,' Alanna says.

'I'm gonna have the choco-vanilla, blueberry and the Oreo, please,' Miki says.

'Gosh, Miki. You barely eat anything and then go wild…'

'You should be careful with that, Miki. In therapy we call that EE,' Carlton says.

'EE?'

'Emotional eating. My therapist and I use letters, as labels can stick. Labels hurt. OK, so I want to clear the air…

I know you two had a weird night working together, wires were crossed and I don't like my ladies arguing. So, what best way to do it than over food?' Carlton smirks.

***

'OMG, I feel like a fat mess!' Carlton says, looking at his plate.

'I feel happy and full and loved every bit,' Alanna says.

'I am stuffed, but I am going to take some lax…' Miki says.

'What's a lax?' Alanna questions.

'Lax. You know what a lax is! Laxative, sista!' Carlton says.

'Oh Miki, don't do that! It's not necessary. You have an amazing body!' Alanna exclaims.

'Look, at least she don't eat cotton balls like the models do!' Carlton says defensively.

'Oh, then it's OK!' says Alanna.

'What's up with you?' he says.

'It's not right to hurt yourself. We have only one shot in life, and our health has to come first,' Alanna says anxiously.

'Mis I-don't-mind-wearing-a-camera-on-my-boobs, stressed-out Annie, it takes one to know one… Give her a break.' Carlton says.

'I'm out of here!' Alanna says as she storms out.

'We hope you had a happy experience at the Waffle House!' the host calls out.

'We don't need you anyway, Queen Latifa!' Carlton screams after her.

***

Driving around LA, Alanna drives past the *Hollywood* sign and through Beverly Hills, going by the crowds of tours outside the houses of celebrities. As she continues on through Bel Air, she drives right out to Santa Monica Beach and pulls in to watch the sunset.

Dear Sally,

I wonder what it would be like to be a star. A true star! Like the old movies. I see more for my future than dancing on podiums in clubs. I want to be a star.

We are the top, the stars on stage,
No one around can take our place,
The kids.
The Industry.
The Industry.
All we do is for The Industry.

We pass through life, day by day,
High and low it's all the same.
Everyone is part of some big game,
Yet when you're near, happiness remains.

My better half is...
Jack, he is the one and only
Why is this so hard?
I just want him,
Right there waiting for me.

Chapter 50

Tweet: *@AStar @Agents Oh, no, oh, no, not me,
I did it my way @FrankSinatra*

Beverly Hills, Los Angeles

Alanna and Pronto, suitably dress turns heads walking into an Industry party up in 'The Hills'. Seeing the pool outside, Alanna jokes, 'I am so tempted to bomb the pool again, but this time I don't think the models and gays in LA would be as kind.'

Pronto laughs. 'Let's wait until later.'

Alanna observes the scene. 'I have never seen so many blonde women bopping. They are not dancing, not standing, they are just bopping. Is this how they do it in LA?'

'No, shorty. I'll show you how they do it in LA once I take you home!' he whispers in her ear.

'Really?' she reacts with a smirk while strutting to the bar.

***

As the night progresses, Alanna meets more agents than she can recall and shows off her curves and dancing skills. Later that evening, she and Pronto move into a private function, where Pronto announces proudly, 'Now Alanna Star is going to sing.'

Alanna sings as part of the show, and all the agents are transfixed by her.

'My better half...' she sings the song until she looks up to see the room of agents. smiling.

'Wow, man. She is good – contract-signing good. Call me tomorrow and we will talk business,' each of them agree.

'Larry here. Call me too.'

'Take my card.'

'And mine, Steve, nice to meet you.'

'Yeah, me too.'

'You may have their cards, but I'm taking you home... Let's bounce!' Pronto says as he leads her out to the valet parking.

***

Palazzo, Los Angeles

Carlton comes in to Alanna's room to see her and DJ Pronto in bed.

'Rise and shine. It's training time!'

'What's up, home boy? Can't ye see we are busy in here?' Pronto objects.

'Just checkin' if you wanted to come for a spinning class before studio?'

'*Hahaha*, we ain't in *LUCE* anymore. I won't be in no classes sticking to no rules,' Alanna says.

'Hell, yeah!' Pronto calls out.

Carlton storms out, banging the door.

Alanna follows him. 'What's up with the slamming doors in my house?'

'Your house? Since when have you bought it?' he asks.

'I pay the bills, so it's my house!' she states.

'Christina pays the bills and you are being a spoilt bitch!' Carlton retorts. 'In fact, other than that rapper, she's the only person you're nice to anymore. If I'm gonna be honest, sometimes it's hard to be around you, as it's all about you, you, *you*! I always love you but sometimes I don't like you. We both know I'm the model, the diva, and even with that I still make time for my family and friends. Like, home girl, when is the last time you called your momma? We are all worried about

321

you!' he adds, more quietly. 'And, sista, you is *so* skinny! Waz up with that? I mean you're meant to be the "real woman" who's got her shit together. Where's the dancer? The singer? The writer? My best friend? You've lost yourself!' Tears spring into his eyes.

'This is me!' she says. 'I am writing an album and I will create a masterpiece. So give me a break if I ain't Mrs Perfect!' she screams.

'I'll give you as long as you need. I'm moving out,' he says as he slams the door shut.

'Gurlfriend, don't mind his moody ass… get back in here and I'll make you smile again,' Pronto calls out.

Chapter 51

Tweet: @CStar @ I came to win, to fight,
to conquer, to thrive.
I came to win, to survive, to prosper, to rise
To fly, to fly @NickiMinaj

Mindy's Apartment, Palazzo
Alanna rings the buzzer. 'Hey, Mindy.'

'Are you free?'

'Are you free?'

'Sure, come in.'

'How are you?'

'I'm good, thanks. You?'

'I'm OK, working through some stuff,' Alanna admits.

'Haven't seen you in a while. Checking if you done much writing, like, do you have anything to play me?'

'Sure… take a seat at the piano.'

Alanna sits at the piano. 'This is something I'm working on.'

She closes her eyes and begins to sing and play simultaneously.

My better half,
You were always there for me.
Through it all,
You're the best of me.
You are my better half, better half, the best half.
Without you I don't think I could last, last, last, last.
You are the only one, only one, only one.
Who I can have, for my life, for my life.
You make it right, make it right, make it right.
You're worth the fight, worth the fight.
I was lost, now I'm found,

When I'm with you I'm flying off the ground.
I can't believe I've met you somehow
My world has changed, it's better, so much better
now.
You're my better half, better half, better half…

'You got a powerful voice. I like this. I like where you're going with this,' Mindy praises.

Blushing, Alanna stands up. 'I had good teachers,' she smiles.

'Do you have an agent?'

'No. No, I had one but we didn't work out. So, I suppose I'm looking,' she says.

'You're an agent sure. I should really ask ye for help. I'm not good at this LA networking thing,' she says laughing.

'It's to your advantage, trust me!' Mindy says. 'Will you get a collection of your tunes written, printed and recorded for me? Also, any demos of your work would be great. I want to play these to people who may like them.'

'Sure, I'm doing some recordings with my friend DJ Pronto so I'll get him to help me out. Give me a week.'

'Take as long as you need to get it right. Yet not too long. It is the Industry, after all.'

***

Alanna and Carlton's Apartment, Palazzo
The buzzer goes. It's Carlton.

'Hey, I was checking in as we have to teach class. You haven't been in a week.'

'Yes, I don't think I'm going to go, after our fight, etc. I can't keep up. Plus, I am working on this demo with Pronto and so I am too tired.'

'What do you mean, not go? They hired you. I got you the job, and it's not fair pulling out when it suits you,' Carlton says sternly.

'I'm having a tough week. Give me a break,' she says.

'What's the point writing albums if you can't even make it to training when you're being paid?'

'Carlton, give me a break! Maybe we are just two different people and you need to let me go.'

'Excuse me?'

'Sorry, I didn't mean that...' she says.

'Look, you act like the world owes you something, Alanna. Why don't you stop the act and start getting out your real talent? Don't you know that I see you writing day and night? You're so much more than this shit! Harry was right; you didn't need Dennis. You're so fucking scared of being happy!'

'I am happy,' she says.

'You could have everything, yet you're wasting it away in clubs with idiots,' he says. 'You used to be real. You're just like my dad.'

'No, I'm not, Carlton. Not everyone is bad. Just because I am tough and need to survive doesn't mean I am a bad person. You have no idea what I've been through. Do you know what it feels like to lose the one person that matters?' she asks.

'Yes,' he says.

'Really? How do you know?'

'Well, perhaps if you took your head out of your ass every once in a while you'd ask me about my dad and my family.'

'Ask you what?' she says. 'You told me your dad wasn't around when you were a kid.' she says.

'Wrong! I told you my dad left us when I was a kid...' he corrects her. 'But you never asked me what happened.

'Well, here it goes. He started like you, a talented jazz musician who made a few bad decisions. Then he got in with the wrong crowd, the wrong manager, etc. No one knows, but we were told he took drugs, had groupies and lost the plot. Momma kicked him out, but he was already gone. He was there but never there. We got a call one day that he had taken an overdose. He got lost in the Industry and never came back to us,' he explains.

'Come here.' She hugs him tightly, with tears streaming down her face. 'I'm so sorry,' she admits.

***

'If you knew how tough it was to work in, why didn't you stay in NYC and do a 'normal' job, then?'

'Because this is what I'm meant to do... ... I have tried it all. Remember I'm years older than you. I've done the hosting, the office jobs, done them all. No matter what, I know I am meant to be a performer. I know that nothing else matters but being on stage, singing, dancing or teaching,' he explains.

'Why are you picking on me then?' she asks.

'I'm not. I just see so much more for you than you do yourself,' he explains. 'I told you to not go with Dennis. I told you about the contracts and you wouldn't listen. You were determined to get rich and famous. What's that about? I mean this place is nice, and it's fun, but it's too much.'

'Then it's your attitude.

'What's up with that? The best stars in the world keep it real and they keep their friends real. Like, why are you friends with Miki? She is a pappz! The only rule I have is don't become friends with people who can make money at your expense. Unless they are a hot hairdresser like MD,' he jokes. 'You are making a huge mistake getting in with that crowd. You'll so freaking talented, you'll meet an agent when the time is right...You're in LA, for crying out loud! Look, I know you are crushed by your sister, but use it. That is in your blood; that is your motivation. Write about it, sing about it, and dance about it, like a proper artist. When my dad died, I created some of the best work of my life. I had good times and bad times, but I always use my experiences in my work.'

'If you're so wise, why did you do LUCE?'

'I *chose* to go back to the UK to travel, get a visa, and have fun... I didn't need to. Same as an agent... I haven't met the right one yet, so I like doing my own thing. I do shows when it suits me. I love my work, but I'll never hurt or stress myself to get ahead.'

Miki, who was sitting outside, comes in.

'So, are you guys, like, having like a domestic?'

'Something like that,' Alanna says.

'Alanna, are you ready to hit class?' Carlton asks.

'Sure, sounds like a plan.' She grabs her bag as they head out of the door.

Chapter 52

Tweet: @CStar
There's something in the air tonight
You know, everyone needs someone to look up to
Why shouldn't it be us? @JohnLegend

Star Studios, Los Angeles

Alanna and Carlton are coming home from studio.

'That was such a great class!' Alanna says. 'Thanks.'

'For what?' Carlton says.

'For everything. I would be no one without you. You've made me a better person,' she says.

'Oh, sista! Don't do this to me. I am T & E so the tears are gonna flow,' he says.

'Let them flow,' she suggests. 'You're an amazing man, and I hope you get this show in New York. I would miss you terribly, but I want you to be happy. I want the world to be happy, and they will be happier when they see you on stage,' she smiles as she puts her arm around him.

'Thank you. That means so much. More than you know,' he says.

'Don't be afraid to fall, Carlton. Not everyone stays down. Like you say, our pain drives us, yet we have to fall to feel the pain,' she says, winking at him.

'You're right,' he admits. 'Not just a pretty face,' he smiles.

'Ditto,' she says back.

Alanna receives a call.

'Hi, Alanna. It's Mindy.'

'Hey.'

'I'm in the office. Look I am calling to say, we've looked at your lyrics and listened to your demos and

328

clips and we are very impressed. Can you come down to the office to talk contracts?'

'Sure, when do you need me?'

'When are you ready?'

'Now!' she says, half screaming as she jumps up and down.

***

U Studios, Los Angeles

Walking into the studio, Alanna smiles at all the platinum albums and posters of stars on the walls.

When she walks up to reception, the lady asks, 'Do you have an appointment?'

'Yes, with Mindy.'

'Oh, you must be Alanna. Please take a seat and Mindy will be with you shortly.'

'Many thanks,' she says as she sits down in the reception.

***

'Alanna this is Eoin, David and Sue', she points to her three colleagues.

'Pleased to meet ye' Alanna responds.

'OK, we know everyone, or most artists, can look great on camera *or* sound wonderful on radio. Yet only a few artists can own the live experience,' Eoin the director says.

'Alanna can. Darling, please sing one of your songs,' Mindy requests.

'Sure.'

She begins.

You're the best of me...

You are my better half, better half, the best half.
Without you I don't think I could last, last, last last.
You are the only one, only one, only one.
Who I can have, for my life, for my life.
You make it right, make it right, make it right.

'Stop, stop, stop! You've made your point. She's remarkable. I haven't heard talent like that in… well, years,' Eoin says as he sits back, impressed. Mindy was smiling, but her face turns serious. 'This is a business, darling. It may be glamorous, but we need artists who keep their head in the clouds but feed on the ground. We need commitment 24/7, especially at the start. But if you work, you get paid. We get contracts. We negotiate. You give us 20% and that's it. No quirks, no catches. We are here to sell your service.'

'Sure, of course,' Alanna agrees.

'We help you, so you must help us and yourself. You need to take care of yourself. No drugs. No drama. You ruin your reputation and you ruin ours. We don't work with people who mess that up,' David the grey haired agent adds.

***

All sitting around the board room table, 'OK, how we work it is that we agree the songs on your album.

To invest we will pay for your first video and you can sign the songs to us. We test the water here and then send you back to Europe to see how things go. If it works out then we will record the remainder of the album and a three-record deal' Mindy states.

'I know it may not appear much for your years of writing and training, but this is the figure we will offer for your first record. This is for an album and the three-

330

record deal. This may go up if you do better, but it won't go down'.

'Jaysus, Mary and Josephine!' she screams as she nearly falls off the chair.

'Take home the contract. Read it. Read it ten times, even. Get a lawyer if you need to. Contracts are legal. We want you to be committed,' Sue says.

'Sure,' Alanna agrees.

'If you're happy we will bring you in for voice training, dance coaching and legalities over the next week or two. We like you together so we want you and DJ Pronto on this track. He will bring in the new edge so leave that with us to negotiate.'

'I am ready. I don't need to go home. I have waited my whole life for this day.'

Where is the feckin pen?

'You can't afford to make any more mistakes in showbiz,' Mindy reminds her.

'I won't. Pen, please!' she says, smiling as they hand over her contract and a pen.

Chapter 53

Tweet: @DJPronto *I'm feeling so good, I knew I would*
Been taking care of myself, Like I should.
'Cause not one thing Can bring me down,
Nothing in this world gonna turn me round
@JenniferLopez

3 Months later, Palazzo Apartments, Los Angeles
Alanna wakes up to the sound of her apartment buzzer going off.

'We are here!' Alanna and Pronto hear from outside.

She pushes her hair back and looks at her iPhone to see it's 5.00am.

'Oh no, my LA Rox trainers are here,' she smiles joking.

'What, why so freakin' early?' Pronto asks.

'Two minutes. Just getting changed!' Alanna calls out.

Within seconds she dashes to her room and walks into her wardroom to throw off her nightdress and get straight into gym clothes.

'Where are you going?'

'My trainers are here. I have the shoot today so they came early.'

'A, it's coming-home time, not getting up time.' He watches her get ready. 'You are smoking hot, Alanna, and getting better day by day. Come here...'

He kisses her on the bed.

'OK, I gotta go!'

Quickly gathering up all the vodka and remnants of her guests last night, she throws these into the bin. With the sound of the buzzer, she lets her trainers in.

'Morning,' Alanna says

'Hey, hey, our Star. Are you ready for spinning?'

They double-kiss.

'Sure, spinning, sounds great. Come in, I just need to get a coffee.'

She lets them in.

'Here's your shake,' the tall dark-haired sculpted male trainer says to her.

They see the glitter all over her face.

'Alanna, were you out again last night? We don't know how you keep up! You have a shoot for the album cover so soon and we need you to get your energy levels up,' the slighter but equally toned female trainer says.

'I'm keeping her toned,' Pronto calls out from the bedroom.

'I am only in my twenties. I am meant to be wild and out all night and working through the tiredness,' Alanna says, winking at them both.

'Yes, she is,' Pronto agrees.

As she hits the button on her coffee maker, she asks, 'So, how are you two?'

'All great. Very busy trying to keep stars on the straight and narrow,' the female trainer jokes.

Alanna fills up all the coffee glasses and, like a waitress, moves back to her 'bar'. 'Espresso shots for us all. One, two, three… knock back!'

'You seem a pro at this,' they joke.

'I sure am!' Alanna says honestly.

***

'OK, Alanna let's go...' they both request.

'One second!' She runs into her room and kisses Pronto.

'Why don't you skip training? I can give you a private session right here.'

'Don't tempt me. I gotta go, today is a big day.'

'I know, I am so happy for you.'

'See you when I'm back... hold off on the shower!' she winks at him.

'Gurlfriend, you can count on it.'

Smiling, she kisses him and makes her way out to the living room. As she grabs her phones and car keys, she moves out of the door.

'Who's that?' they ask.

'My new man,' she says, linking arms with her trainers. 'You may know him.'

They move outside and through the paparazzi to their cars. Alanna very calmly gets into her car, smiles and follows her trainers in convoy.

***

Alanna comes back soon after training. Pronto sees her sweaty in her Lycra. 'Damn girl, you always looking fine!' Pronto says, wearing only his boxers while drinking coffee at her marble coffee bar. 'Come here. I have something for you!'

She moves over to the kitchen and he kisses her and lifts her onto the counter.

'I want to kiss you all over, every single inch of your body, starting here,' he kisses her nose, her cheeks and moves down to her chin, then her neck, but his arms remain around her back to keep her from falling. He slowly pushes her back on the counter and starts to kiss her neck, then he moves down to her belly button and slowly back up her chest. He removes her top and kisses her inch by inch. She leans back on the bar breathing heavily.

Suddenly she rips off her bra.

'Keep going!'

'Girl, I just got started.'

She screams, 'I want you so bad!'

'I want to…. get you all washed up so bad,' he says, laughing as he throws her over his shoulder and carries her to the shower.

Dear Sally,

I am in a fairytale.

For the first time in my life I feel alive.

No pressures.

No family expectations.

No keeping up appearances.

The press LOVE me, or at least they don't abuse me any more.

My fans LOVE me.

Men LOVE me.

I look better than I ever have.

I have money, heaps of it.

I have a great place in West Hollywood. I also helped Carlton get one in NYC so we can always be close.

I am dating DJ Pronto. I swear, I didn't even think it was possible to move in the ways he moves in.

Over here, anything goes. I love that.

I'm recording a new song with him. It will be amazing!

Oh and guess what? I am going to Europe soon so I'll see our family.

Life is perfect.

I miss Jack but he is with someone else so what can I do?

Do you think he misses me?

X

Chapter 54

Tweet: *@AStar* *@DJPronto*
Strike a pose
Vogue, vogue, vogue @Madonna

Photoshoot, Rooftop, The Standard, Los Angeles
As Alanna walks out onto the rooftop in leather shorts
and a studded bra with lace over it, there are cameras,
lights, and make-up stands set up everywhere.

Carlton goes through the rail... 'What to wear?' he
says.

'Away! Get away! We have to style Pronto and
Alanna first,' the overly sensitive stylist called Rian
screams.

'I am the choreographer,' Carlton reacts.

'I don't care if you are the President. Get your club
hands off their clothes!' Rian insists.

***

'MD, I'm so happy you made it over,' she says,
hugging him.

'OMG, sista, you are just so teeny. What's
happened?' MD calls out.

'Stress and having a man like him,' she points to
Pronto.

'*Hahaha.* Go you!' he laughs.

'Anyway, you're behind the camera, so indulge. We
have food, drinks anything you need,' Alanna says.

'Darling, this your big day! Don't be worrying about
anyone else,' MD reminds her.

'Whatever, Trevor. You my home boy,' Alanna
says, smiling. 'Come meet my agents.'

'Mindy, Sue and David, please meet MD, the man
you flew from Ireland for me.'

'Pleased to meet you,' he says.
'Likewise!' they say in unison.

***

After an hour or so of make-up, the shoot begins. Alanna both sings and mimes to her song.

My better half,
You my baby,
You the one,
You're mine.
You're my light,
My light,
My light,
My only light...
(Pronto raps, with Alanna singing.)
She's my light, so bright, you can't miss her coming your way,
Yet, she's mine, my shining lady, the one for me, she's filled with love for all to see.
Every day, day, day, she's in my sight, no matter what anyone will say.
She's the only one through the dark skies, skies, skies, that will last for infinity.

***

'OK, Pronto, we need you to come back on camera,' calls out the director.

Alanna jealous seeing Pronto flirting with the dancers calls out 'Pronto, didn't ya hear the choreographer? You're needed here!'

'Sista, *please*, you can't diss me in front of my crew,' objects Pronto.

'Your crew? Don't talk to me like that!' Alanna erupts.

'You ain't my woman!' he screams back.

'What? What am I, then?' she asks.

'This is showbusiness. You fronting, yet we ain't go no rings on. I am too young to be chained down. Chill out, biatch, I ain't chained to you!'

'Chained? You fecking prick! You can fly all you want, coz after this I will walk out and you'll never lay a hand on me again.'

'You wouldn't leave DJ Pronto' he calls out.

'Yes, I would. I AM THE STAR, NOT you…

Oh, and thanks for helping me write my next song: *The Biggest Prick*. Actually, I take that back: *The SMALLEST Prick.*'

His face is blushing.

The entire rooftop erupts with laughter.

***

Alanna and Carlton's apartment, Palazzo

'OK, gotta run, we have to make the Awards' Alanna says.

'Please can I borrow your laptop?' Miki asks.

'Sure…Why don't you have my iPad' Alanna says.

'Sista, for someone who is journalist, you never have yours working. I think you use it more than A.'

'We gotta run as we have a flight,' Carlton says.

'I want to send you some of the photos from the shoot' Miki says.

'Don't sell them,' Carlton says.

'Will only be two minutes,' Miki says.

The buzzer goes.

'We gotta go sista' Calrton says.

'Look, keep it. I have another one and all my things backed on *EverNote*.'

'Wow, you're so kind!' she says calmly as if expecting this response.

They all double-kiss each other.

'See you in a few weeks,' Alanna says to Miki.

Over at the palazzo courtyard, Miki smiles with an unusual smirk, air-kissing Alanna...

'The whole world will see you and your dirty work in a few weeks you foolish girl' Miki calls out while waving at Carlton and Alanna as they move further into the distance.

Chapter 55

Tweet: @CStar I'm from New York,
New York, New York @AliciaKeys

JFK Airport, NYC
'There she is, get her…!'

The paparazzi chase them out of the airport.

'Carlton!' Mel calls out.

'Over here!' Alanna and Carlton see Mel waving over.

'You're as tall, dark and handsome as ever,' Carlton's mom says, referring to his skinny jeans, biker books and cotton YSL top.

'Momma, you're as fierce as ever! Now, come on, let's go see Lani's new NYC home.'

They all walk past the paparazzi flashes and towards the car.

***

Alannas, apartment, Brooklyn, NYC
Walking into the penthouse, Carlton and Alanna see the food laid out in the apartment, white leather couches, and a modern interior with a view that is priceless.

'Wow, this place is unreal!

'What's up, home girl?'

'Alanna I feel like I knows you already!' Mel says hugging her tightly

'She is my sweet lova for life!

'Let's eat,' Carlton requests.

They all sit down around the table, facing the view.

'We is so happy that you have a friend like Lani who will let you live with her.'

'Alanna, we moved homes a lot during Carlton and Mel's childhood, mostly government housing, so you

can't imagine what it's like to see him in a nice place...
well, your place,' Mel says.

Alanna watches them talk and sees how close they
are. 'You guys are so sweet. Honestly, it's so rare to
see families so happy.'

I miss my family. I miss Brendan.

***

'I want to make an announcement. Everyone, please
raise your glasses...' Alanna says

'Sista, I hope this ain't a proposal! My brother bats
for the other team,' Mel jokes.

'Hahaha, no, not quite. Well, since I met Carlton, he
has made me a better person and not being able to live
with him will kill me and I know how he hates to be
alone. I want him to be happy. So, from today, I want
to give this home to you three. I want it to be your first
home together, a home based on love, happiness and
success' Alanna calls out.

The three of them look at Alanna, each speechless.

'I will call the agent and have this transferred into
your names. It means more to you three than it ever
will for me. So, let's make a toast to your new home.'

The three of them burst into tears.

'Oh, I am sorry for upsetting you!' says Alanna.

'No, no, this is the kindest thing that anyone has
ever done for us,' Carlton says as he gets up to hug her,
then Mel, then their mother.

'Lord, bless this child. She's an angel.' Carltons
momma calls out.

'Amen!' they call out.

***

MTV Awards, NYC

As Alanna and Carlton move over the red carpets in rock-chic outfits, they wave at the crowd and the devoted fans. Whether they are their fans or not, they are there to support one common love: music.

As soon as she arrives, Alanna sees Mindy looking very glam in red.

'Mindy, you look incredible' Alanna announces.

'Alanna, we have to ask you, do you know a journalist called Miki? Well, she has written a book about you, and has threatened us with a big sum or else she will release it.'

'What have you told her?' Alanna asks.

'Nothing. We need your consent on anything of this nature,

'What the fuck is going on? How would this girl get her material? Sorry for my language but seriously' Mindy says

'I don't know. She has used my iPad a few times, but everything is locked. Unless she cracked my codes?'

'Would she have any of your songs?' Mindy asks.

'No, it's mostly diary stuff, but there may be a few pieces of songs,

'I feel sick. I can't believe this!' Alanna says.

'I can,' Carlton says. 'It's her job to sell information on stars.'

Alanna now looks very panicky.

'You need to stay calm…

'We have all of the top producers inside. This is your time to shine. Don't let this girl ruin that for you!' Mindy says.

'We will sort this,' Mindy assures her. 'I just can't believe you never told us the truth. It is so sweet you were dedicating your diary and this album to your twin. This is such an amazing story Alanna' she announces.

'It's not usually a conversation starter,' Alanna says sarcastically.

'Sure, let's go inside. Leave this with me,' Mindy says.

***

MTV after-party, Meat Packing District, New York
'Hey Carlton, where are you?' Alanna asks.

'I am outside the bar, getting a cab home,' he says.

'Without me? He better be worth it!' she jokes.

'I didn't want to tell you face to face because I would cry too much, but I've made it.'

'What do you mean?' she asks.

'I got signed to the *Priscilla Queen of the Desert World Tour*, starting in Broadway.'

'Ah!' she screams.

'Ah!' he screams.

'Ah!' she screams again. 'Tell me all!'

'I met a choreographer at an event and he was like, you is fine, you gotta be mine. I didn't know but I went back to a party and the casting director was there. Then we became friends. Well, he is pretty fine and he loved me. I loved him. It was love…'

Knowing him too well, she has to ask, 'OK Carlton, what actually happened?'

'OK, Christina was at our show and she got me in touch with a casting director she knew in NYC. So I have done some auditions and I made the cut. I am the lead! So I am moving back to New York in the next few weeks. I don't know how I feel… happy, sad, excited… I just know already that I am going to miss you.'

'Carlton, this is your dream. This is why you came here and left your mum and Melanie, so enjoy this

343

moment. We will always be friends and I will be your biggest fan.'

'I will fly straight back after my trip to Europe and we will celebrate'

'Promise? Friends for life? ' he asks.

'For life,' she says.

Chapter 56

Tweet; @*Jack My Better Half by*
@*AStar YouTube*

Bristol Airport, United Kingdom
Alanna lands in Bristol and is met with two bouncers who usher her out to meet a lady called Jenny.

'Hi, Alanna. Mindy had to go back to sort your book and business, so I am your assistant in Europe. Well, wherever you are,' Jenny says in a soft American accent. She has pale skin, brown hair and wears a navy suit. 'Feel free to call me Jen.' She smiles to show her natural charisma.

'Thanks, Jen,' Alanna says.

'Oh, here's a call from Mindy.' She says handing her the phone.

'Darling, in a nutshell, we have curbed Miki's book release of your work. We saved the stress by buying the rights. In fact, the suggestion of this to the media has created a sob story and has added more hits to your release. You're in the top ten. Congrats – I knew you would be. Next thing, Pronto has been on and he is sorry and wants to give it another try. We ignored that – next!' she says, slightly laughing. Oh, and I've taken a look It's a beautiful collection of your journey to now. We love the story, and we think you should release it.

'Miki has been removed from the Palazzo, so don't worry that she would be hanging around you,' she assures Alanna.

'Hope you like your PA Jenny, she's a sweetheart,' Mindy states.

The paparazzi are flashing everywhere.

'Saved the best to last, guess what?' Mindy says.

'More news, What?' asks Alanna.

'Stateside, we have spoken to the producers at *Ellen*, who may want to interview you. We have mentioned the book, the show, your album, your journey in the Industry. She loves your story. Also, in the UK we have Graham Norton, Jonathan Ross and some other breakfast shows have been in touch. You are *so popular*! I knew everyone would love you! I wanted to say congratulations on behalf of myself and U Music. We are very proud of you. You'll get the contracts this week,' she explains. 'Enjoy your gig. We shall talk later.'

***

Alanna makes a phone call.

'Jack, I'm here. I can't wait to see you later! Guess what? I didn't want to tell you, but I am playing at Glastonbury!'

'Oh my God... The lads and myself will be front row!

Amazing, Alanna. You were always amazing' Jack says.

'I've missed you so much. It's ridiculous,' Alanna admits.

'I can't keep up with you and your LA life' he states

'Sure, I can't believe you've won Player of the Year. That's mad! Why didn't you tell me?' she asks.

'Yes, sure, I've been keeping the head down. No wild red-haired ladies here to distract me' he jokes.

'Ha ha, you are funny!' Alanna remarks.

'You sound American, Lani.

'OK, gotta go. Annabel is calling me,' as she hears a lady calling in the background.

'See you later' Jack says.

The phone cuts off.

***

Bristol Airport to Glastonbury Festival, United Kingdom
'Alanna! Babe, I missed you!' MD says as the helicopter is moving closer to Glastonbury.

'MD, I missed you!' Alanna says.

'You hair is a state, but you look fab.'

They have wardrobes of clothes from Rian and Lulu will meet us there.

'You will look like stunners,' he says, smiling 'as always'.

As the helicopter moves through the air 'Jaysus, I have butterflies!' MD says.

'Wow, this is super-cute!' Jen says.

They land down and move into T-P village filled with crowds, colourful people and campsites.

Moving backstage, Alanna and MD see DJs, etc. Alanna sees Jack and everything turns into a blur thinking of the song she is about to sing to the crowds and the man she wrote it for;

You are my better half, better half, the best half.
Without you I don't think I could last, last, last last.
You are the only one, only one, only one.
Who I can have, for my life, for my life.
You make it right, make it right, make it right.
You're worth the fight, worth the fight.
I was lost, now I'm found.
When I'm with you I'm flying off the ground.
I can't believe I've met you now.
My world has changed, it's better now.
You're my better half, better half, better half...

She runs to Jack, and her bouncers come around her.
'Wow, darling, you look...'

Right then a stunning blonde steps forward.

'Superstar A! Meet my girlfriend Annabel.'

'Hey, Annabel.'

'Hey,' Annabel says, looking to the ground, uninterested.

With no response, Alanna feels a lump in her throat and everything starts to spin.

I love Jack, what have I done?

'Come on, Lani. We have a show to run,' MD calls out.

'I've come all this way and he has someone else.'

'You've come here for yourself, so enjoy every minute. People wait their whole lives to play here, so don't let a man or anything stop you having fun!' MD says.

'You're the best! You really are! Let's get some drinks!' she says leading him towards the bar.

***

Sitting at a table of men drinking, Jack comes over.

'Lani, are you OK?'

'I don't know. I missed you, Jack.'

'Jaysus, what bad timing, sure. Annabel and myself are looking at moving in together.'

'You're all around the world and I need a lady who wants to be close to me. Just like me ma. *Hahaha.* Annabel, she is best friends with one of the girls who Jean is engaged to. Like you say, it works, it's simple. It may not be perfect, but maybe there is no such thing!'

'Gay Jean? Yes, all so simple!' she says sarcastically.

They look over at Annabel dancing in hot pants.

'What a classy girl!' Alanna says bitchily, then starts crying. 'I want to be with you. You're the only one I can be myself with. I wrote a song about you.'

She storms off.

***

Alanna walks onto the stage as if she was born to do this, doing her best to ignore to Jack with his arms around Annabel.

'Hello, Glastonbury! I hope you're all having an amazing time,' she calls out.

The crowds roar back.

'Thank you for having me. I am very excited to be playing at my first Glastonbury.'

She is in a bubble-tube top and fitted trousers with stiletto-type chunky heels, her hair poker-straight with plaits tight against her head.

It was only you.
Always you,
Only you,
My better half,
My only true half...
Love you for life!

After the gig, Alanna goes back to her caravan and writes a song with tears streaming down her face.

I hate that I love,
I hate to feel this way,
So together yet, so broken away.
If I had done this or that in another way,
Would I be feeling this feeling of missing you each day?
I hate that you love her,

349

I hate that it's not me,
When it used to be us,
Together happy endlessly.
If you looked inside you would see and feel what I do,
We would together create a love each and every day.

Or is it all a waste?
Is it over? Am I wasting this space?
I hate that I feel this way,
I hope this feeling will soon go away.

Chapter 57

Tweet: @*AStar on The Late Late Show launching her single My Better Half.*

Dublin Airport, Ireland

Alanna hears the young guy beside her say, 'Ma. Ma? Ma! Would'ja bleeding look? It's yar woman from de telly. She's bleedin' massive. Jaysus, Ma, would'ja run over 'n get her autograph? The lads in work would love it.'

'Would'ja ever grow a pair and do it yourself? You're well able.'

'No, it's grand. I'm fine. I was just saying. I don't even want it.'

'You're a bleedin' tool, you are sometimes,' the lady says.

The middle-aged lady moves towards Alanna, her bouncer and Jenny with a pen and paper.

'S'cuse me, miss. Can I have yer autograph for me son?' she says.

'See him over dere… he's too scared to ask you!'

'No, I'm not!' he screams over.

'Sharrup, you!' she says, smiling. 'He's still a boy. He really is. You know yourself how kids are… No matter what age they are, they never change. Always mammy's boys.'

Alanna forces a smile, exhausted from all the tours and wanting to get home to her own family.

Signing the autograph to 'Tim', she calls him over for a photograph, knowing how much it will mean to the mother and son.

***

Alanna grabs her designer luggage and with Jenny they move out to customs, she takes a deep breath, knowing an array of photographers will be waiting for her on the other side.

'RTE Studios, please,' Jen asks the driver.

As soon as they are moving, Alanna looks to her *Evernote* journal and starts to write

Now I know why I'm here,
All the mistakes, happiness.
Up until now,
They made me better, showing me how to live for now.
Now I know that I must be here and be just me.
Sit still and look around at all I see.
A life of endless possibly with love behind me.
Thank you to you, my loving friends and family.

***

RTE Studios, Dublin, Ireland
Sitting on the orange velour couch in patent heels, a tight black dress with chic make-up and flowing curls, Alanna looks around, carefully taking in everything. Within the brightly lit crowded studio, she notices all eyes on her. Seconds later, the cameraman counts down, 'Three, two, one...'

Alanna takes three deep breaths.

'Tonight's guest, an Irish-born lady of many talents, having recorded various shows, both TV and online, is here to launch her first solo album,' says the slim, mousey-brown-haired presenter named Bryan. 'Welcome on the show, Alanna.' He has a distinctly Dublin accent.

'Thanks for havin' me,' Alanna says, smiling back and enticing him to continue.

'A true home-bird, her album has launched worldwide, and this is the start of many interviews in LA, London and New York. She chose Ireland for her first interview. Tonight she will help give us a glimpse of her star-studded life,' he says, smirking.

'Alanna, please give us music lovers a quick snapshot of what to expect in your album?'

'A Star is a soulful, R 'n' B, hip-hop album, with some techno overtones mixed in by various famous DJs. It is eclectic.'

'Eclectic, just like you, perhaps?' he responds rhetorically. 'So, tell us, what was your favourite moment on your rocky road journey to stardom?'

'Well, I don't know. It is very hard to say, but I believe my top moment is now my first album being released. Nothing can beat the feeling of hearing your work being played all around the world. Seeing and hearing people appreciate your work... it is indescribable.'

'On your album, you have thanked many people, including your best friend Carlton, your ex-fiancé Harry and your brother Brendan, to name a few. Can you tell us more about each of the guys?'

'Carlton is and will remain my rock – the most inspiring man I know. Since I met him, he makes me a better person and I would not have made it here without him. He wanted to come this evening, but at the moment he is working shows in Broadway in New York. He is destined for great things, and so deserves to shine,' she confirms.

'Being a star, it makes sense that you collaborate. Would you ever work with Carlton?'

'We have already worked together many times, and he is featured on my album. He also choreographed my first video and there are talks about collaborating in the near future. We will always remain close, as friends and in work' She states.

'Tell us about Harry? He is a famous tycoon, so together that must have been an exciting mix?'

'Yes, we had lots of fun. Harry too is a wonderful man – one of the best men I have ever known, but we were not meant to be. C'est la vie.'

'Is it true you broke up due to the viral show that was released?'

'We broke up for various reasons. If the truth be told, when I met Harry I was naïve and made some mistakes. We both got hurt and now it is in the past. He has since engaged and I am happy for him.'

'Lastly, Brendan, tell us about him'

'Brendan, he is my little brother. I love him for life,' she says emotionally.

'So, how does it feel to get a number-one album?'

'Amazing. What can I say? A dream come true. Yet there are so many people involved – for this to happen it is such a team effort. I can't thank my agents enough. I will continue to – I am a Kerry lass, after all – keep my feet on the ground,' she smiles.

'With all your publicised experiences with agents, would you ever consider becoming one yourself?'

'Never say never' she says.'

'Like many stars, you have been publicised for losing lots of weight since your move to Los Angeles. In such an image-conscious industry, do you feel the pressure to be thin?'

'I was always slim, but a little curvy, and lost weight due to training more. I accept myself. Whatever way I am. I keep well away from stereotypes.

'Sadly, though, already I have seen enough girls and men suffer with eating disorders, using drugs and other desperate measures to keep their image up. It's not right to hurt yourself just for success. My parents brought me up to keep it real.' She says seriously.

'You are known as a bit of a party girl and have been linked to many famous stars, in both music and sport. Can you let the interested men know if any of the rumours are true?'

'I have lots of male friends. I love music. I love to dance. I love to party. People are going to talk whatever I do, so I just rise above it. I promise ye'll be the first to know if I do settle down,' she says flicking her hair back over her shoulders as if to say she is moving on.

'In such an intense industry, do you feel it is more difficult to sustain relationships?'

'Yes and no. I think it depends on each person and couple entirely. I'm single and having fun now, which suits me.'

'Did you ever at any point consider marrying an Irish man and returning home to live the "simple life"?'

Yes, yes, YES. SIMPLE LIFE WITH JACK!

Yet, as advised by her media officer to 'retain as much as privacy as possible', she continues carefully, 'I did have a chance to be with a wonderful Irish man a few years ago, but I made choices to move away. Also, my best friend in London is an Irish man. Ye never know,' she winks.

'All the time with my job I am meeting wonderful guys, but as I say, I am having fun and am enjoying my work' She smiles.

'You seem very open-minded, and nowadays so many young stars have families young. Would you plan to have children?' he asks.

'Yes, definitely one day, but now... well now it is not my time. I am focusing on my career and all I know is that the right guy will slot into that,' she says matter-of-factly.

'Speaking of children, you have done a vast amount of charity work for children, particularly for those kids with autism?' Bryan reminds her.

'Yes, growing up with an autistic brother, Brendan, gave me huge insight into the talents and challenges that autistic people face on a day-to-day basis. They are truly misunderstood, and I wanted to give Brendan and others a chance. Mainly to provide them the dignity that they deserve,' She responds.

'In line with your charity work, since a very early age you have been and still remain a devout Catholic. You speak openly about this faith, so you must feel everyone needs a faith in life?'

'Yes, I believe we all need faith. Many times, I have burnt out or I was off course in life. I always struggled with saying "no", as I loved my job so deeply. But there are times where you can get lost within the hype. When I felt that way, I always found solace in my faith and the belief that there was someone guiding me other than my friends and family.

'Faith is something I can always rely on. Around the world I would as much as possible attend Mass or at least light candles for my family and friends. Faith, in my eyes, is key to living a full life.'

'Well, you seem like you have your two feet very firmly on the ground. Are your parents proud?'

'I've never asked them, but I am sure they are equally proud of all of their children,' she says modestly. 'I am fortunate to have the most wonderful parents, both of whom are watching tonight, as well as my brother Brendan. He will be looking at this now so I better do a wave out,' she says, waving at the camera.

'Speaking of family, you lost your twin sister at the tender age of eighteen. Tell us what happened?'

'On our eighteenth birthday she was killed in a car accident. It has and will always remain tragedy for the family and the community. It makes me appreciate every day and be fearless.'

'Many people have sold you out to the Press. How

did you cope with things like this?'

'Well, they clearly weren't best friends, were they?' she laughs sarcastically. 'At a certain point in your life, famous or otherwise, you take a reality check. If you can count three or four wonderful unconditional friends, you are fortunate. Mine... well, they know who they are.'

'Being "a star", do people treat you differently when you return home to Ireland?'

'I treat people the same as they treat me: with respect. I go home each year for Christmas and Sally's anniversaries, along with events for my autism work, so people were always kind to me. I see everyone as equal and so see what I do as my job. Most people in Ireland do too. In America more, there are funny instances, but you have to laugh and get on with it.'

'What is the funniest thing a fan has ever done?'

'I was lucky that I don't have too many alternative fans. But I couldn't repeat it on live television,' she laughs.

'Oh, go on,' he entices her.

'Let's just say it involves some funny outfits, some chasing and security being called,' she laughs.

'Well, Alanna, thank you again, but that's all we have time for. We wish you all the best with your album 'My Star', which is on sale worldwide. Alanna, our Irish star, everybody!'

As the sound of the audience clapping echoes around the room, Alanna sits smiling and waving out to the crowd.

'Coming up after the break, we are joined with tonight's final two guests, Des Bishop and the Irish movie director Neil Jordan, while Alanna is going to perform the first track from her album. Please join us then. See you after the break.'

The camera cuts, Alanna is led off the set. She looks

into the audience, suddenly stopping as she recognises a familiar face.

'No, no way. It could not be him,' she whispers under her breath while the host continues to make idle chat as he directs her backstage to Jenny and her crew.

Chapter 58

Tweet: @AStar You're Beautiful
@MariahCarey@Miguel

The Royal Hotel, Killarney, Ireland
'Jack, I am so happy you're here. I can't believe it. I can't believe you flew in!'

'Well, ye can make it big in LA, but when you get on the Late Late... well I tell ye, that's when you know you've made it!' Jack jokes. 'I had to come. Ah, Jaysus, when you told me that you loved me... I mean come on!' He kisses her.

'I am going back to LA in a few hours,' she says. 'Ye know, I don't want to leave yet, but I have to leave to go back and sort contracts...'

'Sure, I just bought the house in LA,' She says, looking upset.

'Look, let's not think about that now,' he says.

'OK, but I will always think about this stuff,

'If you had my love, would you always cherish it?' she says.

'Always. I love you,' he admits.

'I love you too,' she says knowing she meant it for the first time.

***

Muckross Lake, Killarney
'Hi Simon,' Alanna says in shock as he walks past her at the lake.

'Hi, Alanna. Saw ye on the Late Late. You were great! Suzie tells me ye're off again?' he asks.

'I'm gonna head back to the car,' Jenny says.

'OK, I'll be back in a few,' Alanna replies.

'Sure, we can go straight to the airport then,' Alanna says as smiles and walks on.

'I have to finish the album, but who knows after that, I think I'm going to come back here full-time,' says Alanna.

'Really? We are good enough for you now? You've lived your high life and now you're ready?' Simon enquires.

'It was never like that,' Alanna responds defensively. 'I had to help with Brendan. I had no choice.'

'Sorry, it's just tough to see you. There were so many times I would have jumped over the moon to know that you would be here, and ye... well, ye never came back. Even when my sister died, you never came back for the funeral. You just left. When Sally died, you left everything. It was like we lost you too.'

'You never thought to come and try come find me?' she asks.

'I wanted you to come back, every day.'

Realising her eyes are welling up, he continues, 'Anyway, I can't stand here and talk about the past.'

'Simon. It is what it is. I left you too, remember. You were my world. You had your family and life. I was alone. You never got on a plane and came to me. It works both ways. So many times I wanted you to come, and then time passed and you never did, so I moved on,' she says, watching him look to the ground.

**

'If you're so sure of my life being so great, why don't you come with me and see for yourself? Take a trip on the wild side. You always play it safe.'

He looked up, confused.

'I am finishing my album back in LA so I need to go back. I have a job, Simon. This is my business. If you're so judgemental, why don't you come visit to see what it's really like? On the other side,' she laughs.

He laughs and smiles the same smile that blew her away over eight years earlier. 'Well, I don't know. It's all a bit mad to just up and leave. You see, I am not mad like you.'

She laughs, 'Mad! I have been called a lot, but mad isn't usually it.' Flashing back over the last year, she realises, 'I can see what you mean, though. Well, how about you think about it? Here is my card and I leave today. I will leave it with you.'

***

They both stand there in silence for a minute or so, knowing that what they have is still there. Whatever it was those days by the lake, they are still there, and this is the only place the paparazzi have not reached.

Looking down at her phone, Alanna realises she is running late.

'I am going to pick up Brendan to say goodbye, so I have to run.'

'Sure, Alanna. I'll think about it and get back to you.'

'Sounds like a plan.' As she moves towards the car, they both wander back through years of memories of their days together.

'Who was that?' asks Jenny.

'An old friend,' she says, smiling.

Chapter 59

Tweet: @AStar @Jack One Love,
One life we've got to do what we should @U2

Dublin to LA
Sitting on the plane, Alanna feels a wave of emotions
surge as she starts to text Jack.

> *Alanna: Jack, I have always loved you too.*
> *I need you with me,*
> *It's so hard to do this without you.*
> *Some selfish part of me wants you to come, drop*
> *your meetings and come to LA.*
> *Even for now,*
> *The rest we can work out.*
> *Romantic ideals, I am sure,*
> *Love you.*
> *Lani*
> *X*

As she sits next to Jenny, she smiles, looking out of
the window and knowing that everything is as it should
be. She continues writing:

> *Dear Sally,*
> *I feel like so much has happened*
> *Carlton and Simon. I am going back to her new life*
> *and a new chapter, yet I need decide what I want. I am*
> *not sure anymore, sister... All I do know is I love music*
> *and I have to follow my heart. The family need me to do*
> *this.*

Alanna's New House, West Hollywood, Los Angeles
As she arrives with Jenny and two bigger bodyguards, there are paparazzi everywhere. Everything seems surreal. She is becoming more and more famous. Yet she writes:

Alanna: Jack, I am more alone than ever.
Please send me strength.
I need you.
Love you.
x

***

Mindy's number pops up on her phone 'Hi, darling, welcome back. Lots of exciting things lined up. I'll see you in studio today. We can run through everything there,' She says as Alanna drops her bag in her door.

Just then she gets a call from her doorman. 'Hi, Ms A. I have a man here. He says he knows you.'

'I've heard that before,' she says jokingly.

'Jack, from Dublin.'

She looks through the screen to see a man. And it's a man she knows.

'Jack? Jack? Jack, what are you doing here? Let him in!' Her hair is all over the place, and although she's wearing no make-up, she still looks pretty as if she was, as she runs to the door towards him.

'JACK!' she screams.

'Alanna,' he says.

'I can't believe you're here,' she says.

'I'm here because you asked me. You never asked me before. I always wanted you to ask me, but you never did. Now I'm here. I got a flight through London. I'm here,' he reminds her. 'And now I don't want to ever leave you.' Since day one, you were always it. I

363

know you feel the same. Carlton has my back,' he jokes. 'He told me you felt the same.'

'Carlton? I will kick his ass!' she says.

'All I ask is if we try... well, that as soon as you have done your things that we try it out. I have my seasons and you have your thing, but we can live together. You can do your work and travel and do what you need to do.'Yet, I need you living with me. I need to take care of you. It's not a nice life to be here alone,' Jack says.

'We are not kids anymore, and I met you and lost you to Harry. I can't deal with losing you again. I just can't do it, Alanna.'

***

'I have never heard you talk so much in all the time of knowing you,' Alanna says with tears streaming down her face.

'It was like all of those moments; travelling to and from different bars, restaurants, in various cities around the world, those live magical moments on television, parties and crowds of people searching for someone when you were here all along.

'It was always you.

'I wish I had told you the truth, maybe I wouldn't have hurt so many people on the way.

'The songs were about you.

'You were always my better half.

'I was just so scared I would lose you... Lose you like I lost Sally.

'They kiss and she looks at him.

'I feel happy for the first time in years. Maybe I have never been this happy' Alanna admits crying as they kiss and wrap their arms around one another.

'I can't believe you're here…' she says, smiling as she gets out of the shower. 'I have to call to Mindy in studio soon, if you want to come?'

'Sure, I would love to!' Jack says.

Just then she sees a call from Mindy coming.

'Hi Mindy. I'm on my way, I have a surprise for you,' she says, smiling.

'Alanna, hey, that's great. Just checking, do you know a lady called Chloe?' Mindy asks.

'Chloe… how do I know that name? Oh yes, I did a casting for her months back.'

'Well, you did a casting for her and then she saw your new site and album. Anyway, the lead has had a bad injury so looks like you're been cast for the movie. This is million dollar stuff. It will take you to a new level of success. How do you feel about this?'

'OMG, OMG…' Alanna drops the phone

'I love it!. Yes, I will do it!' Alanna shouts at the phone, which remains on the floor, while Jack watches in fascination as she jumps up and down.

'OK, great, I wanted to ask you before you got here in case you felt pressured. Let's talk when you get here,' Mindy says.

The phone cuts off.

'Are you ok?' Jack asks.

Trying to gasp for air, she calls out

'I've just been picked as the lead for a dance movie!' She has tears streaming down her face.

'Darling, I have never been so happy for you!' he says, hugging her tightly. 'You truly are A Star!' He kisses her.

Alanna walks out of her bedroom in a tight black dress and heels with red lipstick.

'Are you ready to go?' Alanna asks.

'Feck me. You're the most beautiful girl I've ever send in me life. *Ever*. One day I'll marry you,' Jack states.

She points to the engagement ring on her hand. 'Recognise this?'

'Is that the ring I bought you? Jack asks

'It's on the right hand, but ye never know?

'Maybe one day, sure we only have one life' she says.

Repeating Sally's famous words, she says walking out the door, 'Let's not try to work it all out. Just live for now and enjoy every minute of the journey,' she says kissing him.

Closing the door behind, hand in hand with Jack, she decides to do just that.

Lightning Source UK Ltd.
Milton Keynes UK
UKOW04f1849070214

226113UK00001B/4/P